THE
RIVER OF FIRE

The third Mary Fox adventure

By
Jonathan Posner

Published by Winter & Drew Publishing

ISBN: 9781739184995

CONTENTS

ACKNOWLE DGMENTS

I would like to thank all those who helped me make this book happen.

Jane Rayner, Maggie Saunders and Angie Chadwick of my Devon Novelists critique group, whose constructive comments helped smooth out many of the rough edges in early drafts – and for constantly challenging me on the history and character motivations; Sinead Kelly for her thorough editing, questions and encouragement (as always).

I would also like to thank the following who read the book in beta, and were kind enough to give me their honest feedback and support: Katherine Jacks, Elizabeth Ducie, Cathie Hartigan, Anna Bruce, Rebecca Dharlingue, and especially Catherine Kirkham-Sandy for her constructive comments on the historicity of the book.

Thanks also to the residents of Pozzuoli near Naples for humouring me as I walked around their streets in May 2024, trying to get the best view of Monte Nuovo. This was the mountain that appeared as a result of a volcanic eruption nearly 500 years ago. If you're wondering why I was there, read on; all will become clear in the end!

Finally, thanks to you for reading this book. I hope you enjoy Mary Fox's latest adventure as much as I have enjoyed writing it!

THE THIRD MARY FOX ADVENTURE
BY
JONATHAN POSNER

DISCLAIMER

No part of this publication may be reproduced, stored or transmitted in any form by any means; electronic, mechanical, photocopying or otherwise, without the prior written permission of the publisher.

Jonathan Posner has asserted his right under the Copyright, Designs and Patents Act, 1988, to be identified as the author of this work.

This is a work of fiction. References to real people, events, establishments, organisations or locales are intended only to provide a sense of authenticity and are used fictitiously. All other characters, and all incidents and dialogue, are drawn from the Author's imagination and are not to be construed as real.

I

THE ONE-ARMED MAN

Late summer 1536, Bishop's Lynn, East Anglia, England

The door crashing open made me glance up from my pie and ale. A man was standing in the doorway of the tavern, staring around the crowded room. One hand was hanging by his side, while the other—was not there. His arm ended in a leather sleeve at the elbow.

I resumed eating; a man with a missing limb was an unremarkable sight in a dockside tavern full of sailors.

But then I looked up again. Something about this man did seem remarkable.

What was it?

He was an ordinary-looking fellow of medium height, with short-cropped grey hair—so why should he cause me concern?

Suddenly my heart seemed to stop. Oh yes, I remembered him now. I even knew exactly why he had lost his arm.

Because of me.

Because I had opened it to the bone with my sword.

Then our eyes met. His widened in a look of surprised recognition. Then they hardened into one of anger. He clearly knew me too, lifting and shaking his stump as if to prove it. Then he leaned across his waist, drew out his knife and, with a determined stare, started towards my table.

Time to get out.

I glanced behind, but there was no other door. No way out of the crowded tavern in that direction. Leaving me with the only option; getting past this armed attacker.

I looked left and right. There were many tables that he must get around. I stood and drew my own knife, then scraped back my chair.

Men were all turning to stare. Some looked at me, while others observed my would-be attacker. There were several laughs and shouts of encouragement. I heard one voice say, "A fight, eh? Great sport!".

"I bet on the one-armed fellow," said another.

"Seriously?" came the response. "A penny says the lad will slip through. He is young and lively."

I ignored them as I moved past. They were wrong about me. In truth, I was no lad; instead, a woman of twenty years, who habitually dressed as a man in order to travel more easily around the land.

But just at this moment, my need was to travel past the one-armed man, who was now only a couple of tables away. He raised his blade high, so the point was level with his hard, staring eyes.

I ran to the side of a small table close to the fire, where a man sat nursing a cup of wine, watching the proceedings with a half-smile. As the attacker came to the other side, I moved round, keeping the table between us.

"Begone, fellow," said the one-armed man to the wine drinker, pointing his knife. "Lest I might cut your throat, dealing with this unnatural scoundrel that cost me my arm."

The wine drinker stood; a tall man in a many-coloured doublet. The attacker made to get around, but it seemed the tall man had taken my part. He blocked the attacker's way.

"I said, begone, sirrah!" the one-armed man snarled as he tried to push past. But instead, the other grabbed his wrist and twisted it until the knife clattered to the floor. Then, keeping hold of the wrist, he pulled back his free hand and threw a tremendous blow at the fellow's jaw.

The one-armed man staggered away and crashed down onto the table behind, sending ale tankards flying and drinkers jumping out of the way.

"My penny looks safe," observed one of the men at the next table.

"Not if the lad had help," replied his companion. "That was not in the bet."

I had little time for their nonsense. I called my thanks to my protector, who was still smiling, even as he rubbed at his knuckles.

"Go, then!" he replied, waving me towards the door. But I stayed where I was, concerned that this 'good Samaritan' had put himself in harm's way because of me.

Behind him, the one-armed man got up and clutched at his jaw. Then one of the betting men—presumably the one favouring my attacker—leant down and picked up the knife. He held it out to the one-armed man, who took it with a grunt, and immediately charged towards my protector.

"Run!" I called, but the tall man must have already had the same thought. He set off round the table, snatching up his wide-brimmed hat as he went.

Arriving at my side, he grabbed my hand and said, "We had better get out!"

Biting back a question as to why it was suddenly 'we', I decided in the moment that maybe 'we' was a safer bet than 'I'.

The door was just ahead, beyond the last few tables. I glanced back. The one-armed man was closing on us.

"Quick!"

We pushed past the final two tables and ran to the door, with the drinkers cheering or booing according to their decided allegiances. As I opened it, the tall man and I exchanged a quick glance of understanding. We both knew what we must do.

We ran out, then immediately stopped on either side of the door, pressed against the wall. As the one-armed fellow emerged like a ball from a canon, the tall man stretched out his foot.

The attacker went flying forward, putting his hand out to break his fall. As he crashed full length onto the cobbles, his knife skittered away over the stones. I pinned him down by kneeling on his outstretched arm. My companion appeared beside me, with the man's own knife and put it to the fellow's neck.

A couple of passing sailors stopped. "What is going on here?" one asked.

I looked up. "This man was attacking us," I said.

The sailor shrugged. "The fellow has an arm missing."

"So not much of an attacker," observed the other.

"He had a blade."

The sailor made another shrug. "Well, 'tis your business, fellow," he said, and they wandered off.

"Come on," I said, pulling on the man's good arm. "Get up."

We took him at knifepoint over to an old warehouse and pushed him roughly inside. He fell back against some barrels, and stared up with a twisted look of loathing.

"Mary Fox," he snarled. "I would know you anywhere."

"I never knew your name," I replied. "You were the driver of that cart when your villainous leader, Jacob Cruddon, double-crossed us in the forest."

My companion gave a surprised-sounding snort. "Mary?" he asked with a curious stare. "A woman? Yet wearing men's garb?" Now I realised he had a thick accent; one that I could not place. I pushed the thought away and gave a small shrug. "It serves my purpose not to be bound up like a goose in the tight bodice of a woman's gown. But mostly, it frees me to go where I please."

"'Tis unnatural," muttered the driver.

"But why were you chasing her just now?" asked my companion, holding the knife to the man's neck once more.

"Seeking revenge," the driver snapped, his eyes locked onto mine with a look of pure hate. "For the loss of my arm." He glanced across at my companion. "This witch opened it up to the bone with her sword." He swallowed hard. "Then it festered and blackened, and had to be taken off."

For a moment I felt a little sorrow for the fellow and his suffering. But then I recalled how he, Cruddon and another ruffian had pretended to offer protection to me and my travelling companions, Sir John Fitzwilliam and his son Robert, while all the time planning to do us foul. So any sympathy was misplaced.

"If you had not conspired with Cruddon to kill me, you would still be whole," I said.

"The same if you had not swung your sword at me," he grunted.

I could see we were getting nowhere. I resolved to tie him securely before he could cause any further trouble. Then we could decide what do with him.

I stood back, looking around the dockside warehouse. Of all places, it should have some rope. Leaving my companion guarding the driver, I walked to a pile of what looked like sails and spars. I was just starting to see if I could find some, when there was a sudden shout from behind me.

I spun round, to see the driver now leaning over my companion, who was on the floor. The knife was in the driver's hand, and he was using all his weight to push it towards the other's chest. My companion was grunting as he pushed back, but the driver had the advantage of being on top, and the blade was making determined progress downwards.

I grabbed a long wooden pole with a heavy metal hook on the end, and ran back. As the tip of driver's blade touched my companion's doublet, I swung the pole hard at the back of the one-armed man's head. It hit him with a loud cracking sound, sending him flying into the barrels.

He slid down the side of one, and was still.

There were a few moments of shocked silence, then my companion got to his feet and said, "Thank you, Mistress Fox. I thought I was in control of him, but he moved so fast. I was watching you, when suddenly he had the knife." He paused, looking very serious. "You saved my life."

"As you did mine, back there," I said, waving a hand in the direction of the tavern. "So I thank you as well."

"This means we are even." He broke into a boyish grin, then bowed low. "Angelo di Luca, of Pozzuoli, near Napoli."

A Neapolitan. That explained the thick accent.

I put down the pole and bowed back. "Mary Fox, of Marchington Manor in Essex," I said. "Although I have no love for the place."

Angelo looked over at the driver. "He is dead? he asked.

I crouched down and felt the driver's neck. There was the flutter of a heartbeat. "No," I said. "He still lives." I lifted an eyelid. The eye was rolled upwards. "But for sure he will be insensible for a good while."

We stepped outside. "What are we to do with him?" I whispered.

Angelo was silent a moment. "We cannot just let him go, for he will seek you out again."

"And we must not kill him," I said. "I have vowed never to kill in cold blood." There was a pause as we considered what best to do. A few sailors hurried about their business, none seeming to take any notice of us.

"Tide is turning," one was saying to his companions as they walked past. "Best to get back on board quickly or we will miss her sailing."

I had an idea. "Wait!" I called out. The sailors stopped and I hurried up to them. "Do you need any more crew?" I asked.

One sailor looked me up and down. He seemed the oldest, with an air of authority that suggested he had command of the men. "You fancy a life at sea, lad?" he asked.

"Not me," I said quickly.

He raised an eyebrow. "You are pressing another man?"

I nodded. "I am."

He gave a sly grin. "One who has wronged you then?"

"Yes." I gave him a conspiratorial smile of my own. "We had a fight and I managed to knock him out. Will you take him?"

He nodded slowly. "For sure, if he can work. We need more men, and will take them whatever they have done. Has he been to sea before?"

"Most possibly," I said, thinking quickly. "He has lost an arm…" I left it for him to draw the conclusion that it had been taken off in an accident at sea. Or perhaps in a fight with pirates.

The sailor glanced at his fellows, as if assuring himself of his decision. "Very well, we will take him. We can have the smith fit a hook."

I led them into the warehouse, where the driver still lay senseless.

"This fellow?" asked the sailor. I nodded. "Right, lads, let us have him." Two of his men picked up the driver.

"Thank you," I said.

"We will take him for you, lad, and perhaps he will have a good life at sea." The sailor fixed me with a stern look. "We do not usually go about collecting men who have lost a fight, but we do need more hands on board." He glanced down at the driver as the men carried him out. "Even if this fellow has only one."

2

ANGELO DI LUCA

Angelo di Luca sat opposite me and removed his hat, then ran his fingers through the long dark hair that curled about his ears. "Tell me of yourself," he said, settling back and adjusting his doublet; a strange riot of reds, greens and yellows that, together with the wide epaulets and large grey padded sleeves, gave him a broad-shouldered look unlike any Englishman I had ever seen.

"What would you like to know?" I asked.

It was a while later, after we had ridden away from the dockside and were settled in a new hostelry in the middle of Bishop's Lynn.

"You said you had no love for the place of your birth," he observed. "We can start with that."

"Marchington Manor?"

"Yes. Why do you hate it so?"

I paused a moment, studying him. Could I trust this man? He had saved my life, as I had saved his. That suggested a bond had been formed, which should have some strength. And he had open, honest-seeming features, with a warm smile and eyes that crinkled most pleasantly. In all my life I have either trusted or been wary of strangers, and will admit I have not always been correct—sometimes with disastrous results. But I decided this time, I would go with my gut feeling, and I would trust Angelo di Luca. For better or worse.

"I was raised by a stepfather who had little love for me," I began. "In fact…" I paused, as the memory of the kicking he had dealt me some years before made a painful return. "…he hated me so much, that he oft said he wished me dead."

Angelo's eyes widened, and he let out a breath. "In truth? That is dreadful. Why so?"

I explained how my stepfather had held an obsessive love for my mother, and had most likely killed my true father in order to win her hand. But then he had lost her when she died giving birth to me. That was something he could never forgive me for, and had made my life a misery as a consequence. So much that I had run away some years ago, and embarked on my life as an itinerant wanderer, wearing mainly men's clothes, and seeking only to help others where I could.

"And you had no stepmother as you grew?"

"Nay. He never married again." My throat grew tight, and I had to take a breath. "I have never known a mother's love," I said when I could continue. "So it has always been my dearest wish to enjoy such a thing. I thought I had found it a couple of times, but in each case, it came with conditions attached—and these I could not accept."

He nodded slowly. "I see. And what were those?"

"That I must marry a man, and lose my true self as a result. I must become his property. His vassal. His obedient servant."

"And this is not what Mary Fox is..." he seemed to struggle to find a word. "...is about?"

"Nay." I shook my head. "I would continue to enjoy my freedom. To give help to others where it is needed."

"Most laudable." He nodded, as if he now understood. "Hence your masquerading as a man—it allows you to travel unhindered."

"Exactly."

"And what name do you use?"

"I have decided on Thomas Richardson." I paused. "Named for my true father, Sir Richard Fox. I have three brothers, Richard, Edward and Henry, but none called Thomas. I decided to take that name, as if to be the fourth brother."

"It suits you well," he said with a smile. "Now, let us enjoy some wine." He waved to attract the attention of one of the tavern's serving girls.

He turned his intense dark eyes back on mine. Suddenly, it seemed as if something was troubling him, as if he was struggling to make a decision. Twice, he took a breath to speak, and twice he seemed to think better of it. Then he nodded slightly, and said, "Mary Fox, you say you like to help others?"

"Yes," I replied slowly, curious to see where this was going. "I do."

"Then you might be able to help me," he said, "or in truth, a friend of mine. She is in the gravest of need."

"Indeed," I said. "What is that? Tell me, so I can decide if I can help."

He seemed to relax his shoulders, as if his decision to proceed was justified. "She is a widow of great wealth in Norwich, who has no word of her son. She is greatly worried."

"I see. She is looking for a man who may find news of the fellow?"

He nodded. "Someone who is able to ask the questions and get the answers."

A serving girl came to our table. "Do you have wine?" Angelo asked. The girl frowned, and it was clear Angelo's foreign accent and strange clothes seemed to worry her. But she said only, "As you wish, master," and swept away with a disdainful flick of her head.

Angelo's eyes followed her a moment, then came back to me.

"And this widow has not charged you to perform this task?" I asked with a frown.

He shook his head. "I am come recently from Pozzuoli. For all my mother is English, and has taught me to speak the tongue as if to the manner born, I know little of this country. The widow would rather have one who knows more than me to make enquiries." Then he smiled again and gave a nod in the direction of the serving girl. "And in truth, one who does not cause the grave distrust of foreigners that you all seem to have here."

I shrugged. "We are not all so narrow-minded. And as you say, your English is remarkably good. You have learned it well." I gave a small smile. "But I do see your friend's point."

"Then you will do this for her?" he asked, with a hopeful look. "And perhaps you will meet her in person, so she can explain her needs in full? I believe also she will make generous payment for your services."

I tapped my fingers on the table as I considered this. After attending the funeral of Prince Henry Fitzroy at Thetford Priory a few days earlier, I had no plans other than to head north. Some time spent in the company of this man, and in helping a needy widow, would be exactly to my purpose. And for all I had a good number of coins in my purse, there was always room for more.

"Yes," I said, "I will meet with her."

—0—

The next day we rode to Norwich.

Angelo made an entertaining companion, telling me stories of Pozzuoli, with its ruins originally built by the ancient men of Rome. "We have the *Anfiteatro Flavio Puteolano*; an amphitheatre that is larger than all but two such places; the Colosseum in Rome being one," he said. "It was the place in Pozzuoli where the Romans raced their chariots, or would put prisoners to death. Wild beasts would attack them for the pleasure of the people." He paused, as if for effect. "The most famous of these was *Santo Proculus*, patron saint of Pozzuoli."

I shuddered. "That sounds awful. I trust this amphitheatre is no longer in use?"

"No." He shook his head. "It was abandoned when it was partially buried by fire that spewed from the *Solfatara* mountain. Pozzuoli sits on the *Campi Flegrei*, an area often shaken by the wrath of the good Lord and endangered by the fire he sends shooting out from under the ground. You may still see the ruins." He laughed, showing excellent teeth. "But no person dies there now."

He was also most enthusiastic about the nearby city of Napoli. "It is the finest in the world," he exclaimed, "greater even than Rome itself."

As we rode, he suggested I should learn some words of his Neapolitan language. It was a challenge I was happy to accept, if it made him feel more at ease in my country. He was a patient teacher, quick to point out how Neapolitan bore many similarities to the Latin I had studied alongside my brothers as a young child. By the time we arrived in Norwich that evening, I was pleased to be able to make a few sentences of the most basic conversation in his native tongue.

"You are a most quick learner," he observed as we arrived in a coaching inn on the outskirts of the city. "I will delight in teaching you more, if you wish?"

"I do," I replied. "You teach well, Angelo." Then I tried it in his tongue. "*Insegno bene.*"

He laughed. "No," he corrected. It is *'insegni bene. Insegno bene* means 'I teach well."

"*Insegni bene,*" I repeated.

"Correct. The endings of the words tell us much about them." He gave me a warm smile as we entered the inn and he asked for two rooms. By the poorest misfortune they had but one shared room remaining. I was about to say we would seek beds elsewhere for the night, when Angelo agreed to the offer. I could do naught but smile and accept.

"You have a problem with this arrangement, Master Richardson?" he asked with a worried-looking frown. "I am sure I am a silent sleeper."

"No, no problem at all," I said, with the brightest smile I could muster. He nodded, as if this was enough for him, and we were shown up to the room.

It was a simple chamber, with no furnishings except two pallet beds and a small fire burning in the grate. Angelo grunted his acceptance, and I resigned myself to preserving my dignity by sleeping fully clothed.

"Shall we have something to eat?" he asked, and I nodded, glad of the chance to fill what I now realised was a grumbling hole in my belly.

We went back downstairs, found a table and ordered some pies and ale.

"This food you eat here in England," he said, staring at the pie when it was put before him, "I would not feed to the poorest peasant in my land."

"We find it most wholesome," I observed. "But tell me, do you not have such pies in your country?"

"We do," he said, pushing his knife through the crust and gazing sombrely at the steaming filling. "But it is not what I would eat."

"Then tell me, what do you have?" I asked.

He speared a piece of the meat and chewed on it with a pained expression, before replying. "We have *atriya*, or *trii*, which are long pieces of dried paste made from the freshest flour and water. They bring out the taste of any foods served alongside. Such as the spicy pressed meats we call *coppiette*, and *focaccia* flat breads baked with cheese and *peperoni* on top that taste…" he put his fingers to his lips. "…*perfezione*."

I laughed. "You make it sound wonderful. I would very much like to visit your country one day and try these for myself."

"I am sure one day you will."

"Tell me more of this rich widow who seeks my assistance," I said, starting on my now disappointingly English pie. "How did you come to be finding help for her?"

He ate some more before replying. "I will tell you this, but first I must explain something." He put down his knife. "There is an heirloom that is precious to my family. A necklace made of silver with many ruby stones, called *il Fiume di Fuoco*—the River of Fire. It has been in my mother's family for many centuries. At the start of this year, my parents decided to visit England, as it had long been my father's wish to see the country of his wife's birth." His face fell. "But sadly, as they travelled to the town of Norwich, *il*

Fiume di Fuoco was stolen from them." He shook his head. "My mother, she fell into a great sadness."

"Your poor mother," I said. It pained me greatly to think of this woman being in such distress. "And what of your father?" I asked.

"He searched many days for the jewel, but with no luck. They returned to Pozzuoli empty-handed. My father was heartbroken that he had lost this precious necklace, and fell into the deepest malaise." His mouth trembled, and I could see he was having to swallow hard to hold his emotion. "It was then that the good Lord decided to call my father to his side."

"Oh no," I whispered. "Your poor mother! To lose her husband as well!"

"Yes. And there is something more. She now approaches her fiftieth birthday. There is a legend, I believe based on truth, of a curse attached to the necklace. Any woman of the family who does not wear *il Fiume di Fuoco* on such a day, will be dead within a month."

"Based on truth?" I queried.

"It was long part of the history of the jewel, that it had such a curse—and no one could say where it came from. But my mother's grandmother..." He paused a moment, then continued. "She was the first of two women that my mother knew who was struck down by the curse. She misplaced the jewel and did not wear it on her birthday. She died in great pain of a sudden sickness within three weeks, for all she was in the best of health before."

"And the second?"

"My mother's aunt. Despite the previous death, she said she had no faith in the curse, so she deliberately did not wear it on her birthday. But it was a grave mistake, for the same happened to her. This time, in a week." He shook his head. "Now the curse is proven, no woman would dare take the chance." He paused again, then added, "It is why my mother insisted on keeping the jewel with her when they came to England; a precaution she must now regret."

"I see." I sat back, regarding him. But I was not seeing his worried face, for his story reminded me of a similar curse. I was seeing a kind lady in her sickbed, ailing because a talisman known as the Broken Sword had been stolen by a young brigand, the son of Jacob Cruddon. The Broken Sword had protected the family from harm for many generations, so as soon as it was stolen, she and her daughter had become gravely ill. And when her husband, son and I had found and restored the talisman, both women recovered in full. "When is her fiftieth birthday?" I asked.

"It will be on the twenty eighth day of January in the year of Our Lord 1537."

"Four months," I muttered. "Little time in truth, to find it and return it all the way to Pozzuoli."

He nodded. "I promised my mother I would do all I could to get her jewel back in time. I found a boat sailing from Napoli all the way to England. I arrived a few weeks ago, and rode hard to Norwich. But for all I asked many men to give me information, they all refused me because I was a foreigner, even though I spoke the tongue like a true Englishman. Then finally I found one man who agreed to aid me. His information led me to this particular widow."

"And she said she would help you, but only in exchange for news of her son?" I suggested.

He nodded with the ghost of a smile. "Yes." He was silent a moment, as if considering whether to add some further information. Then he nodded. "She asked me to find her a suitable person to seek this out."

"Well, I am pleased to help, if it will secure your mother's life," I said. "Indeed," I added, "I have knowledge of restoring just such a precious object. I will do the same for you."

He smiled. "You would do this thing?"

"Of course." I gave him a warm smile. "And back to this widow. Where does she live? Will we meet at her house?"

He shook his head. "No. She would have you see a grave that is relevant to her son's disappearance. She would meet you in the graveyard of All Saints Fybriggate…" he stumbled slightly over the pronunciation, which made me smile. "Then you can begin the task."

We finished our meal, then sat by the parlour fire indulging in some idle chatter, until I found myself unable to stifle a yawn.

"You are most tired," Angelo said. "We must leave well before sunrise tomorrow. The widow has said she will wait at the agreed place each day at dawn, until I can bring her someone to help with the task. You should go to bed."

"I will," I said. "Are you also coming up now?"

He shook his head. "No, I wish to sit here alone, with thoughts of Pozzuoli, my mother and my father."

Leaving him staring into the fire, I made my way up to the room.

3

THE WIDOW IN THE GRAVEYARD

Just before dawn the following morning, Angelo and I set off. A weak sun was inching above the eastern horizon as we reached the main street. The heaviest mist was revealed, covering the land in a cold, oppressive cloak. The few buildings we could see looked as if they were but shadows of their true selves.

"Your English skies are as difficult to see through as your English customs," observed Angelo, his voice sounding disembodied and flat in the fog.

"We have only low marshlands between us and the sea," I replied. "Thick mists oft roll in, especially this early in the morning."

Angelo gave a small shiver. "It is as cold and damp as the rest of your weather." A dog barked somewhere. He cocked his head to one side, as if listening, "And do you notice how this heavy air makes sounds hard to place?" he asked. "That dog could be anywhere; it is impossible to say."

We rode on for a few more minutes, until I felt we must soon be near our destination.

A woman was walking along the lane with a couple of fat geese waddling behind. "Can you tell me how to reach All Saints in Fybriggate?" I asked. She looked up at me as if I were soft in the head. "This is the very lane you seek." She pointed ahead. "A few yards more and you would not be asking, but seeing it for yourselves."

"Thank you," I said with a thin smile.

Sure enough, a high flint wall soon appeared out of the mist, then the lychgate of a church. We dismounted and secured our horses on rings set into the wall.

As we walked through the gate, a figure in black seemed to emerge like a spectre from the greyness. We got closer, and I could make out that it was wearing a woman's hood and cloak, and was standing by one of the gravestones alongside the church. On her other side was a freshly dug grave with the earth piled all round and a shovel standing proud.

"Is that the widow?" I asked. Angelo nodded, then gestured for me to walk over.

I made my way to the figure. The woman had her hands clasped together and a large canvas bag secured to her waist. Her gown was all black, and her hood had a dark veil covering her face. She also wore a heavy black cape over her neck and chest. For a moment I wondered why she chose to obscure herself so, but put the thought from my mind as I stepped up to where she stood. I felt Angelo walking behind me.

"I have come to help in your quest for information on your son," I said, stopping before her.

"Indeed, so you have," she replied. Her voice was soft, and had a slight East Anglian burr. "Your name?"

"Thomas Richardson, at your service," I replied, sweeping off my cap and bowing. "And you are?" I asked as I replaced it.

She slowly lifted the veil so I could see her face. She was perhaps one or two years short of reaching fifty, and had a look that was unremarkable... except... except... There was something about her that seemed vaguely familiar...

"Thomas?" she whispered. "Thomas Richardson?" She shook her head, almost as if in sorrow. "I think not." She was silent a moment, her eyes burning into mine. "Nay, I think 'Mary Fox' is more appropriate."

My blood turned to ice as I stared at her.

Now I knew her—from a doorstep in Ipswich, and from the sound of her voice when I was hiding behind a pile of logs in the courtyard of her house. It was over two years earlier, but I knew her well.

"Yes," she said. "Joan Cruddon, widow of Jacob."

Jacob Cruddon. The father of the brigand who had stolen the Broken Sword, and who had sworn to kill me. Yet who had been executed as a traitor, after kidnapping the King's son, Prince Henry Fitzroy.

I made a move to run, but my arms were suddenly grabbed from behind, and my sword was drawn out of its scabbard.

"I am so sorry," Angelo said in my ear.

He had played me false!

"Let me go!" I snapped, struggling against his grip. What a trusting fool I had been!

"Oh no, Mary Fox," Joan Cruddon said, coming forward and putting her face right into mine. "I have waited for this moment for too long. I shall not let you go now."

"This whole thing was a trap," I said, writhing against Angelo's hold, then turned my head towards him. "You used the attack by the driver as a way of gaining my trust. Did you set that up as well?"

"Nay. It was just a fortunate opportunity."

"Which you used against me."

"I am only doing this because I need the information she promised on my stolen necklace. Truly, I am sorry."

"Are you?" His words were like a knife in my heart. "Really?"

"Much as I hate to end this pleasant conversation," Joan Cruddon cut in with a twist of sarcasm, "but I have you at my mercy, Mary Fox, and I intend to make best use of this."

I turned back to her. "To find out about your son?"

"Indeed no," she replied with a cold smile. "I know precisely what happened to him. You killed him, Mary Fox. Just as you killed my husband." She put her hand to my chin and pushed my head round so I was staring into the black depths of the open grave. "Just as I am going to kill you and dispose of your sorry carcass down there."

She stood back, then reached behind the gravestone, coming up with a cocked crossbow in her hand. She took a bolt from the bag at her waist and slotted it into the weapon. I tried again to release myself from Angelo's grip.

"Let me go!" I repeated. "You are mistaken about me!"

She ignored this and held the bow so close that I almost had to cross my eyes to see the tip of the bolt.

"I have waited many weeks for this, Mary Fox," she snarled, her voice now hard. "I am not mistaken."

"You would kill Master di Luca too?" I demanded. "Even though he has followed your bidding? At this distance the bolt will pass through us both."

She frowned, and it was clear from her expression that she was giving serious thought to killing Angelo as well. Then she shook her head and said, "You, di Luca, throw her in the grave as we agreed."

"For the reason we said?" he asked, and I detected a note of hesitancy in his voice.

"Yes, yes," she replied in a dismissive tone. Then she raised the bow a little. "Or I will test her theory that one bolt will kill you both."

"But you said…" Angelo muttered.

"Do it!" Joan Cruddon snapped, "Or you will ne'er see the jewel!"

Angelo pushed me along the gravel path until I was balanced on the edge of the pit. "I really am sorry," he said, then held me so I could see nothing but the dreadful blackness before me. It seemed so deep that I must surely be injured from the fall alone.

But that would be of little consequence, I thought, as I struggled to keep my footing on the loose earth. Once I was down there, Joan Cruddon would have me captive and could shoot her infernal weapon at will.

I shivered in fear as I stared across at her twisted smile. In that moment I knew exactly what was her intent. No quick and merciful death from the first bolt. Instead, a series of shots to wound only. Where first? An arm? A leg? All four limbs? Then maybe the belly—but even that may not kill me.

No, death would finally take me in screaming agony as she piled six feet of suffocating earth on top of my wounded body. I thought I would retch as the true horror of her plan for my suffering became clear.

She raised the weapon and pointed it at us. "Throw her in, di Luca, as we agreed!"

But Angelo hesitated.

Joan Cruddon's face suddenly turned red. "Throw her in!" she screamed.

But still he hesitated.

This was my chance.

I muttered to him, "You are not as sorry as I am," then swung my heel back hard, making contact with his shin. He made a yelp and relaxed his grip. I gave a twist, and in an instant, I was free. With a single bound I leapt across the mound of earth at the corner of the grave, then scrambled to the relative safety of the next gravestone.

There was the crack of a shot and the crunch of a woman's foot running across the gravel. Then the creaking sound of her winding the bow back, before another shot snapped into the far side of the headstone. It sent stone chips flying.

I crouched low. How soon before she circled around my hiding place and tried again?

I needed better cover.

I peered through the mist. I could just make out the next monument along. It seemed to be a substantial stone block with a tall obelisk above. Better than this small headstone. If only I could get to it.

I flinched as another bolt slammed into the slab. I swear it even leaned an inch towards me with the force of the impact.

Just how close was she? I had no wish to find out.

There were but a few seconds before she re-armed the crossbow. Keeping down, I ran for the obelisk, forward rolled and came to my feet on the path behind the stone block beneath.

Another monument was close behind, just visible as a grey shape. I glanced back, then ran softly to its cover. A large headstone was my next target, and after that a further monument.

"Come out, Mary Fox," Joan Cruddon called. Now her voice seemed disembodied; as if she could be anywhere.

I stayed silent as I crouched down. Some words were carved into the stone by my head; *Requiescat in Pace.* I shuddered. That was what this woman wanted for me—but not to 'rest in peace'. Rather, to die in agony.

"I said, come out!" Her voice echoed in the stillness of the thick morning mist. There was the crack of the crossbow, and the sound of a bolt hitting stone.

I shuffled further round, my foot kicking a loose stone. It was a rough piece of flint, just smaller than my fist. But it skittered on the path with a sound like a thousand drums.

"What was that?" She was close.

There was a creaking sound and a click. She was winding back the bowstring again. "Then you leave me no choice, Mary Fox," she snapped. "I still have many bolts remaining in my bag. Enough to make sure one of them finds its mark. I'll send you to hell for what you have done to me." There was the rustle of skirts and the crunch of a foot on the gravel path. A pause. "Art a witch, Mary Fox? Have you conjured up this blanket of mist so I cannot find you?"

A movement caught my eye, and I spun round.

It was the treacherous Angelo di Luca, a sword in his hand.

I backed away as he moved towards me, the blade raised.

I glanced back. Could Joan Cruddon have reached the other side of the monument?

If so, I would be surrounded.

Angelo came closer.

I would have to make a run for it...

"Wait!" he hissed. "I mean you no harm."

I froze, giving him a hard, silent stare. His words could hardly be believed.

"She promised to help me get the necklace," he whispered as he lowered the sword, then crouched at my side. "But I warrant that was a lie, just to make me trick you. She used me."

"You betrayed my trust." I hissed back.

"Please, please forgive me," Angelo whispered, his eyes fixed on mine. "On my mother's life, it was not by my will."

But how could I forgive such betrayal? Then I bit back a sharp retort; he did look genuinely contrite.

"Maybe," I whispered. "But only if you will truly promise to help me."

He turned the sword in his hand and offered it towards me, hilt first. "I will," he breathed. "Take this, it is yours," he paused. "And run me through if I ever play you false again."

With a quick prayer that I was doing the right thing to trust him this time, I grabbed the sword.

Angelo drew his knife from his belt, as we stared into the thick grey air.

I thought I caught a movement to my left.

I spun round, pointing my sword into the fog.

I froze as something pressed into my neck. Something cold and hard.

"You look the wrong way, Mary Fox," said Joan Cruddon, her voice loaded with malicious triumph. "Stand up, the two of you."

We did so, as Joan stepped back so she could cover us both with the weapon. "Drop the sword, Mary," she ordered, pointing the crossbow at me.

I let it clatter to the ground, but in my other hand, I gripped the piece of sharp-edged flint I had picked up.

"You, di Luca. To my side."

Angelo swallowed hard. "No."

She was silent a moment, and I could see her considering the possibility that he might have changed allegiance. "Do you defy me?" she asked.

"I do."

She swung the crossbow, so it pointed at him. "We had a bargain. I said I would help you find the stolen necklace."

I took a small step away from Angelo. "But I assume it was in truth stolen by your thieving husband, Jacob Cruddon?" I asked.

"Christ's wounds!" Angelo exclaimed, and she looked across at him. I took the opportunity to take another step away.

She shrugged. "I may as well say now. Yes, Jacob stopped some foreign travellers in a wood and relieved them of all their possessions. The necklace was the best piece of all, so he decided to keep it."

"She said she only had news of it," Angelo muttered. "She told me she would give me help in finding where it is."

I took another step away, then said with a grim smile, "Oh, that she can." I paused. "She can tell you exactly where it is. Because she has it about her own neck even now." Joan Cruddon put a hand to her throat, confirming my suspicion that she was covering up the necklace with the heavy cape. Otherwise, why wear such a strange garment? I made another step. "I am guessing that Jacob gave it to you, and you wear it every day." A further step. I was now more than a couple of yards away from where Angelo was crouched down. "Your husband is gone, but you have no intention of returning it."

"You have the *Fiume di Fuoco?*" Angelo stood, putting his hands on his hips. "You have had it all the time? You have lied to me about this as well?"

Joan raised her chin and looked down her nose at him. "It was necessary, to make sure you would bring the girl to me."

"You are as much a thief as your traitorous husband!" Angelo snapped.

"Well, that is of no matter, for I shall kill you both, one after the other, and throw your sorry carcasses into yonder grave."

I took another step away.

Joan Cruddon swung her crossbow over to me. "Stay still, Mary Fox!" she snapped. "Why do you keep moving aside?" She raised the bow. "I can kill you from much greater distance than this."

I said nothing, but glanced briefly across to Angelo. He nodded, seeming to understand my purpose.

He drew his knife from his belt. The movement distracted

Joan Cruddon so she swung back at him, allowing me to take a few more steps.

I was now far enough away that as she held her gaze on Angelo, I was fully outside her line of vision.

"That would be bad for you, Joan Cruddon," I said. "Whichever of us you shoot first, the other will have time to step forward and kill you before you can re-arm."

She waved the bow at each of us in turn, frowning as she appeared to realise that I was now far enough away from Angelo for this to be correct.

The flint stone felt solid in my hand.

"Then what?" Angelo demanded. "You would put me to death first?" He brandished his knife. "As Mary Fox has said, she will run you through."

"Mayhap I must take that chance." Joan Cruddon raised her weapon again. "Indeed, for you would be most inconvenient if you stayed alive." She lifted it higher and took aim. "I am sorry, di Luca, but it needs to be this…"

She got no further, as I snapped back my arm and hurled my flint directly at her.

By God's good grace my aim was true. The stone caught her directly on the forehead. She fell back, discharging the crossbow so the bolt flew harmlessly over our heads, then she hit the ground with a cry.

The crossbow clattered to the gravel just behind her.

Immediately she rolled onto her side. She grabbed the weapon and started to swing it round.

But before she could re-arm it, Angelo was on top of her, his knife ready.

I gasped as he raised the blade high, then brought it down with a sickening thump, deep into her side.

Joan Cruddon reared up with a fearsome yell, throwing Angelo off like a piece of chaff. He fell to his back with the knife still in his hand, now red with her blood. She gave another cry, then put her hands to his throat. I ran forward to pull her away, but suddenly her body jerked upwards, as if she were a marionette whose string had been pulled.

Then she flopped down with her full weight on top of Angelo.

There was a silence, broken only by the sound of him struggling to breathe. "Get her off me!" he gasped.

I took hold of her shoulder and rolled her away onto her back. Immediately Angelo drew a great breath, which ended in a fit of coughing.

Once he was able, he pulled himself up onto one elbow and looked down at Joan Cruddon.

"Dead?" he asked.

I nodded. With his knife now embedded deep in her chest, there was little doubt.

He got to his feet, and we were silent. Joan Cruddon's cold eyes were still open, but they were now dull and lifeless, fixed eternally on the sky.

"She would have tried to kill us both," I said eventually.

We stared down at the body.

"I was not aiming to kill her," he said. "She fell on my knife."

"I know," I said.

He bit his lip.

"There is an open grave close by..." I said slowly.

He nodded. "I am thinking the same." He looked at me. "But first, there is something I must do."

He leaned over her, grasped his knife and, with a look of determination, pulled it out. It came away with a sucking sound that made me feel sick to my stomach. Then he made a cut down the cape at Joan Cruddon's neck, letting the two pieces fall away to the sides.

Again we stared down, but this time it was not death that drew our attention.

It was the magnificent fiery necklace she wore.

It was formed of a wide crescent shape, made of tiny, burnished silver chain links and set with many rubies. There were four on each side of a central stone. This stone demanded attention for its size alone. It was perhaps twice as large as the nail of my thumb, and pointed down to the natural valley of her chest. Two smaller stones were placed either side of the main one, then three larger rubies on each side. All were coloured the deepest, purest red.

Angelo gave a deep sigh. *"Il Fiume di Fuoco"* he whispered. "The River of Fire. I have it back at last."

4

BE ON MY GUARD

It was a while later that we finished shovelling the earth into the grave, covering over the mortal remains of Joan Cruddon and her crossbow.

We stood back, patting the dirt off our hands. Angelo said the requiem in Latin, finishing with the sign of the cross and "Amen."

"Amen," I echoed, making the sign as well.

There was a long silence as we stared down at the earth. Then Angelo looked up at me. "This Cruddon woman," he began with what seemed to be casual indifference, almost as if he was remarking on the weather. "In the graveyard, she told us that you had killed both her son and her husband…"

I looked him in the eye. "In neither case did I set out to cause their death," I said. "Yet if I had not, both would have killed me."

"You were defending yourself?"

"Yes, I was." I felt he needed further explanation. "The son was a brigand who had stolen the Broken Sword—a valuable talisman—and died on the end of my blade. It was not by my intent, for he ran forward as I held my sword up for protection. For this, the father sought my death, until he was executed for a treason he so wilfully committed."

"I see." His eyes held mine, as if searching for the truth. "And as God is your witness, Mary Fox, your conscience is clear in this matter?"

"It is," I replied. "And yours should be also," I added. "For if that woman had got to her crossbow, she could have killed either one of us. Or both, even." I paused, seeing once again as Joan Cruddon scrambled for her weapon. "That is, if you had not plunged your knife into her side."

He frowned, as if deep in thought. "You have been instrumental in the death of three members of the same family." He raised his head with a troubled look. "We must hope there are no other sons, uncles or cousins who seek further revenge."

"By all the Heavens," I said, appalled at the possibility of yet more murderous Cruddons coming after me. "I do hope not."

He took an old cracked leather pouch from his belt, and carefully put the necklace inside. The bag was decorated with some faded swirling patterns. He noticed me studying them. "These are the markings of the Saxons who first created the jewel," he explained, as we made our way out of the lychgate to our horses.

A few townspeople were walking to and fro along the lane, but none paid us any notice. I mounted Hestia, my faithful mare, and wheeled her round to head out of Norwich. I glanced back over the wall into the graveyard, and stopped as another thought struck me. I had not realised that while we had been busy with the shovel and the necklace, the mists had finally cleared. We were now in bright sunshine, and the monuments we had fought around were plain to see. As was Joan Cruddon's new resting place; the dark earth looking as fresh as a new-formed scar.

"Angelo," I said as he settled into his saddle and gathered his reins. "What if a man has ridden past and looked over this wall? He might have seen any part of what occurred here."

"No, no—it was the thickest fog…" He faltered to a stop, as he realised the same as me. He frowned. "Then we must fear not just members of that woman's family, but perhaps the guardians of the law too? A constable coming for us?"

I swallowed hard. "Yes."

"Then the sooner we are gone from this place, the better it will be." He gave his horse's side a tap with his heel. "Come, let us make haste." There was a flurry of dust as he cantered away.

Instead of following him, I held Hestia back. She pawed at the ground with a snort, as if she felt the urge to follow.

"We must not draw attention to ourselves by charging away," I explained, and she nodded. I patted her neck. "You understand me so well," I whispered, and she gave a small whinny in reply.

A moment later, Angelo must have realised he was alone, for he reined his horse back. I trotted up to his side and explained my concern.

His eyes narrowed, then he nodded. "For sure, Mary," he said. "You speak the truth." He smiled. "I will have to expect such common sense from you if we are to travel together."

"You would have us become travelling companions?" I enquired with a raised eyebrow. "Really? Until a short while ago, you were part of a plot against me." I nudged Hestia forward as if I would walk on alone. He did the same. We were now riding together, our knees almost touching. "In truth," I said, "how do I know I can trust you this time?"

"For sure you can," he replied with a serious-looking frown. "We both have reason to be cautious of the other. But it is better if we stay together, for now we are both in the same danger." He pointed at the sword at my waist. "And I have said you can run me through if I ever play you false again." He paused. "And I meant it."

I did not feel ready to answer this.

As we rode on in silence, our knees brushed together, and he smiled at me. I looked quickly away, suddenly unsure how to respond.

I gave him another quick glance sideways. There was little doubt he had a strong profile, and a noble-looking brow. And his hair did curl about his ear in a most pleasing way... but no! I must be firm. I had resolved to travel alone, and ultimately, that I must do. I should not be distracted from my purpose by this man who had tried to trick me.

No, I should be wary of this—very handsome—Neapolitan...

A sudden thought struck me. "When we shared a room last night, you were well aware that Joan Cruddon was planning to kill me the following day?"

"No, Mary Fox, I did not know that. She told me that she only wanted to frighten you—to throw you in a grave and leave you there a while to realise your errors, before I would be able to pull you out."

He rode on in silence a moment, then he looked hard at me, "I am no murderer," he said, "but maybe a simple fool for believing her lies." He shook his head. "If I had known the truth, I would never have agreed to assist her—even for help in finding *il Fiume di Fuoco*. And…" he paused, looking unsure of himself, then slowed his horse to a stop.

I stopped as well, giving him time to say what was on his mind. "Mary, the more I was with you, the more I realised that the Cruddon woman was mistaken. She told me you were a godless sinner; one who must learn a lesson. She made me believe you were more evil than Satan himself." He patted his horse's neck as if this helped him to think. "But that was not what I saw when we were together. I saw someone who lived only to help others. Someone who made the effort to start learning my language, making me more comfortable in your land. And…" again, he faltered to a stop.

He looked confused, so I raised an enquiring eyebrow, but he seemed as if he would not say what was on his mind. He urged his horse on. As we walked, I decided to let him say more, if or when he was ready.

We passed the last few cottages at the edge of Norwich and emerged onto a forest path. The autumn sun had now reached its highest point, flashing golden beams between the trees as rooks cawed in the high branches.

A thought struck me and I took a sharp breath. If I was found alone and accused of Joan Cruddon's murder, I would undoubtedly hang for it. For who would believe the word of an unnatural girl disguised as a boy? And if some hitherto unknown and vengeful member of the Cruddon family found me, what chance would I have on my own?

That meant it would be better to stay with this man, as he had proposed. To trust that he was now telling the truth, and his remorse was genuine.

But I must remain cold to his charms, and be on my guard at all times.

"I would thank you for throwing that stone, Mary," he said, breaking into my thoughts. "For it saved my life."

"And once again I thank you, Master di Luca, for saving mine," I replied. "With your knife."

There was another period of silence.

"Mary," he said. "I have a suggestion for you."

I said nothing, but hoped my raised eyebrow was enough to make him continue.

"We are both in danger, so I say again, we must travel together. And England is no longer safe for us, so we are best to leave the country as soon as we can. I had planned to ride to Plymouth where I first landed, and take a boat back to Pozzuoli, but now I think it would be better to leave more quickly. Better to sail across to the Low Countries, then make the journey down to Pozzuoli over land. I must return *il Fiume di Fuoco* to my mama before her birthday."

He turned in his saddle and took my arm.

"I have been giving this some thought, Mary Fox. Let us travel to my home together. Come with me to Pozzuoli." He swallowed hard. "You said you wanted to see my land. Well, now you shall."

5
MIO AMORE

Angelo and I arrived in Yarmouth later that evening, having decided to make as quickly as possible for that port rather than the larger, yet more distant, one of Harwich.

But as we dismounted in front of a dockside inn, the reality of our situation overtook our earlier optimism. "We have no certainty of a passage to the Low Countries from here," I observed, looking at the ships moored along the dock. They all seemed too small; suited only to sailing on inland waterways rather than crossing the open seas. "Belike we will need to go to Harwich anyway."

Angelo nodded. "Maybe we will," he said. Then he brightened. "But we should not make any hasty decision. Perhaps a ship to suit our needs will depart in time. We can stay out of sight until then." He glanced at the hordes of seamen coming and going along the dock. Some were hurrying along with their canvas kit bags slung over their shoulders, while others were walking at a more measured pace, talking and laughing together. "There are few who will remark on two more men in a busy place like this."

"We should get rest tonight, then start asking about ships in the morning," I said, as we went inside.

The inn was one large room, crammed with sailors eating, drinking and shouting. After a simple meal, we were shown up to the only dormitory; a room the same size as the tavern below, laid out with rows of pallet beds stretching away down both sides.

I gave a small sigh as we found two at the far end that were empty. "As in Norwich, I am going to have to sleep fully clothed with no privacy." And my chest was going to have to remain bound tight a while longer.

Angelo indicated the few sailors who were already asleep, each a lumpish shape huddled under a thin blanket. Some feet could be seen poking out in shoes, and the occasional back still in a rough shirt and breeches. "Sleeping in their clothes seems to be normal for these men."

"I suppose so." I said as we put our bags down on the hard straw mattresses. I wrinkled my nose. There was no escaping the noisome smell of unwashed bodies, and the rasp of heavy snores. "Let us hope we can be away soon."

After a night of very little sleep, we rose with the dawn and went down to break fast in the crowded tavern.

"Tell me," I said, as Angelo cut himself a slice of gammon, then added some bread and a piece of cheese, "how did the man you found in Ipswich know to direct you to the widow?"

He broke off some bread and chewed it, his eyes holding mine. "My father made enquiries after he and my mother were attacked," he said once he had finished. "He gave a description of the leader of the robbers to a constable. The man I found was the same constable. He knew immediately who I sought from this description."

I traced my finger from my forehead to my cheek. "A scar running from here to here?" I asked. "And a milky white eye?"

He nodded. "A man called Jacob Cruddon—that we have both suffered from, it seems."

"A brigand and a traitor," I agreed.

He took a drink of ale. "I should have realised," he sighed, as he put his tankard down, "if the man is a villain, his wife is also likely to be one."

I gave him a thin smile. "I could have told you that." For a moment I was back in the courtyard of the Ipswich house, hiding while the Cruddons had a chilling discussion on what harms they would do if they found me. "But surely," I asked, frowning as a thought struck me. "If the constable knew Cruddon, why did he not apprehend him at once for the theft?"

Angelo gave me a rueful look. "He seemed most reluctant to do this." He took another drink of his ale. "My father made a guess, that this Cruddon was too wealthy and too powerful to be touched, especially when it was only foreigners who had been robbed." He paused a moment. "And my father was told that is was possible that *il Fiume di Fuoco* would have been broken up already and sold, so there was little point."

"But you thought maybe not, and you would try to find it yourself?" I suggested.

"This is true. I arrived in your town of Ipswich, and was told where to find this Cruddon. But when I came to his house, I was met only by a woman in black who said she was his widow."

"And she told you the necklace was sold," I guessed. "But she offered to help you find the buyer?" He nodded. "So long as you helped her in return, by finding me and bringing me to the graveyard?"

"Correct. You have it." He looked me up and down. "She described you well."

"But why use a different town? Why say it was Norwich?" He gave another smile, as if challenging me to work it out for myself. After a moment I replied, "Ah, yes. If you said a widow from Ipswich wanted my help, I would be suspicious that it might be her. Joan Cruddon."

"You are a clever girl, Mary," he said, a little too loudly.

"Shh!" I hissed. "Here I am a man. You must call me Thomas."

"My apologies, Master Richardson," he said, his eyes twinkling. He leaned forward. "Tell me," he asked softly, "do you ever dress and behave as a woman?"

"It is not my wish," I replied. I leaned forward myself, so our eyes were but a few inches apart, and I could smell his musky scent. His soft lips curled upwards under his beard. For a brief moment, I wondered how it would feel if I leaned in a little more and pressed them to my own. Would he pull back, or would he welcome them? Would they part under mine? And what then?

I gasped and sat back. What of my resolution to stay cold to his charms? No. I must be firm. There must be no place in my heart for him.

He sat back also.

"As I said," I whispered, "here I am a man."

Then I frowned. Where was the troubled look all men seemed to have when faced with such apparent unnaturalness in a woman? But his open expression showed little sign that he had such a concern. "Does it not bother you?" I whispered.

He laughed, showing white teeth. "Certainly not! Why should it?"

"Men think it against nature." I paused. "Against God."

"Then such men are stupid. I have said, I see the woman in you anyway. You have good reason for such behaviour. The priests, they say God is to be feared. But I say 'no—God is good.' He must see this and understand."

I thought back to the men who had tried to win my heart—Sir Reginald de Courtney, Robert Fitzwilliam and Marcus Kytson. All keen in their own way to re-make me as their ideal woman; all seeing me as a potential wife and mother, if only I would conform to their vision of how a woman should present herself. Yet here was this man, who I had known but a few days, prepared to accept me for myself.

"So, you would not seek for me to grow my hair and wear uncomfortable gowns?" I wanted to be sure.

He sat back and shook his head. "No. Not at all. For then you would not be true to your feelings. You would not be you." Then he whispered, "*Mio amore, Maria.*"

I tried to answer, but no words came. It took little Latin to know what '*mio amore*' meant.

My love.

—0—

After we had finished breaking fast we stepped out onto the dock. This was to find the harbour master, and gain information on departing ships—but in truth, my thoughts remained fixed on what

Angelo had just said.

'*Mio amore, Maria.*' The words circled around like autumn leaves swirling in the wind. What had he meant?

I glanced across at him as we walked. His head was held high and he had a firm expression, as if he knew exactly what we must do together. He must have seen my glance, as he looked back at me with a slightly distant smile, as if his mind was elsewhere.

Maybe I was putting too much weight on his words? Maybe it was my understanding that was mistaken? How could I, a girl who had lacked a mother's advice all her life, and who had passed herself off as a boy for much of the last few years, know what a man might say to express his true feeling? And a foreign man at that? Yes; that was it. Perhaps this was just his impulsive Neapolitan way of expressing nothing more than a passing friendship.

I had resolved to keep him out of my heart, so friendship was all we would have. Of that I was certain.

But withal, it was good to know I had found someone who would accept me without trying to change me. Who could see the woman inside, without me needing to wear women's garb. Who would see Mary Fox as an equal, not as a weak-willed woman.

For I had never truly been accepted.

Not by my stepfather, who had hated me from the moment of my birth and my mother's early death. Nor by my three older brothers. They had seen me as a plaything—an amusing little girl who would be a boy like them; one they could teach to fight with a sword. That was until my skills exceeded theirs, and they joined my stepfather in pressuring me to fit the traditional role of the woman of the family; one they could use as a pawn in their chess game of marriage and advancement.

Was that what being a woman in a family meant? It seemed so; for there had been other families that I could have been accepted into. The Fitzwilliams had offered me the warmest welcome—but in return I must marry their son Robert and be mother to his many desired children. The thought made me feel sickened. How long before I, too, died of child-bed fever?

Then there was Lady Kyme, the parent of Prince Henry Fitzroy. She had almost become a true mother to me. But I began to realise that her love rested on my marrying her childhood friend Marcus Kytson. And again, how long before I died giving birth to his children?

Which is why I had said my farewells each time, preferring instead to keep my own company. I had decided I would seek only the gratitude of those I could help, before moving on once again. That way I could keep myself safe from those who would change me. Those who would make me fit their own expectations.

But what of my wish to be alone? Here I was, throwing my lot in with this tall foreigner; a man who now called me '*Mio amore, Maria.*' Heading for his country, where I would be a foreigner myself.

I nodded for my own reassurance. I would stay there a while before heading back to England, once the hue and cry over the death of Joan Cruddon—if there was one—had died down.

Once again, I would say farewell to a man.

That was settled.

With renewed confidence, I stopped an old sailor and asked for the harbour master.

"You will find him just there," the man said, pointing at a small hut just inside a warehouse of stores.

"I thank you sir," I said, and led Angelo across the cobbles.

The harbour master was a small man with chipped wooden teeth, very little hair and skin like tanned leather. He was sitting at a desk made of an old door spanning across two barrels, and was using a dirty quill to scratch some notes into a large ledger. "Good sir," I said, "we seek passage to the Low Countries. Can you tell us if there is a ship bound in that direction any time soon?"

He looked up from his ledger. "The Low Countries, you say, young master? Lemme see, lemme see." He ran his finger down one of the columns on the ledger, then licked it while shaking his head. He turned the page and started down the next column. He stopped and looked up. "Hmm. There is this one. It is called the *Jozefien,* under Pieter de Vries. She is coming in from Den Haag, scheduled to arrive in three days. I expect she will take on a new cargo, then most likely make the journey back to Den Haag two or three days after." He looked a little further down the column. "If you miss her, then there is also the *Jacobus* docking two days later."

"The *Jozefien* sounds perfect," I replied, then paused a moment. "Will she take horses, do you know?" I was not going to leave my Hestia behind if I could help it. I had done so once before, and only found her again by good fortune.

He shrugged. "Most likely." He glanced down at the ledger. "She is a floot—big enough, I would say."

I had heard of these *Fluyt* ships, designed by the Dutch especially for carrying cargo.

I gave thanks to the harbour master, then followed Angelo back out into the autumn morning sunshine.

"Three days," I observed. "All we must do is keep our heads down until then."

He gave a small chuckle. "I am sure we can, Master Richardson."

6

AN OFFER OF HOSPITALITY

After the three days, Angelo and I emerged from our self-imposed hiding in the tavern and boarded the *Jozefien.*

We had spent the time working on my learning of Angelo's Neapolitan language, and I was becoming ever more proficient. I found it easy to understand the Latin beneath it, so comprehension came quickly. As before, I made mistakes on the endings of the words, but Angelo was patient in his corrections, and by the evening of the second day, we were able to converse with more freedom.

"You are doing well," Angelo told me. "With some practice we will have you talking like a native one day. You just need to learn the names for all the things you talk of."

"Keep pointing them out," I said.

"I will," he said. And he was as good as his word; as we left the tavern and walked the horses to the *Jozefien,* he kept pointing to objects and giving me their names, which I repeated. By the time we had gone aboard, I was feeling more and more sure of my command of the language, and eager to keep learning.

"You must talk in my language as much as you can," Angelo observed in English as we walked across the deck. "I will press you to use the words in my tongue, rather than the ones you are used to saying. This way we will make your learning faster."

After making sure the horses were content in their stalls down below, with plenty of mash and water, we went up on deck. "Remember, here I am Thomas," I whispered, using Neapolitan rather than English, as we leaned on the rail and gazed across the harbour towards the open sea beyond. "Not Mary. Or even Maria." I gave Angelo a serious look as I considered my words in his language. "A woman is aboard ship be considered poor luck."

If I had expected him to respond with his usual irreverence, I was pleasantly surprised. "I agree," he said with a serious nod, once he had corrected my clumsy grammar. "Although I warrant the Dutchmen here have less superstition than your typical English sailors—but it is better to be safe than sorry." He stared out across the water a moment, then turned to me. "You say this with feeling. Have you poor experience of such sailors?"

I took a deep breath. "On one voyage I was near thrown overboard when my secret was made known," I said, picking my words in Neapolitan. "And on another I was not exposed, but the ship hit bad luck indeed. She lost a mast in a storm." Saying this brought back bad memories of *The Margarita*. I swallowed hard. "And a good man lost his life."

He put a hand over mine, then withdrew it quickly when I gave him a look of warning. "I hope you do not blame yourself for such ill-fortune?" he asked. "I do not think you share such superstitions?"

"Nay," I muttered, glancing down at his hand. It gave a small twitch, as if he considered replacing it but managed to stop himself. "I do not," I added.

There was a slightly uncomfortable silence as we both gazed across the harbour. It was a mass of scows, wherries and skiffs moving about the water, like ants making frantic activity across a patch of earth. I glanced across at Angelo.

"Do you feel any sorrow at leaving England?" I asked, seeking perhaps to take our conversation into safer waters.

He threw back his head and gave a deep laugh. "Nay," he chuckled. "It is a land of one-armed men, one-eyed thieves and their lying, murderous widows. Why should I feel sorrow at leaving it?" He turned to me with a raised eyebrow. "But you, Ma... Thomas... it is your land. Are you not full of sorrow?"

I stared across the water. A small skiff was leaving the safety of the harbour for the open seas, leaning sharply into the waves as the wind snapped into its gaff-rigged sail.

"I have never before ventured beyond England's shores," I said, "and for sure, I am apprehensive." I turned to him. "It is a step into the unknown for me."

"But you do have the look of a young man who seeks adventure."

I searched his eyes to see if he was making fun of me. But his slight frown seemed to suggest otherwise. "Young man?" I asked softly, turning back to the harbour.

The skiff tacked across the wind with a crack of its sail and leaned the other way.

"Yes…" Angelo said. "If I had not known in truth I was seeking a girl when I first found you, I would have thought it were so. You play this part well."

"Yet you say this does not concern you?"

His eyes creased into a smile; one I was beginning to recognise as his regular manner. "I have said this already. No, it does not." His hand twitched again. "But it concerns you—and greatly—to be taken as a man?" He paused. "Why so?"

How to explain this? Should I even try to tell him what troubled me so deeply? But a quick glance at his concerned look told me he would understand. I took a deep breath. "From the youngest age, I was cast as the woman of the house. It was not a role I wanted, nor even understood how to perform. In fact, I tried hard to be like my brothers. Or better, even. I learned to become more practiced with a sword, and shoot an arrow straighter."

I paused a moment to see his reaction. But he was silent, with his eyes fixed on mine, so I continued. "When I was told I must cast off boyish pursuits and marry a much older man, one who would use me even more harshly than my stepfather, I ran away." I drew a breath to steady myself. "And perhaps I have been running ever since."

Again, he was silent, seeming to encourage me to keep going.

"I have met a number of men," I said, "who have sought to change me into their ideal woman. It is not my wish, and it troubles me that this is the only way I can be accepted…" I faltered to a stop and stole a glance to see how he was taking this.

He nodded slowly. "I understand. But I must tell you, it is not a problem for me. God, he looks at you and I believe he sees a good person. The clothing you wear; the cut of your hair," he shook his head. "These things are not of consequence." He looked across at me. "If they do not trouble the good Lord, why should they trouble me?"

I wanted so desperately to put my hand over his; to show him how much I valued his honesty. But the many Dutchmen moving about the deck behind us would most likely see it as two unnatural men and cast us ashore. I only said, "You put it so clearly. Thank you."

—0—

The following afternoon the *Jozefien* docked in the Netherlands port of Den Haag.

It was a hive of activity, just like every port I had seen so far; but this one boasted many more ships than I could possibly have believed. I stood at the rail as we came slowly into the dock, gazing in wonder at the deep forest of masts, spars and furled sails that seemed to extend as far as I could see on either side. Ropes sounded like volleys of arquebus fire as they cracked against masts in the breeze. Men of all sizes and colours swarmed up and down rigging, balancing on spars and running along decks, all calling out in so many different tongues that I was put in mind of the story of the Tower of Babel. I caught the sound of some words that I recognised in English and French, but mostly it was that hoarse, guttural tongue of the Dutch that I had heard so much on the *Jozefien* as we had made our way across the—thankfully calm—seas from Yarmouth.

Dutch was a tongue I had found difficult on my ear. I had spent much time on the voyage standing at the rail, keeping well apart from the sailors and their ropes, listening to their calls and doing my best to make out what they were saying. I had decided

54

that the *grootzeil* was the main sail, and when the order came '*het grootzeil trimmen*', it was to draw it in tighter, to make better way from the wind. The well-built fellow standing at the whipstaff, pushing it one way or the other to make the ship steer, was referred as '*Meneer Stuurman*'—leading me to conclude that '*Meneer*' meant 'Mister'.

I had been standing at the rail earlier that morning when a well-dressed man with a stone-grey beard came across and stood at my side.

"You are Englishman, *ja*?" he asked.

I nodded, swept off my cap and bowed. "Thomas Richardson, of the county of Essex."

He did the same. "Pieter de Vries, Master of the *Jozefien*."

I had seen him earlier, standing at the upper deck rail issuing instructions, so I had assumed he was in command, but this confirmed it. I waved a hand across the wide expanse of deck. "She is a fine ship, *Meneer* de Vries." I hoped I was right about the word's meaning. "Thank you for allowing my companion and myself passage."

He smiled. "You speak *Nederlandse taal*?" he asked.

I shook my head. "No, but I have been listening, and, I hope, learning a few words."

"It is a fine thing in a young man, to listen and learn," he said, nodding slowly. "I respect that." He paused a moment, studying me carefully. "I saw you when you came aboard yesterday and booked your passage with one of my officers. You were with a tall, dark-eyed man." It sounded like a question; as if he were casting a net for information.

"Yes, Master di Luca. He is resting in the cabin we were allocated below."

"I see. And what is your business in Nederland—you and Master di Luca?"

"We are travelling through, on our way to the Kingdom of Napoli."

He raised an eyebrow. "That is a long journey."

I shrugged. "Indeed. But we have four months—enough time."

"And you will stay in coaching inns or taverns along the way?"

"Yes," I replied. "As we find them."

"Then you will surely become tired of such hostelries." He paused. "Sadly, travellers are not well served by these places in my land."

I thought of the one in Yarmouth, and decided not to tell him that the hostelries in England must surely be worse than anything in the Nederlands.

He nodded, as if he had reached a decision. "You have been welcome guests on board the *Jozefien*. Most travellers are wearisome folk, who treat the ship as a nuisance, but I see you and Master di Luca have spent much time up on deck, enjoying the air and treating my sailors with the greatest respect. You will allow me to continue the hospitality for at least the first night or two of your long journey? I invite you to stay as my welcome guests in my house in Den Haag."

I looked out across the rail to the far horizon. If I said 'yes', I was sure Angelo would also agree. No doubt as master of a fine ship, Pieter de Vries's house would be extremely comfortable. And how much better than sharing a room in a lowly tavern? There would be plenty of opportunities for that over the next months.

"It would be most kind," I said. "Are you sure?"

"Our Lord bids us offer hospitality to those in need," he said with a serious look.

"Then we are honoured to accept."

7
ENTRAPMENT

Pieter de Vries's house was a fine place. It was tall and narrow, like the houses crowded on either side, and was painted a deep burnt ochre. The front wall seemed to rise up beyond the top floor and was shaped like a plum pudding with curved sides and white copings.

"That is called a gable," de Vries said, as we halted our horses and I stared up at the roofline. "They are most common on houses here." I glanced along the row, and could only agree—almost every house had such a gable. The only exception was the one directly beside de Vries's house, which was the last of the row. It was only a single storey high, and had a more normal pitched roof facing edge-outwards, with a deep inward curve to its profile. A round window was set into the wall just below the eaves.

"That is where the horses are stabled for all these houses," de Vries told me. "Come," he added as we dismounted and a groom came out to fetch our horses, "I am most anxious to introduce you to my family."

Just as he turned to usher us into the house, there was a yell from behind us, followed by many voices cheering. We all turned, to see a man in black pulling at a ragged-looking girl, who was down on her knees. He was holding one end of a rope, with the other end bound round the girl's wrists. She was perhaps the same age as me, with matted hair uncovered, wearing only a torn and filthy grey shift. He yelled again; something in Dutch which I took to be an order to get up, then gave the rope a sharp pull. The girl's arms snapped forward, and she fell onto her face. The crowd of men and women who were following gave another cheer, as the man in black pulled once more on the rope. This time he dragged the girl bodily across the cobbles.

Instinctively wanting to help, I started to move towards her. De Vries put a hand out to stop me.

"Please, *Meneer*, let them alone," he said quietly, but with a hard edge to his voice. "This is a girl accused on the strongest evidence of witchcraft. She is being taken to the square to be burned."

"God have mercy," Angelo said.

"She is beyond God's mercy," de Vries replied. "Witchcraft is the work of the Devil. Such unnatural women must be burned." Then he smiled. "But it is no matter. These things are dealt with and that is the end of it. Come," he added, as if the scene in the street was naught but a mild diversion. "As I said, I would like you to meet my wife and daughter."

I glanced at Angelo and got a reassuring smile. Then he shook his head as if to say, *you must forget this; it is none of our business.*

I took a breath as we went in, trying to clear my head of the scene outside. As Angelo said, it was none of our business. But for all that, it disturbed me greatly that these people were so ready to see witchcraft in unusual behaviour.

Heaven only knew what they would make of me if they found out I was not the man I claimed to be.

On that disturbing thought, I followed de Vries inside.

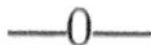

The parlour walls were painted in an even heavier shade of the same ochre as the outside. A dark table stood in the middle of the room, with two chairs on each side and a carver at the end with turned arms. A fine twisted-stem glass and a pewter platter were placed before each chair, all glinting in the bright light that streamed in from the single window. On one wall was a tapestry showing a ship at sea, looking remarkably like the *Jozefien*. On the opposite wall were two portrait paintings; one of a stern-looking man and the other of an even grimmer-looking woman, both in austere clothing. A plain wooden cross hung above these pictures, and more crosses hung on the other walls.

A door at the far end opened and a woman walked in. She was wearing an elegant peach gown with large embroidered shoulders and full skirts. Her hair was greying under her felt cap, but she looked as if she had such a great joy for life that it gave her a more youthful appearance.

"Pieter!" she exclaimed, coming up to him and giving a small curtsey. Then she stopped as she noticed me and Angelo. She asked him something in Dutch, which I took to be a question as to who these two strangers were.

"*Meneer* Richardson and *Meneer* di Luca," he replied. Angelo and I both removed our caps and bowed. "*Meneer Richardson is Engels, en meneer di Luca is Napolitaans*," he added as his wife made the same curtsey to us. "My wife, Jozefien," he said.

She smiled prettily, and it seemed clear to me that she had not a word of English. I glanced at the tapestry—wondering if it was just a coincidence, or if the *Jozefien* ship was named for his wife. From the look of pride on the master's face, I guessed it probably was.

Jozefien held up a finger, as if to say, 'wait a moment', then went out again. A shout came from beyond the door; "Adriana! Adriana!" This was followed by some Dutch words that sounded as if she was summoning this person to come down.

There was the sound of a foot on the stair, then Jozefien came back in, followed by a slight girl in a similar style of gown. The girl had her head lowered, so I could see nothing but the top of her uncovered auburn hair. She walked up to Angelo and curtseyed. He bowed, then she turned and looked me full in the face.

Adriana de Vries was maybe fifteen or sixteen years old. Her skin had a delicate, almost ethereal look, as if an angelic spirit had come down to earth and been recast in the finest porcelain. "Thomas Richardson," I said as I bowed, "at your service, Mistress de Vries." Her bright blue eyes widened briefly, and her lips parted to show perfect white teeth. "*Meneer* Richardson," Adriana whispered as she gave me a curtsey, then dropped her head again and stepped back to her mother's side. She looked up quickly as I replaced my cap, then away again as she saw I was watching.

Pieter de Vries said, "Please, we will now eat." He rang a small hand bell. Then he indicated where we should each place ourselves, before standing at the head of the table. A moment later a girl in a black dress with a white cap bustled in with a carafe. She served us each with wine, before giving de Vries a little bow and leaving again.

"We prefer to eat plainly, in recognition of the simple life of our Lord," de Vries observed. "And we will now say grace." He glanced at one of the crosses on the wall, then bowed his head and spoke quite a few words in Dutch, ending with 'amen'. Angelo and I joined with Jozefien and Adriana in saying 'amen', and we all sat.

De Vries took a sip of wine. "Our choice is simple; bread, cheese, mutton and fruits of the season. I trust that will be acceptable?"

I glanced at Angelo, hoping this would not start him on one of his condemnations of non-Neapolitan foods—but thankfully he stayed silent, although I fancy there was a small twinkle in his eye. "Of course, that is most welcome," he said.

"We are grateful for your kind hospitality," I added.

The maid returned with a platter containing the foods de Vries had mentioned, including what I took to be a cheese wrapped in a smooth red waxy cover. There was also a bowl piled high with apples.

Once we all had food on our platters, Adriana turned to her father. "*Wat zei meneer Richardson?*" she asked, looking back at me while winding a finger in her hair. De Vries answered her, and there was some further conversation in Dutch between the three of them.

While they spoke, Angelo leaned in to my ear. "I may be mistaken," he whispered, "but I rather think that young Adriana finds Master Richardson of some interest."

"By the Heavens," I replied in the same low tone. "I do hope not."

The Dutch conversation stopped, and de Vries looked across at us. "My wife has asked where you are headed, and I have said it is to the Kingdom of Napoli." He smiled at us both. "My daughter now wishes to know how long you will stay with us, before you start on your long journey?"

I took a sip of wine and Adriana again gave me a shy glance. Angelo replied with the mock-seriousness that he seemed to use when he was, in truth, being quite mischievous, "We have no need to be hasty in starting," he said. "And I am sure Master Richardson will agree, it will be most welcome if we can enjoy your kind hospitality for a few more days."

Naturally, Master Richardson did not agree, and the thought of becoming the object of a young girl's unwelcome fixation left Master Richardson feeling quite cold. But there was little I could now do, so I just smiled, muttered something about that being most kind, and took a long draught of wine to settle my nerve. Was Adriana really showing interest, as Angelo had said? Certainly the way she looked at me suggested some level of regard...

Adriana said something to her father, and he raised an eyebrow. She said it again, but this time with more force. He frowned, and replied with what appeared to be a denial. Then Jozefien added her part, which seemed as if she were endorsing her daughter's request. De Vries looked at each in turn; his wife with a stern set of her brow, and his daughter with a look of girlish hope. Then he gave a small sigh, as if this was not the first time he had been overruled by his women. Perhaps it was the sigh of a father used to indulging his daughter's every wish. He nodded slowly and said something back in Dutch. He turned to me, just as I took another drink of wine. "My daughter has made a request," he said, with an almost apologetic smile. "She has a keenness to learn some words of English. She asks if you will be kind enough to give her some lessons while you are here."

I forced myself to swallow the wine before replying, lest I spray it in shock across the table.

But it was Angelo who answered, before I could gather my

breath. "Certainly," he said with a smile. "Master Richardson has a gift for language. He has even spent time learning to converse in my Neapolitan. I am sure he will be delighted to help Mistress de Vries take a firm hold of his English tongue."

—0—

I tapped my finger on my chest. "My name is Thomas," I said carefully. Then I pointed at Adriana. "What is your name?"

"Mine name ish Adriana," she replied, with equal care.

"It is 'my' not 'mine'," I explained. "My name is Adriana," I said it slowly, emphasising each word.

She gave a small girlish giggle and punched me gently on the shoulder. "You is not Adriana!" She tapped her chest "I is Adriana!" She pushed her finger into my arm. "You is boy."

I sat back beside her, easily resisting the temptation to put her right on this as well.

It was the third day since we had arrived, and this was now our fifth lesson. I glanced across at Jozefien. She was working on some embroidery in the corner, as she had for all the previous sessions. Much as I understood the need for a chaperone, my concern was more for her to protect me from Adriana's advances, rather than the other way round. The girl was now taking every opportunity to make physical contact—either with such playful punches on my shoulder, or with a hand on my arm. It was hard not to admonish her, but I was not sure if such behaviour was acceptable in the Netherlands. And because I had not reacted immediately, Adriana was now taking every opportunity to touch me. Heaven knows what young Dutch girls are taught, but surely no English girl would behave in such a way?

The first session had started on an uncomfortable note, with neither of us being able to make ourselves understood, and for a brief moment I thought perhaps Adriana would abandon this foolish notion of English lessons. But Jozefien had fetched Pieter to help interpret, and through him I was able to establish some

62

basic communication, especially as many Dutch words sounded similar to their English counterparts. Gradually we became less dependent on him, and by this lesson, he had excused himself and left us to it. Without him there, Adriana had become even more confident, turning from a nervous little mouse into a more assured young woman.

One who thought it perfectly acceptable to punch her teacher on the arm.

Jozefien had her head down over her tambour frame, stitching carefully. Eventually the silence between me and Adriana must have filtered through, and she looked up with an enquiring expression. She said something to her daughter and Adriana replied. Jozefien nodded, smiled warmly at me, then went back to her work.

"*Mijn mama…*" Adriana began.

"My mother?" I suggested.

"*Ja, ja…* My mother… she ish *blij…*" she made an exaggerated smile, showing her perfect little teeth.

"Happy?" I suggested. I pointed at a smile of my own. "Happy."

She nodded. "My mother ish happy… that you… learn me English."

I shook my head. "…That you *are teaching* me English," I corrected her.

"*Ja.* And I am happy too," she leaned over and put her hand on my arm, then smiled up at me. "That you are teaching me English."

I took a breath to stop myself from flinching, then carefully moved my arm away, picking up one of the glasses on the table. "We must now learn some more words," I said, desperate for some diversion. "This is a… goblet."

She put her hands together on her lap and gave me a look of such purity and innocence that I struggled to stop myself from laughing. "Goblet," she said, nodding with exaggerated seriousness.

"Well done," I replied with a smile.

It seemed that she could not keep her mask any longer. She clapped her hands and took the glass from me. "Goblet, Mama!" she exclaimed. "*Dit is een* goblet!"

Pieter came in, and she held it out to him. "*Een* goblet, Papa! *Geen beker maar* goblet!"

"In English, Adriana," he said. "Are you saying that this is not a *beker*, but a goblet?"

"Yes, Papa!"

Pieter took it. "I must thank you, *Meneer* Richardson," he said. "My daughter seems to be enjoying these lessons greatly." He put the goblet back on the table. "I only wish I had your knowledge and skill as a teacher. Unfortunately my English is too basic. I fear I would give her all the wrong words."

"Your English is excellent, Master de Vries," I replied, as if that might prompt him to take over the role of teacher. But he smiled vaguely and said something to his wife. She nodded, put down her embroidery, said a few words to her daughter and followed him out of the room.

Adriana and I were now alone.

Surely she would not take advantage of this?

She gave me a slow, calculating smile that sent a chill through my bones.

"*Meneer* Richardson," she began. "I am happy you teach me English. I am like this very much." She moved closer.

"That is good," I gasped, shuffling my chair away. "You are learning well."

She pushed her own chair back towards mine. "I am like *you* very much, *Meneer* Richardson," she whispered. "Thomas. You are first real man not boy I meet. I am most happy with this."

She put her hand over mine. I gave a small yelp and snatched it away. Her touch had scorched me, as if it were a flame.

But whatever Dutch girls are taught, it seems they are not informed how to understand social signals. Adriana appeared to take this as me being coy, as if I were some callow youth myself.

Instead of retreating, she moved even closer.

She pulled my head round so we were only a few inches apart.

She smiled again, her eyes narrowing with a burning intensity that was truly frightening. It was as if I was staring into the eyes of a wildcat; one about to leap on an unfortunate mouse.

A moment later, that is exactly what she did.

Suddenly her lips were clamped over mine.

I tried to get away, but with surprising strength for such a slight girl, she held my head firm as she pressed down. My struggles seemed only to encourage her, for she kept up the pressure, her lips working against mine. Try as I could, I was not able to push her away.

There was a sudden high-pitched woman's scream. "Adriana!"

The girl pulled apart, her eyes now seeming consumed with panic rather than passion. She sat back, her face flushed red, as her mother came up.

Gone was the smiling woman of before. Jozefien de Vries's face was a twisted, bloodless mask. For a few moments, she stared in silence, her eyes snapping at each of us in turn.

It was like a dam building up the pressure of a flood.

Then, with sickening inevitability, the dam burst. And like the waters cascading over the breach, a string of screaming accusations broke over her daughter in an angry wave. As they did so, Adriana's head sank lower and lower.

Eventually Jozefien seemed to run out of invective. She ended with a question, her hands on her hips. At this Adriana looked up, gave a strangled-sounding whisper, then lifted a trembling finger.

And pointed at me.

I felt the hairs on my neck stand up.

I stood as well. "I am sorry, Mistress de Vries, but..." was as far as I got, before Jozefien released another long string of Dutch at me. Then she screamed towards the door, "Pieter! Pieter! *Kom hier nu!*"

Without having the words to defend myself, I could only wait for Pieter.

There was an excruciating silence; a truly painful scene. I was glaring at Adriana, while her mother was doing the same at me. The girl herself did not return my stare; appearing instead to study the toes of her slippers with great interest. After what seemed like an age, there was a growl in Dutch and Pieter came in. He was closely followed by Angelo, who looked at me with a raised eyebrow.

De Vries demanded something of his wife, who seemed to repeat her accusations, pointing at me. He turned to his daughter and asked something of her. She just gave him a small nod, but said nothing.

Then he turned to me.

"Richardson," he snarled, "I find you have made a great abuse of my hospitality. My daughter says you have forced yourself on her, like a filthy beast. Like the very devil himself." He glared at me with a curled lip. "What of this, Richardson?"

I opened my mouth to reply, then stopped. What could I say? That his daughter was both a wanton and a liar? It would be my word against hers—and it looked as if in her own house, she would be the one to be believed.

I closed my mouth again and said nothing.

I caught Angelo's eye over de Vries's shoulder. He gave a small shrug—as if to say this was indeed an impossible situation, for if we revealed the truth of who I really was, this god-fearing family would no doubt have me arrested for being a witch. And we had already seen what the Dutch did to those they accused of such practice.

"If we were at sea," de Vries was saying, "I would have you held secure while we decide what is to be done." He tapped his finger on the table a moment, then he seemed to come to a decision. "And this is what I will do. Come, you." He moved round the table and took hold of my sleeve, then pulled so sharply that I almost fell. "Come, I say!"

He dragged me past Jozefien, who looked away. Adriana continued to stare downwards. Only Angelo caught my eye, giving me a small nod—I hoped of reassurance that he would think of something. He had better—if he had not encouraged Adriana to have me as a teacher, none of this might have happened.

De Vries pulled me along the passageway to a small door. He drew back the bolt and opened up, to reveal a pitch-black room down a few steps.

He threw me inside and slammed the door shut.

As I tried to stop myself falling headlong, there was the sound of the bolt being locked.

I was alone in the darkness.

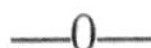

The room was, I believe, a cellar and a cool store for the household foods. Once I had found my feet and regained some small amount of composure, I made an exploration. It did not take long, for it was no bigger than five paces in each direction. My fingertip search revealed that each wall was composed of a set of shelves. Some held large, round objects with a waxy surface that I took to be the cheeses we had been served at each meal. Others had breads and bowls of apples. On one wall there were shelves containing only earthenware flagons—presumably wine and ale. At least I would not starve or want for drink.

I took an apple and ate it as I considered my position.

Adriana's childish decision to avoid her parents' anger by blaming me had clearly been accepted. But it might not stand up to scrutiny, for she had been pressing down on me when her mother came in, not the other way around. Belike Jozefien would recall this when she gave it more thought, and maybe come to the conclusion that her daughter was not as innocent as she made herself out to be. But then again, maybe not. Maybe Adriana had wanted to be caught in such an indecent position. Heaven forbid she had actually planned the whole thing?

Then there was Angelo. Would he make a strong argument on my part, as he seemed to indicate? To make amends for his mischievous connivance? The truth of my masquerade as Thomas would surely reassure him that I would hardly have been the instigator of the whole unfortunate incident. But would he be believed, any more than I would have been? At least he should try. Perhaps his argument would make Jozefien recall what she had really seen.

On that thought, I decided I should at least sit down, lest I may be in this place for some time.

There was a part of the wall that had no shelves, so I settled on the floor with my back to it and finished the apple.

The flagstones beneath me were painfully cold, so I got up and made another fingertip search of the shelves. Eventually I came upon something soft, that had the roughness of a folded sack. Further exploration revealed there were several of these. With a small grin of triumph, I used them to make my bottom a little less cold, and settled against the wall.

As I stared into the darkness, there was nothing to distract my mind, other than the heavy smell of breads, meats and cheese.

I had a sudden thought. These were the family's regular foods. Someone would need to come down and fetch new provisions in no more than a few hours. Then I would either be released, or maybe have a chance to make my bid for freedom.

On that thought, I must have drifted off to sleep.

—0—

A sudden metallic noise made me come awake. While I was trying to understand where I was, the door swung open and the light of a candle filtered down.

As I struggled to my feet, my predicament came back to me.

The candle flickered down the steps, illuminating de Vries's stern face as a series of harsh shapes and sharp shadows. It gave him the look of an evil gargoyle.

He stopped at the foot of the stair and held the candle up. I could now see how small the cellar was, and how the shelves were

68

tightly stacked with food and drink.

"Richardson," he growled. "Jozefien and I have discussed your actions, and we have reached a conclusion as to how we must proceed."

I said nothing, dreading to hear.

"We could have you arraigned and cast into jail," he continued. "And I was first of the mind that we must do so. But my daughter made a plea for some clemency."

How good of her.

"I also considered pressing you onto my ship for the next voyage. Perhaps a life at sea as a lowly seaman might teach you not to impose yourself on defenceless girls." He gave a mirthless laugh. "But your companion *Meneer* di Luca spoke well against that idea. So no, we have decided that there is in truth, only one true action we can take."

Again, I remained silent.

"This is not ideal; indeed, I must say it sickens me, but both my wife and Adriana approve. So I have agreed that this is what will happen." He took a breath. "You have forced yourself on my daughter. You have violated her sanctity, as well as my honour." He paused. The candle flickered, almost as if it was also affected by my supposed actions. "We are taught in the bible that this results in two necessary outcomes," he continued, his voice flat. "The first is that you pay me fifty pieces of silver."

He stopped, so I found my voice.

"And the second?" Although I fear I recalled from past sermons on the book of Deuteronomy what this would be.

He gave a deep sigh. "The second," he said, "is that you will be married to her tomorrow."

8

ANGELO'S PLAN

I was left in the cellar for what seemed like many more hours, until de Vries returned and led me upstairs to the parlour, where Adriana, Jozefien and Angelo were waiting. I found myself blinking owlishly as the afternoon light streamed in through the window, and was acutely aware that I presented a sorry sight after my time in captivity. I brushed my hands down my jerkin, as if to remove any possible dust or cobwebs, or perhaps even a stray spider that had managed to escape with me.

Adriana looked down, with what I hoped was some measure of contrition. But then she looked up and I was surprised to see she had an expression of triumph on her delicate little face. Her lips were parted, and her pale cheeks were unusually flushed. I caught her eye and gave a small frown, to make it clear that I was fully aware of her lies, and could not—would not—countenance such a brazen act of entrapment. I expected she would again hang her head, but instead her lips parted further, and she gave me a wicked little smile.

The wanton child had played me for a fool!

Her smile broadened at my reaction, sending a chill down my spine. I could see now that my suspicions in the cellar had been correct; she had indeed planned the whole thing. She had most likely sought to entrap me into this appalling marriage as early as that first day, when she had initially asked me to teach her English. It was the perfect opportunity to get me alone, once her mother had trusted me enough to leave us.

Her eyes narrowed and her pink tongue darted out and ran across her top teeth. She was telling me plainly that she had won; that I had become the answer to whatever girlish fantasy lived in her head. I gave a small gasp at this obvious lack of propriety. No English girl would behave this way—at least not any that I knew.

Although to be fair, I did not know that many.

I turned to Jozefien, seeking any understanding that none of this was my doing. But her normally open, friendly face was clouded over, as if another thunderstorm was building.

I bowed and took off my cap. "Mistress de Vries," I began, preparing to say something along the lines of how my sorrow at (supposedly) causing this situation was tempered with my joy at becoming her son-in-law, when she held up a hand.

"*Meneer* Richardson," she said; the words snapping out as if nails were being scraped down a washboard, then she followed it up with a stream of Dutch.

I looked round to de Vries for a translation, although in truth, I could guess the meaning from the depth of her frown and the way her foot struck the floor with almost every word. She was saying that I was far from her ideal son-in-law, and the circumstances of the betrothal were not as she would have wished them for her only daughter.

De Vries took a more practical approach. "Richardson," he snapped, and I noted that I no longer qualified for the honorific '*Meneer*', "now we have agreed on this course of action; one which I note pleases only God and my daughter, we will carry it through on the morrow. Then you will be wed, and we will try to accept you into the family." He paused, observing me as if I were a piece of grime on his shoe. Then he seemed to force a thin smile. "Who knows, perhaps one day you will prove yourself worthy of this honour, and even become father to my grandchildren."

There was a small snort from Angelo, which he tried to cover with a cough. He had one of his amused smiles; and it seemed clear that he was not taking this dreadful situation seriously enough, despite his part in its cause. I shot him an accusing look. However bad things were now, they would be many, many times worse once my truth was discovered—as it must surely be at some point. The thought of Adriana expecting her conjugal rights and discovering that her husband was in fact a woman made my blood run cold.

And that alone was not as bad as what would come next; being dragged, bound and wretched, to the market square, where a pyre would await me.

De Vries took his wife and daughter to one side, and they started talking fast in Dutch. Angelo used the opportunity to put his hand on my shoulder. "I have a plan," he whispered. "You must do exactly as I say, and we can get away from this."

My heart leapt and I gave him a nod. "What must I do?" I asked.

"Wait. Just agree when I make a suggestion."

I nodded again, allowing a small flutter of hope to rise in my chest. De Vries came back. "We must make this official," he said. "You must offer Adriana a *knottedoek* of coins. Adriana, fetch a cloth. I will need to knot it myself, as Richardson is not used to our ways." Then he said something in Dutch, which I took to be the translation, and she scampered off, returning shortly after with a square of white linen. Her father spread it out on the table. "You need a few coins—three will do." I reached into my purse and took out three coins. Adriana's eyes opened wide at the sight of all the gold, and I could see she was calculating just how rich I was.

"Place them in the middle." De Vries then made a complicated knot, securing the coins inside. "Now give this to Adriana. If she accepts it, then you are officially betrothed."

I handed it over to the girl, hoping against hope that she might now refuse it, but I was not to be so fortunate. She took it in one hand, while the other was clasped to the middle of her chest. "*Ja,*" she breathed, "*Ja, ja.*" There was a small cry from her mother, which I took not to be one of joy. Then Adriana reached up and gave me a small kiss on the cheek.

"It is now official," her father said.

"Then let us men go and celebrate," Angelo suggested. "We must drink to the health of the happy couple." He gave me a small, but significant glance.

"Absolutely," I agreed.

"And I suggest we leave the womenfolk to their own plans for the morrow," Angelo added. "*Meneer* de Vries, is there a tavern nearby, where we can celebrate with a drink?"

"That is indeed a good idea," replied the Dutchman. "The women will have much to do, and I would know more of my new son." He gave me a thin smile. "There is a tavern close by. Come, and I will lead you."

We left the house and stepped out onto the street. I took a deep breath, seeking to clear my head after my time in the cellar, and the shock of finding that my customary man's garb had led me to this awful situation. How had I made such an impression on Adriana, that she so quickly decided to entrap me into marriage? In truth, I must have appeared as a confident young man but a few years older than her. Perhaps I just happened to fit whatever girlish notion she had of the ideal husband. Most unfortunate, that I was in the wrong place at the wrong time. Pretending to be a different person.

With luck, Angelo's plan would be the way to get us out of this.

I looked up and down the street. We were on one side of a canal, with a bridge around a hundred yards to our left. De Vries set off at a fast pace, with Angelo close behind. I caught him up, and tugged on his sleeve. He slowed down until we were a few feet back.

"What is your plan?" I hissed.

"You will see. Just go with what I say."

De Vries looked round. "It is not far," he said, and crossed the bridge. We followed him down a side street to a building which looked just like an ordinary house in a similar row as de Vries's. It was two stories high and topped by the same gable roof. He climbed the steps and pushed open the door.

Inside, it was similar in layout to his house, except that the parlour was much bigger. It was full of tables, with men sitting at each. They all had large heavy-looking pewter tankards in front of them, topped with hinged lids. They were pulling back with their thumbs on the lid to open it every time they took a drink.

I glanced enquiringly at Angelo. He gave me a smile, which I took to be one of reassurance, as de Vries took a seat and bade us sit on either side.

A hard-faced woman in black appeared, and de Vries ordered drinks. Then he settled back in his chair. "I am aware that this match has come as a surprise to us all," he began. "And I have made it plain it is not to my liking. But after what has happened, it is as God has ordained. His word is very clear on this point, and to go against His will would imperil all our souls. So we must accept that it is for the best." He took a deep breath. "So now, *Meneer* Richardson—Thomas—tell me of yourself."

I gave him a tale of my upbringing as near to the truth as possible, except that I told it as the story of a boy not a girl. Angelo watched me closely as I talked, his amused smile never far from his mouth.

The beers arrived just as I finished, bringing a welcome opportunity to end the dryness that formed in my mouth while I talked. But when I moved my hand towards the tankard, Angelo gave me the tiniest shake of his head. He was telling me not to drink.

"I see." De Vries pushed his thumb on the hinge of his tankard and took a long draught. "And you told me aboard the ship that you and *Meneer* di Luca were headed for the Kingdom of Napoli?"

"We are… were," I corrected myself, realising that it would no longer be seemly for a man to abandon his new wife so readily.

Unless, of course, he must.

"Indeed." De Vries took another draught. "Then I assume *Meneer* di Luca will continue his journey without you?"

Angelo gave him an easy smile. "Naturally, *Signore* de Vries. I would not dream of depriving the delightful *Signorina* Adriana of her new husband's company." He patted me on the arm. "It is of no matter, Thomas. I will go on alone."

My mouth was now so dry that I could feel my tongue sticking to the roof. I glanced at Angelo then at my tankard, and again got the smallest shake of his head.

Then, with a rush of relief, I realised what his plan was.

It was for de Vries to become drunk, while we stayed sober. Then we might have an opportunity to escape! But surely the man would suspect something if we did not touch a drop? I narrowed my eyes at Angelo, then glanced again at our tankards, trying to tell him that we must at least drink something. By good fortune he seemed to understand me, and he raised his own tankard.

"*Signore* de Vries, let us drink the health of your fine daughter and her betrothed, Thomas Richardson. May they have a long and happy life together."

De Vries pushed back his lid and downed a long, deep draught. Angelo took what I thought to be the smallest sip, for all he made a great show of drinking, wiping his beard and putting his tankard down with a flourish. I did the same, glad of the chance to free my tongue from its captivity. The beer had a crisp, nutty flavour that was quite pleasant, and which I found refreshing—but it was clear now that I must not drink anything more than the tiniest amount. Not least because even the smallest drop was making my head start to spin.

Angelo clapped de Vries on the back. "You are also to be congratulated, *Signore,*" he said. "For your daughter has made a good match in young Thomas here." As the Dutchman turned his head to give me a long look that spoke not so much of the quality of the match; more of its distaste, Angelo swapped their two tankards. "Your health!" he continued, and drank the toast. "I suppose," de Vries admitted with another frown in my direction, but then he picked up his tankard and drank with us. He did not seem to notice that his drink had miraculously replenished itself; by good fortune, and no doubt the weight of the pewter and the fact of the lid, he most likely felt little difference.

"Tell me," Angelo asked when we were once more settled.

"How are you not again at sea in your fine ship? For sure," he added, "it was our good fortune to enjoy your hospitality. But unexpected."

I gave him a small frown; concerned that he was perhaps over playing his part. Never had hospitality been so little enjoyed. Surely de Vries was not yet so drunk that he would overlook this blatant untruth? But perhaps the strength of this beer was having the desired effect, and the comment seemed to pass.

"She is my ship, not owned by any other. So I have decided that after every second sailing, I will take a few days to be with my family."

"But does it not cost you in lost trade?" I asked, mindful of my stepfather's anger if a voyage in one of his ships was delayed by even a day. De Vries nodded. "For sure," he answered. "But God grants me enough to live in comfort."

"Then you are good at trade," Angelo observed, drawing the other's attention away so I could change tankards with my own. "That is something I have not yet mastered."

"*Ja*,"

Angelo raised his beer. "I drink to you, Captain, for you have made your trade and your life fit neatly with each other."

When we all drank, de Vries seemed to drain his completely. Angelo waved briefly at the hard-faced woman, and indicated more beers. Shortly after, three more tankards were placed before us. De Vries got through all of his, and, by some further unseen changes by me and Angelo, most of ours as well. At one point he had to stagger off to find the jakes, allowing us to refill his tankard from our original ones as well.

It was clear when he made his unsteady way back to our table, that all the beer was having the desired effect. By the time he finished the tankard, his speech had become slurred, and it looked as if lead weights were now attached to his eyelids.

It was time to make our next move.

9
COLD, DARK EYES

Angelo waved at the hard-faced woman, and when she marched across, he handed her a few coins from his purse. She grunted something in Dutch as she pointed at de Vries, which I took to mean we should get him home. Angelo and I stood either side of him, lifted him by the arms, and marched him out of the building.

Once we were outside in the cool darkness of the night, it took little effort to find a quiet doorway in which to sit the now sleeping de Vries. He slumped down where we placed him; his head lolling to one side. There was even a snore as we glanced about to ensure we were unobserved, then made our way quietly back to the bridge.

"I warrant he will soon be found and returned to his family," Angelo muttered as we hurried back along the canal-side to the house. "But with luck, we will be far away by then." He stopped and put his hand on my shoulder. "We must get the horses if we are to make good our escape." I nodded. The thought of abandoning Hestia was too much to consider. "As quiet as you can when we get to the stables, Maria," he whispered. "The house is right beside. If we are overheard, then all will be lost." I nodded slowly, the reality of discovery now making my belly feel leaden.

What if we were found, skulking like thieves in the night for the horses? This time, I would not be thrown into a convenient cellar; one full of food. No—the constable, or whoever the Dutch had in such a position—would be called, and it would be a gaol cell for me, or even the stocks. I shivered. And with that would come my unmasking as a woman—and no doubt the forced march to the town square and the stake.

I felt bile rising in my throat.

Then we must not be overheard.

We arrived at the house and stopped. The windows seemed like eyes watching us approach. Some even had candles flickering in them. I grasped Angelo's sleeve, and pointed at the shadows to the side of the building, where it met the smaller stable. Treading with care we each made a quick run to the safety of the darkness.

The stable had a pair of large doors at the front, which I was concerned would be too noisy to open. But before I could hiss to Angelo my fears, he was already standing by them, easing up the latch.

"Shh!" I cautioned, but he had it open, and I had not heard a sound.

He opened the door by the merest fraction, and again he did this in total silence. As soon as it was wide enough, he slipped inside, and I followed.

"I applied some grease to the latch and hinges earlier," he whispered, closing the door and dropping the latch on the inside into place, securing it again. "While you were in the cellar. I told the family I needed some air and was taking a walk. I also took our bags and hid them here. Look in the straw at the back of the stall."

"I am impressed," I whispered back.

In the dim light of the round window above, I could just make out some ten different stalls, each with the head of a horse just visible over the door. I glanced back at Angelo. "I know not where is my horse," I muttered.

He gave me a slightly self-satisfied smile. "I also made it my business to find out earlier," he replied. "She is in the first stall to the left."

I made a soft whistle. His planning seemed even more thorough than I had first thought. "And I suppose you made sure they were well fed and watered?" I asked, with my head to one side.

"As it happens, I did." I could hear the smile in his voice

"I see." I resolved to congratulate him properly once we got away—assuming we were able to do so. "Then let us make haste," I said.

"But make no noise." He pointed to the house. "Those

candles suggest there are people who are not yet abed."

I made my way to the first stall and studied the fastening on the outside of the door. Hestia's head appeared beside my shoulder, and she gave a little whinny of greeting. "Shush, old girl," I muttered, stroking her nose. "Got to keep quiet." As ever, my clever Hestia seemed to understand me well. She nodded her head.

The lock was one of those barrel and bolt affairs; one that can make the noise of a thunderclap if you withdraw it too fast. I took a breath, then lifted the lever and pulled it back as slowly as I could. I could see Angelo doing the same two doors further along.

At first it slid with ease, and I resolved that I would soon be inside with my beloved Hestia.

Then it stuck.

I pulled it with as much force as I thought necessary, two, three times, trusting I could stop it sliding too fast if it freed. But it refused to move. So I applied a little more force.

It suddenly shot back with a sound like a hammer striking an anvil.

Angelo looked across at me in horror, as there was the sound of a window being pushed open. We froze. A voice called out in Dutch.

The window closed again, and I let out a sigh of relief. But Angelo shook his head and gestured at me to close the bolt and come to him. I did so and scampered over, then we crouched into the deep shadow of a recess behind the last stall.

It was not a moment too soon, as the door opened, and a candle cast a glow just beyond our hiding place. A male voice—I presumed a servant—called out what sounded like a challenge in Dutch.

Angelo pulled me closer to him in the shadows. I could feel the warmth of his arm around me, and his breath on my cheek.

There was the sound of steps in the straw and the light wavered, as if the searcher was walking further into the stable. Closer to our recess.

One yard further, and we must be seen.

I held my breath and offered a prayer to almighty God to keep us hidden.

The light grew stronger. The voice repeated the challenge—so close now that we could almost be face to face.

I dug my nails into my palm; our discovery was now a certainty…

Outside, a cat meowed.

The light stopped.

Then it withdrew. The voice said something in Dutch, and I caught a word that sounded like 'cat'. The speaker seemed to be accepting that the noise was made by the animal.

There was the sound of the door opening and closing again, then silence. We waited a few long minutes, then looked cautiously out from our hiding place.

We were alone.

This time the bolt slid back quickly and silently; no doubt eased by its recent use. Hestia was moving about in her stall as I opened the door, making noise with her hooves. In the dim light I could just make out her saddle and bridle hanging on the wall. She gave another small whinny. "Shush!" I stroked her on the nose again, then waited a moment with my heart thumping, lest she had been heard. "I am pleased to see you as well," I whispered. "but shush, please."

As quietly as I could I eased her saddle off the bar on the wall. Then I lifted it onto her back and secured it. Now the bridle. I lifted it slowly off its hook and put it on, my fingers fumbling with the buckles in the dim light. After what seemed like an hour but was most likely only a minute or two, I had it done up. Finally I found my saddlebag in the straw and tied it on securely.

I stood back. Hestia was ready.

No time to find a mounting block, so I put my foot in the stirrup and pulled myself up as best I could, then grabbed the reins.

Angelo walked past my stall, leading his horse.

There was a loud creak as he opened the door—wider this time so the horses could get through.

The window opened again, and a shout came from above.

"*Presto!*" called Angelo. I urged Hestia out of the stable, just as Angelo swung into his saddle. Hestia and I emerged into the night at a trot—the fastest I dared go on the rough cobbles. As we rode past the de Vries house, a man in a rough smock appeared, holding a lamp above his head. Jozefien was beside him in a nightdress, and I caught her eye as we went past. She looked furious—and maybe slightly relieved?

Then we were beyond her, making our way alongside the canal. Free and clear!

I could feel myself grinning broadly as Hestia made a good pace behind Angelo's horse. Now I could breathe easy once more; clever Angelo's plan had worked, and I could forget the horrors of yet another marriage being forced on me; one as awful in its own way as the one my stepfather had tried to put me in.

There were very few people as Hestia and I rode through the town centre, so thankfully our progress was relatively unhindered. Except for one man; a plainly dressed young fellow, who had to leap out of the way as Angelo came directly towards him. Unfortunately for this person, avoiding Angelo put him directly in my way. It all happened so quickly; one moment I was riding along; the next I had to pull Hestia up sharply or I would have ridden the man down.

Hestia came to a slithering stop, just before she would have struck him. I looked down in the blue light of the Autumn moon. The man's face was white, no doubt with the shock of almost being ridden down. Then he looked up at me, and his face turned from shock to anger. "Pardon," I said, hoping it would be understood in Dutch. But there was something in the way he looked at me that strongly reminded me of another person.

I shook my head to clear it. Surely it was but a coincidence; how could I possibly know a random stranger here? I gave Hestia a gentle kick and we set off after Angelo, leaving the man staring after me with ill-concealed disgust.

Once we were clear of the city cobbles, we were able to make faster progress, and pushed the horses hard for a while. Eventually, Angelo reined in his horse and pulled up at the side of the path.

I trotted up beside him, Hestia's flanks steaming in the moonlight.

"The next town is called Amsterdam," he said. "But I say we do not stop there, but go around it. We can make better progress during the night." He settled his horse, who was throwing its head up. "I was told there is a town beyond by the name of Breda. We can be there in the morning and travel in with others, then be lost among the crowds." He observed me a moment, as his horse dropped its head and started nibbling some grass. "That fellow I almost rode down back there…" he began, then faltered to a stop, staring at me. "What ails you, Maria?" he asked. "You look as if you have seen a spectre."

"I think have," I whispered. For now I knew exactly why the young man had been so familiar. The curve of his cheek; the set of his cold eye. I knew where I had seen it before.

In a misty graveyard in Norwich.

It was no coincidence that this young man was in the Nederland.

He was related to the widow.

Yet another of the Cruddon family.

Seeking us for vengeance.

IO

HIDING IN PLAIN SIGHT

As we rode on, Angelo tried to dissuade me from believing the man was another member of the murderous Cruddon family—despite being the first to have suggested this back in Norwich.

"They would have to have found the body of the widow very soon," he observed, in Neapolitan. "Then followed us to Yarmouth…"

"Which would have been easy," I replied in English.

"How would that be in my own tongue?" he asked with a smile. "You will need to be able to converse with ease in Pozzuoli, Maria, so you must practice at all times."

"There would have been a funeral already planned for that grave on the day," I said in Neapolitan, picking my words with care. "So the body would have quickly been discovered. Then, people would start asking about the events of the morning. You are most colourfully clothed, and I am a beardless man. I warrant there would have been no shortage of passers-by willing to identify us in Norwich, and I am sure we passed a few travellers on the Yarmouth road."

I thought on other ways we could have been followed, as we had blundered around like a pair of thoughtless fools, laying a trail even a child could understand. "And what of the old fellow in the warehouse? The one who told us of the *Jozefien*? He also talked of a second ship arriving soon after. I warrant he would have been as free with his information to our pursuer as he was with us. The second ship would have been the one the young man took; arriving only a few days after us."

"I see." We rode on in silence a moment, then Angelo said, "If indeed you are correct, what then?"

"Enquiries at the docks will no doubt have shown that the captain of the *Jozefien* returned to his house with two travellers matching our descriptions. So it would have been easy to follow us there. I warrant that Jozefien and Adriana will lose little time in telling the young man sorry tales about us." I had another thought. "And Pieter de Vries too, once he has woken and found his way home."

"Then we must be on our guard," he said. "At all times." He hesitated a moment, chewing on his lip as if he wanted to add something further.

"What is it?" I asked.

"We must become different people." He cleared his throat. "You are correct; my Neapolitan garb is distinctive, and you are well marked as a beardless man. We need to change." He gave me a significant look in the moonlight, and in an instant, I could see where he was headed."

"You suggest I become a woman again?"

He gave a slow nod. "I do. If you are correct, this Cruddon person seeks us as two men. He may be working for himself—driven by a desire for vengeance. Or maybe he serves English justice, and seeks to arrest us for the murder of Joan Cruddon, and take us back to England by force. So he if he finds two men answering our descriptions, he will be a grave threat to us. But if he comes across a man and his wife, that would be different. If we do not draw attention to ourselves, then we can move more freely."

So it was that the following day in the town of Breda, I found myself waiting in a room above a tavern, while Angelo went to find a place selling clothing for women.

I paced up and down as I waited. How would I feel once again dressing as befitted my true nature? It was not something I did often, for how could I run, ride and fight in a cumbersome gown? But that was when I was alone, and had only my own wits and sword to rely upon. Now, at least I had Angelo, and was finding myself increasingly trusting his judgment.

I ceased pacing, as the thought struck me. I had not considered for a moment that it had been Angelo, not me, who had devised and executed the plan to escape the de Vries family. I had simply followed his lead, and done as I had been instructed. Something I would never have considered with Marcus Kytson, when I had to play the part of Prince Henry Fitzroy. Or with Robert Fitzwilliam, when we were returning the Broken Sword. No, in those situations I had relied only on my own scheming, and ensured the men followed my instructions.

Yet here I was, following Angelo's plans, and about to struggle into a women's gown.

I resumed my steps. If becoming a woman again meant we could avoid the attentions of yet another murderous Cruddon, then so be it. I must do what had to be done.

There was a tap on the door; a special pattern of knocks we had agreed. I unlocked it to let Angelo in. He had changed his colourful doublet for a plain Dutch one, and was carrying a large bundle wrapped in linen. His long Neapolitan hair had been trimmed back in the more severe Dutch style, and his beard was less full.

"I have secured this," he said, unrolling the bundle to reveal a black crossover bodice, a white undershift, a red kirtle with white lacing across the front, a brown overgown, woollen stockings and a pair of leather slippers. He had also bought a wide-brimmed straw hat complete with a white cotton coif, and a pot of rouge.

"Do you need assistance?" he asked with a cheeky smile.

"I think not," I said sternly. "You can wait downstairs. "

When he had gone, I looked over the clothing. Then I took a deep breath and started to unlace my man's doublet.

—0—

An hour or so later, I stepped daintily out of the room and made my way down to the tavern. I was careful to hold up my skirts as I descended the stair, lest I trip over them. With my hair in the coif, the laces of the hat firmly secured under my chin and a little rouge applied, I was sure I was as unlike Thomas Richardson as it was possible to be.

Angelo was at a table in the corner with a heavy-lidded pewter tankard, facing away from the room. Something made him turn as I approached, and he saw me. But there seemed to be no recognition, and he turned away again.

Suddenly his head snapped back; his eyes as wide as saucers.

"*Buon Dio!*" he breathed, then stood as I smoothed my skirts and took my place on the bench beside him, ensuring I had a good view of the room. "*Santa Maria—Madre di Dio!*" he said with an enormous smile, "I could not have believed it possible!"

I raised a casual eyebrow, as if to say that this was nothing special. "Do you not offer a lady a drink?" I enquired in English.

"In Neapolitan, Maria," he insisted.

I repeated it again in his language, while twisting in the tightly laced bodice; my ribs unused to such pressure. "Although belike this lady has little space to accommodate it," I muttered, before attempting a smile myself.

Angelo gave a chuckle, then waved at an old man in a dirty white apron who was weaving among the tables with a tray of tankards. He asked for a beer, pointing at me. The man looked me up and down, said something dismissive, then walked off. I stared at his broad retreating back. "I am not used to being treated as a woman," I said. "It is hard to accept that I no longer command the respect usually given to a man."

Angelo nodded. "Indeed so." He paused, staring at me. His smile faded, to be replaced by a furrowed brow. "For sure, Maria, it is remarkable how a single person receives such diverse dealings if a man or a woman. I had always thought it normal for the two to be treated differently—but now I see it through your eyes…" He shook his head. "I begin to understand how it must be to experience such a thing."

We talked on for at least another half hour, seemingly ignored by the serving man, who moved around the tables, failing to look in our direction at all. Eventually, I stood up and grabbed hold of his arm as he passed. *"Een bier, alstublieft,"* I stated, repeating words I had heard de Vries use the night before. The man's lip curled, but he nodded and ambled off with what I considered a calculated lack of haste. I sat again, pleased at least that I had asserted myself.

A few minutes later he returned with a half-size tankard and thumped it down in front of me.

Opening the lid and taking a sip, I wondered at his strange behaviour. Why was he so antagonistic towards me? Then I glanced around the room and noticed something strange.

I was the only woman in the whole place.

There were upwards of thirty men in the room, but no other women. I glanced enquiringly at Angelo. He looked around and seemed to understand. "Mayhap there is some holy day celebration, and the women are meant to be at home preparing food?" he wondered.

I gave a deep sigh. "I cannot do right here in the Low Countries," I said. "If I am a man, then I am under threat of discovery and possible accusation of witchcraft. And if a woman, then I am seemingly out of place, and just as remarkable." I sat back and folded my arms in protest.

Angelo touched my shoulder, then pointed briefly at the door. "But for all that," he said, "you are not alone." A woman, similarly dressed to me, had just come in with a grey-haired man. Where my kirtle was red, hers was blue, and she had a strap around her waist with a purse attached. She was maybe ten or so years my senior; lines radiating out like sunbeams from the corners of her eyes, which suggested she was a person more used to smiling than making a frown. This was proved true when her eyes swept the room, and she spied me. She broke into a broad grin, then gave me a look of knowing companionship, as if we women must band together against adversity. I smiled back and nodded to show I understood. She looked away, and started to follow her companion towards an empty table.

A small bald man in a brown jerkin got up and moved with purpose towards the woman. As he reached her, a knife suddenly appeared in his hand. Before I could shout a warning, there was the flash of the blade, then he was past her. He pushed open the door and was gone.

So was her purse.

Without thinking I was up and running for the door. How dare a cutpurse commit theft in such a blatant manner! Bursting out into the street, I looked left and right. The small bald man was hurrying away on foot. I lifted my skirts and ran after him, my soft leather slippers making little sound on the cobbles.

For all that, the man must have heard me, and looked round as I came up behind him. I had the brief impression of a pair of wide eyes in a dirty face, then he increased his pace to a run.

I did likewise, and soon we were both running at our fastest.

The man had little chance to outrun me. He was short of stature and stockily built, and I warrant, some twenty years older. Within a few strides, I had caught him again. I flung myself forward, my arms reaching for his waist. This knocked him off balance and he fell forward, landing heavily with a grunt. And with me clinging to his back like a barnacle to a ship.

As soon as he was down, I snatched the woman's purse, leapt to my feet, and set off back to the tavern.

I allowed myself a quick glance over my shoulder as I ran, lest he was following. But he was sitting up on the cobbles shaking his head, seeming in no hurry to get up and come after me.

I made it back to the tavern and pushed open the door—to be met with a silent stare from every man in the place. And the one other woman. Taking a deep breath to steady myself, I walked up to her and held out the purse.

She said nothing as she took it, but continued to give me a look of total amazement.

Then a single man somewhere in the room made a slow clap of his hand. I glanced over my shoulder, lest it was Angelo, but he was sitting still, although wearing his customary amused smile.

Another man started clapping, then another. Soon the whole room had joined in. Someone added a cheer. This prompted others to make further cheering, which then became shouting and whooping. Men came up and struck me playfully on the back, and some made exclamations in Dutch. A tankard was pressed into my hand, and I took a small drink.

Angelo came up and led me back to the table. He sat me down, then placed himself beside me. He leaned in and spoke directly into my ear.

"So much for not drawing attention to ourselves, Maria."

II

THE SHY WOMAN

The woman's name was Marike Cuypers, and by good fortune, she spoke passable English.

Once all the clapping and back-slapping had died down, she and her husband Clement Cuypers came to sit with us. Angelo introduced us as Luca and Maria Ceretti. He explained that we were returning to his home in Rome after our happy wedding in England. He told how I was the English bride promised to him by my merchant father, who had trading connections with Rome.

I sat silently while he poured out this tale, simply smiling and nodding as each new revelation about my supposed past emerged. Occasionally I pulled open the lid of my tankard and took a sip of beer, mainly to cover my surprise at a new outrageous claim made by Angelo di Luca.

So we were married? I supposed that made sense—or why else would be travelling together as a man and woman?

And the ceremony? Ah, yes. That had been in a beautiful country church near Norwich, surrounded by my delightful family. In the sunshine. Of course. How delightful.

And we were to live in Rome, where we hoped to start a family. For sure. Why would we not?

Although the marriage was arranged, Angelo—no, sorry; *Signore* Luca Ceretti—had been struck with love the moment he had first caught sight of his beautiful bride. How fortunate.

I watched as he added each new untruth on top of the last, like layers of filling in a pie. His eyes were sparkling, as if lit by the brightest candle from within. He was enjoying this opportunity to build a fantasy. And the more he built it, patting my hand and occasionally bolstering his point with a little stroke of my cheek, the more I realised something.

He wanted it to be real.

He was simply telling the story that already lived in his head.

Sure, his actual home of Pozzuoli was now Rome, and Luca had become his Christian name not his family name—but these were just incidental lies compared to the big one; that we were a married couple and deeply in love.

I took a long draught of my beer as I tried to come to terms with this revelation.

He had let slip the words *mio amore Maria* back in Yarmouth, and at the time I had been surprised; not just that he had said it, but also that we had known each other but a few days. So now, here he was, telling Clement and Marike—two perfect strangers— that he had been struck with love when he first saw me. Could I doubt that he was telling them the truth of what was in his heart? But—had he not also said in Yarmouth that he accepted me as the person I am? It was what made me think him different to the other men; the ones who wanted me as their compliant wife and mother to their children.

I bit the inside of my cheek as a disturbing thought occurred.

Now that he had seen me as a woman, was that no longer true?

Could I trust any more that he accepted Mary Fox for the woman she was, not the one everyone seemed to want her to be?

"…Is that not a kindly offer, Maria, my love?"

I forced my attention back to the room. Angelo was looking at me expectantly, as were Marike and Clement. "Hmm?" I asked.

"Marike here has said that in gratitude for your bravery in wresting her property from the cutpurse, they would be honoured if we spend a day or two as guests in their house."

I shot him a concerned look. Had he taken leave of his senses? The last time we had accepted Dutch hospitality, we had been lucky to escape. And now he was doing the same again? "Should we not be setting off for Rome, my love?" I asked. "Not making an imposition on these good people…"

"Nonsense, Maria," Marike interrupted. "It is no imposition at all. It is the feast of *Allerzielen,* when we offer prayers for the souls of those who have left us in faith, and are now at peace with the Lord in Heaven. We could not bear the thought of you travelling on such a day, when you could be celebrating with us."

I could see that there was no way we could now refuse, so I nodded with as best a smile as I could manage.

—0—

"What in Heaven's name were you thinking?" I hissed at Angelo as I untethered Hestia from the tavern stables. "Accepting hospitality again? Look where it led us last time."

"I had reason," he replied. "If the man you saw really is a Cruddon, then he will be expecting us to be making all haste towards Napoli. So he will do the same, presuming to catch us up. I warrant if we stay a few days with these people, then he will get ahead, giving us the advantage of being behind him."

I said nothing more as we followed Marike and Clement to their house, leading the horses on foot.

Of course, Angelo was correct; I could see that. Having this possible Cruddon ahead of us meant he would be pressing forward, expecting to find us around every possible corner. That meant we could proceed carefully, and perhaps even follow any trail he might leave, just as he would do for us. We could even make plans to ensure we would not cross paths.

On that positive thought, I made my way through the streets of Breda, until we arrived at a row of gabled houses and Clement showed us where to stable the horses.

The house he shared with Marike was much the same size as de Vries's, but seemed better furnished. As with the house in Den Haag, the parlour had a table for dining, but there were also two high-backed chairs before the fire and a small pedestal table beside each one.

"Welcome to our home," Marike said. "I hope you will both

95

enjoy your time here."

For a moment I was tempted to enquire if she had any impressionable daughters, but then I realised that even if she did, Maria Ceretti, wife of Luca, would hardly raise even the briefest flutter in any young girl's breast. I took a breath and smiled at Marike.

"This is most kind of you," I replied. "I am sure we will."

A girl in black came in and gave a small curtsey. "Else will show you to your room," Marike said, then added something in Dutch. The girl, Else, nodded and indicated for us to follow.

I looked at Angelo as we were led up the narrow stairs. *Room?* I mouthed at him. *Just the one?*

He gave a small shrug, as Else pushed open a door to reveal a well-appointed bed chamber with a single box-bed in the centre. There had been such a thing in the de Vries house; like a miniature room with a bed inside and a door for access, although this was brightly painted with coloured patterns, while the de Vries one had been plain, bare wood. A cheery fire was burning in the grate. Else curtseyed again and withdrew.

"We may be married in the eyes of our hosts," I observed once she had closed the door, "but not in the eyes of God." I pointed at the solid wooden floor. "I will take the bed. You can sleep there." If I had expected him to protest, I was mistaken. He shrugged again, and said, "As you wish."

He pulled open the box bed door and sat on the mattress. With a small sigh he leaned back, supporting himself with straight arms; his feet swinging. "Although I do seem to remember that we have shared a bed chamber before."

"Angelo di Luca," I said firmly, "we will maintain the pretence of being married for Marike and Clement, but behind this door, I would have you respect my maidenhood and keep your eyes—and your thoughts—firmly to yourself."

—0—

We stayed three days and nights with the Cuypers, which we both thought was enough time for Cruddon to get ahead of us. By good fortune our hosts were most welcoming, and it was generally a time of relaxed conversation, good food and fine wines.

Except, that is, on the first night, when Angelo and I retired to our chamber. I was mindful that he had readily agreed to sleeping on the floor, so I thought there was nothing more to be said on the matter.

After we had bid each other good night, I sat on the bed and pulled the door closed, then struggled out of my clothing in the dark. It took me a little while to undress by feel alone in a seated position, but eventually I was down to my chemise.

There was a creak of floorboards outside the bed, and a couple of rather obvious sighs, as if he was a mummer on stage and playing to the highest gallery.

I ignored him, pulling off the chemise and patting round the covers beside me, until I found the linen nightdress that Marike had so kindly offered. Conscious that I was now completely unclothed, while a hot-blooded Neapolitan lay only feet beyond the bed walls, I fumbled with the new garment to get it on as quick as I could. But it was dark inside, and the more urgently I tried to get it over my head, the more tangled I became.

There was a particularly loud creak of the boards.

I froze, with my head now stuck inside a sleeve. Was he standing up?

There was a tread on a board, then another.

Was he now coming towards me?

"Stay away," I snapped, although I fear my words were lost in tight linen stretched across my face. "Stay away," I repeated.

"I have a concern for your safety," he said, his voice so close that he must have been right beside the door. "It sounds like you do battle with a fearsome demon in there."

"I am perfectly well, thank you," I said, using both hands to try and pull up on the sleeve. But it would not move.

"If you say so," he replied.

I tugged harder. Suddenly the sleeve came free, and I gave an agonised yelp as it raked over my nose.

"Are you sure?" he asked, and I could hear the smile in his voice. "It sounds as if the demon is winning."

"All ib webb, I can abbure you," I muttered, rubbing my nose to relieve the pain. "Good bight."

There was a creak as he settled back. I had another attempt at identifying the sleeves and neck, and eventually managed to pull the nightdress on.

Wriggling down under the covers, I rested my head on the bolster.

Silence descended on the room.

No sounds of movement came from the floor. Was he still there? I gave a small gasp. Perhaps he had gone out while I struggled with my garment? Perhaps he was even now sitting downstairs taking wine with Clement. I strained my ears. Or was that the sound of him breathing?

I lay staring up sightlessly up in the dark, unsure if I should look out and check. But what if he was right there, and found my concern most amusing?

I put my hands behind my head, and determined to stay put. His business was his business; not mine.

Was that a sigh?

Was that his breathing?

Not my business.

I turned over, thumping the bolster to make a dip for my head.

"My money is on the demon," came his voice.

"Be quiet, Angelo," I snapped. "I have no interest in your thoughts on this. Good night."

"*Buona notte*, Maria."

—0—

The following day we attended the *Onze-Lieve-Vrouweker* in Breda—or Church of Our Lady—to celebrate *Allerzielen*, which in

England we would call All Souls. It was a large, almost cathedral-like building, with a main tower so high it could be seen from many streets away. The service was in Latin, so I was able to follow it with ease, and I took some comfort from the familiarity of the event.

There were many people in the church, and I glanced around continually, searching the faces of the men for any sign of the young fellow I thought to be a Cruddon. But none of them had the same curve to their cheek or set to their eye that had so strongly reminded me of the widow Joan.

I was able to relax further, as I felt all but invisible amongst the womenfolk. All wore the same or similar clothing and hats to my own, so it was hard to tell one from another.

Over the following two days, Clement showed us around the town. This included another trip to the church to marvel at the memorial to Engelbert the First of Nassau, the overlord of Breda, who had died some forty years before. It was a magnificent stone monument, resplendent with carved figures, including that of Engelbert himself in the garb of a Roman soldier. Angelo was particularly interested in this, and was keen to understand why this man wanted to be seen as a Roman, but Clement either did not know, or had not the English to explain.

"You ask this?" a heavily accented voice said beside me, and a tall Dutchman stepped forward. "It is believed Engelbert sought the legitimacy of Rome, because his claim to the lordship of Breda came only through his wife Johanna of Polanen. He therefore wanted to validate himself by other means."

"I see. Thank you, *Meneer*," Angelo replied.

The Dutchman nodded and moved away, holding the arm of a slim female. I took her to be his wife, for she clung to him with such intensity that it was almost unseemly. I was curious to see how she might look, but she kept her head down and did not allow her face to be seen under her hat. They walked over to the main doors and stepped out while we were still entranced by the monument.

"That was most helpful," Angelo observed, as we made our own way to the doors and into the cold autumnal air, then set off back to the house.

A couple of days later, we bade our farewells, and rode out of Breda.

"I suggest we make first for the Duchy of Milano," Angelo suggested.

"Why so?" I asked.

"It is on our way," he replied, "and will be a welcome stop after we have crossed the snow-capped Alps."

12

SHARED BODILY WARMTH

The going was easy over the next few days, as we passed through the flat lands of the Low Countries.

The Dutch people on the road and in the taverns gave way to the Flemish, and then to the Germanic Saxons. As we rode into these people's lands, the terrain started to become more hilly, with the occasional climbs for Hestia and Angelo's horse to manage. For the next few days these climbs were then followed by an equal drop back to the flat plain, which provided a welcome relief and seemed to please Hestia.

I wanted to make sure she was well fed and rested, so insisted to Angelo that we avoided travelling for around one day in every four. At first, I was concerned lest Cruddon was somehow still behind, and might then catch up with us. But Angelo insisted that the man must be ahead—so reassured me that every time we stopped, it would allow us to put even greater distance between us and our pursuer.

We pressed on, and after around ten days, passed through a Germanic town called Konstanz. There, we came across a lake of breathtaking beauty. It was so lovely, that I felt I could spend the rest of my life enjoying its shores, until Angelo sought to remind me of our mission.

"We must return to Pozzuoli and restore *il Fiume di Fuoco* necklace to my mother before her birthday on the twenty-eighth of January next year," he insisted, patting the leather bag attached to his saddle.

"Very well," I said, getting up and brushing grass off the split riding skirts I wore. "Then we will keep moving."

A few days later we passed into the land of the Switzers.

Now we were climbing again, but this time there were no corresponding drops once we had crested a rise. Now we were just climbing. All day. Every day.

And it was getting colder. At my insistence we purchased some heavy furs and boots, as well as blankets for the horses. I was soon grateful for this, and Hestia seemed so, too. I made sure to keep her well covered, and whenever we stopped, I secured additional mash and water once I had rubbed her down.

A day after we had started climbing, we came across snow clinging to the tops of tree branches and clumps drifting up the side of the path. Very soon these clumps became more widespread and regular, until the whole landscape was made white by settled snow. Every one of the trees was covered, and the path we were following was crisp and white underfoot. The horses did not seem too worried by this, but carried on plodding along the path, their hooves making round shapes in the snow.

Most times we were the only travellers on the path; we did occasionally see others coming down from the opposite direction. Mostly these were heavy-set Switzers, their beards reaching to their waists and their cheeks reddened by the wind and snow. We enquired as best we could about taverns up ahead, always concerned lest we had no place to sleep. Some spoke much the same language as Angelo, so were the most helpful. Through them we were able to ensure we found a place to stop and rest each night. These taverns were always made of stripped tree trunks pegged together, and had heavily pointed roofs that held a perfectly formed blanket of snow. These reminded me of the icing our pastry cook used to add onto cakes and marchpane, so perfectly did they sit on the roofs.

The taverns themselves were generally warm, with large fires burning merrily in the hall and in the bed chambers, and it was a pleasure each evening to come inside and warm ourselves before a blaze.

We maintained the story that we were husband and wife. I could imagine how badly these dour Switzers would react to a man and woman travelling together who were not wed.

At first, we kept to the same sleeping arrangement as we had in Breda, with me in the bed and Angelo on the floor. But that all changed after we had been climbing the mountains for a few days. It was already dark when we found a tavern for the night, and this one seemed more full of travellers than we were accustomed. The landlord apologised, but said he only had one room remaining, and it did not have a fire. Would we accept it? Angelo looked at me with a raised eyebrow, and I gave a small nod in reply. We had our furs, so I thought we would be able to keep warm.

I was wrong. Despite remaining fully dressed and burrowing under the blankets, the cold seeped into my bones, and I felt as if I were made of ice.

If it was bad for me in the bed, it must have been a thousand times worse for Angelo. He was trying to sleep under a thin blanket on the floor. His shivering was loud enough to hear, although he made no complaint. But once the shivering became the chattering of teeth, I could bear it no longer.

"In Heaven's name, Angelo," I said, "must we both suffer this cold alone? If you promise to behave as a true gentleman, you can share my bed."

I had scarce finished this little speech, before he was beside me under the covers. I lay behind him and held him, choosing not to complain about his weight trapping one arm.

It seemed an age, but eventually his teeth were still, although he continued to shiver a while longer. I wondered if I could distract him, and moved my free hand up to his cheek. I gave it some slow strokes, thinking it would take his mind from the cold. This seemed to work, and gradually the shivering stopped. Now I could feel the warmth coming off him, as we huddled together under the blankets. I even found myself becoming drowsy.

"*Grazie*, Maria," he muttered. "You are better than a warming pan."

I gave a sleepy giggle, then added without any thought, "A warming pan? You will have to do better than that if you wish to woo me."

There was a silence that seemed to stretch forever, as these words hung in the air between us.

"What is that, Maria?" he said eventually. "We are but travelling companions, as you have made so clear. Would you wish for something more?"

Now I was wide awake. Why in Heaven's name had I said that? Had I not vowed to keep my distance, and avoid allowing Angelo anywhere near my heart?

"It was but a figure of speech," I said, moving my hand away from his cheek. "I meant nothing by it."

He shifted round and turned to face me, allowing me the opportunity to withdraw the arm that he had been lying on. "For sure?" he asked, and I could see a frown in the dim light. "It seemed real enough to me."

"Well that is the truth of the matter."

He turned over again. "If you say so," he muttered. "If that is how you see it."

"It is," I replied wanting to bring this unfortunate discussion to an end.

There was another long silence, and I wondered if he had fallen asleep.

Then his voice came out of the darkness. "You wish for me to move back to the floor?"

"And have us both freeze to death?" I asked. "No, stay here."

He grunted with what I thought was agreement, then shifted slightly, as if he were settling for the night. I turned away from him, but stayed close enough that our backs were touching, and settled as well.

Soon his breathing became regular, and there was even the occasional snore.

But sleep would not come for me; not while my thoughts were tumbling about my head like leaves in the wind.

Why did I say such a foolish thing? I had vowed to keep my distance from Angelo, yet here I was, talking of being wooed and sharing a bed with him like a wanton. I flinched in horror. How must God see me? As a loose woman? But then—only if I was breaking His Ten Commandments?

I went through them from memory, quickly going over the first four with a feeling of relief. These I had not broken. So far, so good.

'Thou shall not kill.' Ahh.

Several deaths had occurred in my past—but God must know I had never deliberately caused one by my own hand, nor would I ever set out to kill in cold blood. Surely that must prevent it being a mortal sin?

Then I came to 'Thou shall not commit adultery.' I glanced across at the shape of Angelo. Was this adultery? I took a breath. Hold yourself, Mary. Neither Angelo nor I were married, so how could it be? Reassured, I went on to 'Thou shall not steal.' My conscience was settled on this one—unless perhaps I had committed the sin of stealing Angelo's heart—but I did not think that was what God meant by it.

Next—'Thou shall not bear false witness.' Ahh. Was I guilty of this? Pretending to be a man? Pretending to be wed? But if that was a sin, it was one committed by Angelo as well. Did that mean it was only half a sin if we were both guilty of it? I turned onto my back and stared up at the dim ceiling. An interesting question, and one I must remember to ask at my next confession.

But back to the matter in hand. Finally, 'Thou shall not covet thy neighbour's oxen.' I could not see how this could apply; Angelo was hardly an ox. But for all that, I did not covet him.

Or did I?

I looked again at his bulk; a dark shape in the dim light.

No, I had vowed to keep my distance from him, and that I must do. Even though he was the only man who accepted me for who I was, and would not seek to change me?

But… Now he had seen me as a true woman, was his heart

still in the same place? He had been surprised, and most definitely pleased, when he saw me in woman's attire. How would he feel when I went back to my usual man's clothing? Would it sadden him? Would he no longer accept me?

Or… perhaps I should stay more as a woman, now I had seen how deceiving one such as Adriana could be so full of danger? And if pretending to be wed was bearing false witness, what then was presenting myself as Thomas Richardson instead of Mary Fox? Was that more of a sin? Even if the reason I did it was to help others?

Angelo moved in his sleep and let out a small snore. I gave his hair a soft stroke, and he made what seemed a contented sound. Like all Christians I may be a sinner in the eyes of God, but this man and I had a mission to return his jewel to his mother. And to keep away from a possibly murderous Cruddon. My concerns about sins seemed less important than such matters, and these should be my main concern.

On this thought I turned away again, and drifted off to sleep.

13

THE EYES OF HATE

We set off again the following morning, having agreed to keep pressing on without any further pause. Although we had been climbing for many days, we now appeared to have reached a level plateau of pastures; open fields of pure white stretching away to the base of the next set of mountains. I imagined during the summer these were tilled by the Switzers, or maybe their animals grazed on the luscious grass that now lay buried beneath the snow. Indeed, there were occasional little huts dotted around the fields, where I imagined the farmers would rest while they were tending their herds.

At first the sun shone out of a clear blue sky. The mountains before us seemed so close that I felt I could almost reach out and touch them; the lower slopes with their soft green and brown fur of trees; above them the flowing slopes of pure white slashed with dark scars of rock. The sharp, jagged peaks cut into the deep blue sky with such precision and perfection that it was as if the finest painter had made the picture.

I wanted to share my wonder at all this beauty with Angelo, but sadly that did not seem possible, for there had been an uncomfortable—and painful—silence between us all morning.

It had started at dawn, for when I had awoken, the bed beside me was empty. I left the chamber and found him breaking fast in the tavern. I had tried to converse, but he seemed too busy eating and I soon gave up trying. It was obvious he was made upset by the casual comment I had made the night before, and I wished that I had held my peace. But the damage was done, and it seemed impossible that we could go back to where we had been before. I would have given anything to have his twinkling smile once again,

107

and get back the playful teasing that I had grown so used to. This silent Angelo seemed so unnatural, and it concerned me that it was a side of him that I had not seen before.

After finishing our meal, we had saddled up and mounted in silence, then ridden out onto the path to resume our journey. Angelo rode slightly ahead so we did not look at each other. Judging by the set of his shoulders and the angle of his head, I rather fancied that he was as upset by this enforced coldness as I. But as a stubborn man, he was not prepared to admit it. I resolved to do whatever I could to help him find a way out of this self-imposed isolation.

After we had been riding for two or three hours, clouds started rolling in from the west. At first they only clung to the peaks, but more arrived to join them, until there was no longer any blue sky to be seen. Then they darkened to a flat, heavy grey, so the original sparkling clear light was quite gone. All the shadows disappeared, and a fog descended, causing everything to become the same dull white. It was soon impossible to make out any feature of the land around us, and all my focus was on making sure we stayed on the path.

Occasionally a grey shape would emerge from the mists ahead. It would begin as an ill-defined form, then, like a shadowy spectre, it would resolve itself into another traveller coming silently towards us. We passed such riders without engaging them in conversation, other than a small nod of acknowledgment

Not long after the fog had first come down, I felt a deep rumble in my belly. Just then one of the herder's huts emerged from the mists beside the path, and I touched Angelo on the shoulder.

"We should stop to eat," I suggested. "That hut would be a good place."

He nodded, so we dismounted and secured the horses.

The inside of the hut was bare, apart from a single bench along one wall. We sat and we took out the wrapped packets of cheese and dried meat that the tavern had provided. The cheese had a slightly waxy texture, with almost as many holes as there was cheese.

"We must ask of the next traveller how far is a place to eat and rest for the night," I said to Angelo, taking a bite.

"Hmm," he replied.

His tone still seemed dismissive, so I glanced sharply across at him. Here was an opportunity to try and end this coldness between us. "What ails?" I asked.

"Naught."

"I think not," I said, allowing some small annoyance into my voice. "You have not said a word all day, and now all I get is 'naught'?"

"There is naught to say," he muttered.

"If you are still cross after what I said last night…"

"Why should I be cross?" he replied. "You made it most clear that you had made a mistake. Naught more than a 'figure of speech', you said."

I put my cheese back in the packet and put my hand on his. Thankfully he did not withdraw it. "Please, Angelo," I said, "let us forget what happened and be as we were before."

"If that is your wish, Mary."

"It is," I said, and we finished our repast and remounted the horses.

I knew enough of Angelo to know we were still a long way from restoring normality, so a few minutes after we started on the path once more, I tried again.

"I am sorry, Angelo," I said. "I should not have said something I did not mean."

I thought perhaps an apology might show I was genuine in my desire to put this right. But before he could reply, two shapes started to emerge from the mist.

"Ahh," he said. "Here are some travellers. We should ask how far it is to reach a place for the night." He held up a hand and said something to them in his Neapolitan tongue, too quick for me to follow.

The travellers came closer, and it became easier to see their true shapes. One was a man, tall in the saddle, while the other was slight, and appeared to be a woman.

They pulled up their horses and the man leaned forward. "What is this you say?" he asked in English, but with a heavy Dutch accent.

I frowned. There was something about the voice that reminded me of one I had heard before. And not too long ago, either. But I could not place it.

I studied his companion. She was sitting quietly in the saddle, her wide straw hat pulled down, so her face was obscured.

No doubt a shy woman, not wishing to say anything, but letting her husband do the talking.

A woman with her hat pulled low…

Then it came to me. The church in Breda, as we studied the monument to Engelbert the First of Nassau. The tall Dutchman and his wife, who had obscured her face then as well. He had answered Angelo's question. That was where I had heard the voice before. I recalled wondering then why his wife was so reticent, and how I had wanted to see her face, but she had made sure to keep it hidden.

Angelo repeated his question, now in English.

The Dutchman said, "There is a tavern about three hours up this road." He turned to his wife, and said, "Is there not, Janet?"

There was a moment's silence, then her voice came from under the hat. "Indeed so, Rutger." It was quite high pitched, but with a hard-sounding edge. "I am sure Mistress Fox and Master di Luca will find it perfectly satisfactory."

I gave a gasp. How on earth did she know our names?

And—why did she have a crossbow secured to her saddle?

But before I could ask, she slowly raised her head. I found myself staring into the coldest ice-blue eyes I had ever seen. Eyes that were full of hate.

There was no doubting who she was. The one I had seen before; clothed as a man in the moonlight in Den Haag.

A deep chill went through me as her eyes narrowed.
They were eyes I had never wanted to see again.
They were the eyes of a Cruddon.

14

THE SHEPHERD'S HUT

I wasted no time in getting away, as I had no wish to find out this woman's intent.

Nor to discover her skill with the crossbow.

"Come, Angelo!" I called, and dug my heels into Hestia's side. My wonderful mare needed no further urging, and broke into a gallop so quickly that I thought my arms would be pulled from my body. Once I had gathered myself, and we were thundering away along the snow-covered path, I looked across. Angelo was alongside; his horse making as good speed as Hestia. I kept pressing my mare forward, then risked a glance back at the Cruddon woman and the Dutchman.

There was no sign of them.

Had they decided not to follow us? Or was the fog so thick that, even though they were close behind, they could not be seen or heard?

I clutched tightly on the reins. Was she somehow aiming her crossbow at our backs?

I decided not to take the chance, and crouched as low as I could over Hestia's mane. "Keep down," I called to Angelo, then glanced quickly back again.

There was still no sign of Janet or Rutger.

A tree rushed past, followed by another shepherd's hut. Then more trees. I looked forward. We had come to a thick copse, and I gave a small prayer of thanks, for at least now we had some cover. Once we were deeper in, and the snow underfoot had thinned out and gone completely, I slowed Hestia. She settled to a walking pace, snorting and blowing heavily, with steam rising from her flanks. I leaned forward and gave her a pat and a few strokes to

113

show my gratitude, then pulled off the path and walked her further into the trees.

Angelo came up beside me. "Was that the one you saw in Den Haag?" he asked. "The Cruddon person?"

"Yes, it was," I replied.

"I thought you said it was a man?"

"It was." I paused, as Hestia came to a stop and found a clump of grasses growing at the base of one of the trees. She started pulling them into her mouth. "But in truth, it seems it is a woman who seeks vengeance for the death of Joan Cruddon, not a man."

"A woman who uses men's clothing to disguise herself as she moves through the land," he observed, bringing his horse to a halt. He made a small chuckle. "Now where have I heard that before?"

He was teasing me; something I had very recently been desiring so greatly. But that was before we had met with the two travellers. Now I wanted to understand the dangers we were facing, rather than be light-hearted. "It is not the same at all," I said.

"How so?" he asked with a raised eyebrow. "If it has the look of a goose, and the smell of a goose—and makes the noise of a goose—is it not a goose?"

"Is that what you are calling me?" I chose to make as if I did not understand his meaning, although in truth I understood it well. How curious to have another such woman as me! It was as if I was looking in a mirror and seeing an evil, twisted version of myself.

This Cruddon woman presented a real threat to us. She was angry, vengeful—and armed with a crossbow. No doubt it was the same weapon, or similar, to the one used by Joan Cruddon in the graveyard. It must have been dug up with the body.

Angelo frowned. "Nay, as well you know," he replied. "But it is of concern, for we have little knowledge if she will come at us as a woman or a man, or if we will even recognise her."

I shivered. Once again, I saw the woman raise her head and fix her hard, evil gaze upon me. So full of vengeance and hate. "I will know her again by her eyes, I am sure of it." A thought occurred to me. "But why did they not come after us just now? We made our escape on the only path; one that they had come along themselves just moments before. Our horses would make clear marks in the snow, so they would have no problem seeing where we had gone, even in the mist. Why did they not follow?"

Angelo's horse dropped its head and started nibbling grasses as well. "I know not," he said, letting go of the reins. He paused. "You know, they had a chance to attack us in Breda." He looked up at me. "They could have knifed us in the back as we stepped out of the church, yet they chose not."

Why had they let us alone? What was their plan? If this Cruddon person was able to be a man or a woman at will, then she was clearly someone who could concoct a scheme. Was it not just hate I had seen in her eyes? Was there a look of sly calculation as well? I nodded to myself; yes, that was it. An idea took hold in my head. "I warrant they do not seek to carry out their evil intent immediately," I said slowly. "Mayhap they want us to be always looking behind, in a state of fear as to what they might do."

"Before they then do it," Angelo agreed.

I pictured them sitting on their horses as we galloped away, smiling as they watched us go. Now they had found us, they could play us according to whatever plan she had concocted, like we were marionettes on a string.

"Then we must change the game," I said. "We must play it our way, not theirs."

"How is this, Maria?" he asked.

"Somehow they were ahead of us," I began, trying to get my mind clear on their actions, and possibly therefore, their plans. "But we could not be found, so they came back. Now they are behind us, and are aware of which direction we are headed. They also know there is a tavern nearly three hours ahead, and possibly no others; so they will expect us to go there." I fixed him with a stern look. "So that is what we will *not* do."

"Are you saying we will be spending the night in the open?" Angelo asked. "You know how difficult it was to keep warm in the chamber with no fire…" His voice faltered to a stop. Perhaps he was also remembering how we had managed to find heat eventually—and how that had ended.

"I am saying we keep riding till after the dawn," I said. "So we are as far ahead of them as we can be by morning. If we rest the horses first, and let them feed on more grass, then they will be able to keep walking through the night."

"And us?" he asked, unable to hide a slight look of disappointment from his face. "How do we keep going?"

"As best we can," I said simply. "It is all we can do."

—0—

Once both the horses were secured to a sturdy tree trunk in the thickest part of the copse, we agreed that the best place to wait until dark was the shepherd's hut I had seen as we came in. On the way there I crouched down at the foot of each tree and cut a slice from the bark with my knife, leaving a bright white scar on every trunk.

"What are you doing?" Angelo asked.

"We must find our way back to the horses," I replied. "Even at night we should be able to see which trees mark our path."

"*Buon Dio!*" he exclaimed. "I would not have thought of that!"

The hut was on the edge of the copse, surrounded by snow. We came up to it by a wide route, approaching from behind so as not to make our footprints too obvious. Angelo pulled on the door, and it opened without protest, so we slipped in. There was a bolt lock on the inside, so he pushed it across.

As with the other hut we had used, this was made of stripped tree trunks pegged together. It, too, was empty apart from a bench seat along one wall, with a window opposite covered in some sacking.

Now we were not moving, I could feel the cold start to work its way into my bones, and I worried that Hestia would feel it as well. She would be spending some hours in the open forest, without being rubbed down or covered with a blanket. But when I

116

said this to Angelo, he made light of my concerns, saying that Hestia was well able to keep herself warm, as she did this in drafty stables every night.

I reluctantly agreed, but could not avoid worrying for my friend's wellbeing.

"Have more concern for the Cruddon woman or her Dutchman finding us," he said. "We should keep a watch, lest they pass by." Then he added, "Or worse, they force their way inside."

I shivered at his words.

Angelo offered to be the first watchman, so I lay on the bench trying to get some sleep, while he stood by the little window looking out across the snowy fields. At first sleep eluded me, as my mind was filled with so many thoughts and fears about our situation, but I must have fallen asleep at some point, for the next thing I knew, Angelo was shaking me awake.

"There has been no sign of them," he said. "It is your turn now."

We changed places, and I took my watch by the window.

I pulled the sacking aside, to get a limited view of the distant path leading into the forest. It was almost lost in the mist, but I fixed my gaze on it, determined to make sure I did not miss any person moving along in the flat afternoon light.

A gentle snore told me Angelo had fallen asleep almost immediately.

I touched the hilt of my sword, reassuringly hanging at my belt. I knew I could fight Janet if I must—in close combat if that was needed. But she had that infernal crossbow. That gave her the advantage.

The path remained empty, as the sky grew darker. No travellers appeared to be moving along it at this time. I took a hopeful breath. No doubt any genuine travellers had found shelter and were settling for the night. And surely if Janet Cruddon had let us go earlier, she was hardly likely to be hunting our trail now that the light was becoming so poor? She would wait until the morning, and try then. And after riding through the night ourselves, we would be a long way ahead…

I stiffened. A distant shadow had emerged from the mist.

It was a horseman, walking along the path.

Was he alone? Now I was looking at a rider, I found myself shaking like a deer faced by hounds. I searched the mist behind the figure for a possible companion.

Then I gave a small yelp. Another dark shadow had appeared close behind. I stared hard, seeking to understand the shape as it moved. After a moment, I was sure it was another rider on a horse. But was it a woman? It was too distant and the air too thick to tell.

They were coming closer. Riding slowly. Were they looking for us?

My hand gripped so tight on my hilt that it hurt.

There was a sound behind me and a touch on my shoulder. "What is it?" Angelo asked, coming to the window beside me.

I pointed silently at the two horsemen who were moving along the path, and were now almost into the trees. He frowned as he leaned forward and studied them. Then he stood back and said, "Switzers."

I looked again. Now they were closer I could see them better, and it was clear that Angelo was correct. They were not a thin Dutchman and a slight Englishwoman, but two stocky and heavily bearded men.

I let out a long breath and my heart slowed to its more usual pace. I moved my hand away from the hilt, opening and closing my fist a few times to relieve the stress.

Angelo patted me on the shoulder. "There. Naught to concern you. Just two worthy Switzers going about their business." He looked out of the window again. "It will soon be dark," he observed. "We can set off once more."

"Thank Heaven," I began. "I was just…"

But I got no further. There was a rush of air and a sudden loud cracking sound, as if a lightning bolt had struck. A flighted crossbow shaft was quivering in the window frame, only inches from my face.

I threw myself sideways, just as another shaft flew through the window and passed between us. It slammed into the bench, exactly where Angelo had just been sleeping.

I dropped to the floor, crouching below the window, and drew my sword. Angelo was close beside me.

"Come out, Mary Fox!" A high-pitched woman's voice came from outside. "I can loose off as many of these bolts as it takes to kill you."

"Nay, Janet Cruddon!" I called back. "Cease this attack. You have no cause."

"My name is not Cruddon," she replied. There was a pause, then her voice came again, "I am Janet Crosse. Joan Cruddon was my aunt. Until you did her to death in Norwich. Just as you did my uncle Jacob, and my cousin John."

"Come out, murderer!" This was a man's voice. So the Dutchman Rutger was with her.

"I am no murderer!" I called. "All their deaths came from their own evil. Not mine."

"You lie!" she screeched. "You will die for what you have done to my family!"

There was another sudden thud and the whole hut shook. I screamed as a wicked iron tip punched through the join between two trunks with a shower of splinters, only a couple of feet from where I crouched.

I moved across to where it had emerged, reasoning that she would be unlikely to aim for the same place twice. Angelo came as well and moved up close to me. He put his hand on my knee without words, as if this was reassurance enough. But I was unable to see how we could escape this madwoman and her crossbow.

I flinched as another bolt hit just where Angelo had been, spraying the inside of the hut with more splinters and shards of wood.

Now it was only a matter of time until she walked up to the

hut and killed us both. We were sheep being made ready for slaughter.

There must be something we could do. In desperation, I looked over at the door. "Can we burst out and reach the trees?" I whispered.

Before Angelo could reply, my question was answered by another crossbow bolt slamming into the side of the hut. I glanced up at the window. In place of the grey light, now there was a clear night sky, with the winter moon shining like the brightest lamp. Janet Crosse would most certainly see us emerging from the shadows, and be able to shoot us at will.

Not a chance we could take. We needed something to distract her attention.

The door was made of loose planks, some of which were so badly worn that there were gaps between them.

That gave me an idea.

I crawled slowly over, and carefully pushed the tip of my sword into one of the smaller gaps. I judged it was around chest height for our attacker. The fit was most tight, but I eased it in as quietly as I could; just enough to hold it firm, but, I hoped, not be seen from the outside.

Angelo came over as well, and must have understood what I was doing. He pushed his own sword into another gap slightly higher up. Then he held it in place.

Another bolt hit the side wall. This one almost came right through, and I shuddered to think what damage it would have done had we still been over there.

"Come out!" repeated Janet Crosse.

"Nay!" I called back. "You will have to come in for us yourself!"

There was a few moments' silence, and I imagined she was working out what she must do. Perhaps she was gesturing to Rutger to play his part.

I was correct. There was the sound of some footsteps crunching in the snow, moving fast towards the hut. Then the door shook, as if someone on the other side was trying to open it.

"Now!" I hissed, and we both pushed our swords hard through the planks.

There was a rattling gasp and a guttural man's voice exclaiming *"Mijn God! Verdomme!"*

And the strong metallic smell of blood.

I gestured to Angelo that we should push the door open and whispered what we must do after. He nodded, and we put all our strength against the door, which opened with great resistance. As soon as it had finally swung outward, we pulled our swords free. The blades came out, and there was the heavy sound of a body falling beyond. Without waiting to see if it was Rutger and he was truly dead, we both ran into the dark night, separated so there was no single target. We each made for the trees.

There was a high-pitched scream from the hut. "Rutger! No!"

The crossbow cracked and a bolt flew past, so close that I felt the rush of air.

"Not hit?" Angelo yelled from further over to the right.

"Nay!" I gasped, just as I spotted one of the scarred trees; the cut in its bark shining white in the moonlight. From there I saw the next marked tree, and the next, until I could make out two dark shapes beyond that had the look of the horses. With relief I ran up to find them both patiently waiting.

I untied Hestia and leapt onto her back. There was a thump of footsteps and Angelo appeared beside his horse, then untied it and mounted. I wheeled Hestia round, and with a glance at the moon to make sure we were headed south, I gave her a quick squeeze of my legs and urged her forward.

Together we galloped through the remaining trees and out onto the moonlit white fields beyond.

15
THOMAS RETURNS

Angelo and I rode our horses through the night.

Fields and forests flashed past as we pushed our mounts with only the briefest pauses to rest. We rode over mountain passes and through Switzer villages, keeping going when we were all but falling asleep in the saddle, and when Hestia's head was hanging low with tiredness.

I kept encouraging her, and it was as if she understood why we were so keen to ride hard; why we must put distance between ourselves and the wrath of Janet Crosse. Each incitement to keep going seemed to give her a burst of energy and she would leap forward with renewed vigour. I made all sorts of promises to reward her; I offered her a long rest, a warm stable and many bags of mash, once we made it over the mountains. My brave friend seemed to respond to each of these.

I prayed I would be able to make good on my promises. I prayed God would see us safe away from Janet Crosse and her infernal crossbow. For we had done naught but add kindling to the fire of her vengeance.

To the deaths of Jacob Cruddon, his son John and his widow Joan, must now be added that of the Dutchman Rutger. I knew not if he was already Janet's husband or even her betrothed, but it was clear from her reaction that he was someone special to her. I imagined how she had landed in Den Haag on her quest to find me and Angelo, then somehow been befriended by the tall Dutchman. Perhaps a deep relationship had blossomed, even in the short time they must have known each other.

A relationship that had then been cut short at the door of the herdsman's hut.

I kept a watch every time we stopped, forcing my tired eyes to search the moonlit path behind us for any possible sign of a following rider. And in truth, I convinced myself that every shadow was Janet Crosse creeping toward us; her crossbow raised, ready to strike. I said as much to Angelo, but he gave little credence to my fears.

"She is not a spectre," he observed, "able to move without making a sound. If she comes, belike we will hear the noise of her mount's hooves, or see her in the moonlight." He regarded me with a furrowed brow. "And we have ridden hard through most of the night." He glanced to the east, where a pink glow was already starting to cloak the tips of the snow-capped mountain peaks. "The dawn is nearly upon us. I warrant she will not have abandoned the Dutchman's body and ridden through the night, but instead tended to his wounds if he still lives, or taken his corpse to consecrated ground if not." He gestured to the south. "No, I think we are many hours ahead of her now, and are like to stay that way if we descend once again to yonder flatlands."

He walked his horse over to me, and put his hand on my arm. "So still your fears, *dolce* Maria, and let us press on. We are but a day's ride to the Duchy of Milano, and I would we keep moving, so we can lose ourselves in the city."

I managed a weak nod, trying to show confidence I could not truly feel. Every time I closed my eyes, I was back in that hut, the crossbow bolt striking the window frame right beside my head. Or spraying out sharp shards of wood so close that it was a wonder I was not hit.

"So, we keep moving, Maria?" he asked. After a moment, I nodded again. "Good." He wheeled his horse round. "We stop for food in the next settlement? Agreed?"

Unable even to speak, I set off behind him.

The evening of the following day, we arrived in Milano. By this time I was all but asleep in the saddle, and Hestia seemed barely able to place one hoof before the other. I had scarcely taken in the end of the snows, but at some point during the day I realised that we were no longer descending through bright white fields, but were now riding through the green pastures and forests of the lowlands. The air seemed thicker, almost as if I needed more effort to breathe, but it was richer with the scent of pine. We even came across a small stream, chuckling over stones. Both Hestia and I lowered our heads into the clear waters, and drank our fill, before Angelo charged both our costrels with two quarts of the precious liquid for later.

We found a coaching inn at the edge of the city. I urged Hestia across the yard to the stables; a distance that seemed at that moment to be greater than all we had travelled in the last two days. But we finally made it, and I slid off her back and unsaddled her, while Angelo did the same for his horse. I gave her a desultory rub down and found a blanket for her back. Making sure she had hay in the manger and water in the trough, I bade her a fond farewell and we hobbled into the inn.

Angelo found the innkeeper and spoke quickly in his native tongue. I knew I should follow with ease, for we had been continuing with my lessons over the past weeks and Angelo had proclaimed I was now able to converse almost as well as a native. But in my weariness that evening the words just slipped past me, like chaff blowing away in the wind.

Angelo said, "Come, wife, there is a room for us. Let us go up and rest from our travels."

It took a few moments for his words to take hold, and I fear I stared at him as if I had taken leave of my senses. But eventually his words formed themselves into some meaning.

He had referred to me as 'wife'. Should I call this out as a falsehood, for it was clearly not true?

Maybe I should. What might be the words to use?

They would not come.

Not with the roaring sound now pounding in my ears.

Then Angelo appeared to jump to one side. I shook my head; he had not moved.

The roaring became louder, as if a wave were coming at me. A wave of blackness.

I let the wave wash over me; for how could I stop it, as everything was becoming dark?

The last thing I recall was collapsing like a bundle of rags.

—0—

Adriana de Vries looked up at me with a broad smile; her small pink tongue playing across her perfect white teeth.

"You may now kiss the bride," said a voice. A clergyman was standing beside us, beaming like a cloth-headed fool. He gave me an encouraging nod, and even waved a hand, as if to make it clear that my duty was to seal the marriage vows with a kiss. Marriage vows? I had no recollection of making any vows—but here was Adriana, licking her lips as if in anticipation. And there was her mother in the first pew, appearing to be both laughing and crying at the same time, while Pieter de Vries sat beside his wife, his head slumped forward and a large lidded tankard in his hand. He looked up slowly and fixed me with bloodshot eyes. Without looking away, he raised the tankard, flicked open the lid and took a long draught. Then he slumped forward again.

"Please, Master Richardson, kiss the bride," the clergyman repeated. "For how else will you seal the contract of marriage than with a first kiss?"

Nay, we have kissed once already! I wanted to say. But for some reason my tongue was stuck in my mouth and no words would come out.

"Speak, my husband," Adriana whispered. "Speak!" She gave me a playful punch on the arm. But as much as I tried, I could still not make a sound. "By Heavens, Thomas," she said, putting her hands on her hips, "what has become of you, that you have no power to say what is on your mind?" I wondered how she now had such good command of English. Had I taught her? She leaned forward and punched me on the arm again. "Speak!"

I cannot! I shook my head in frustration. She gave me a most unladylike scowl and shook my shoulder. "Maria!" she growled, "Maria!" She shook it even harder. "Maria, in Heaven's name!"

How did she know me as Maria? And why had her voice become so deep?

"Wake up, Maria!" she said, and now her voice was no longer hers, but Angelo's. "You have been asleep near on a full day! Awake please, *dolce* Maria!"

I opened my eyes.

Angelo was standing over me, his hand on my shoulder.

"Where am I?" I whispered. "I was in church and had just been married to Adriana..."

He gave a small laugh. "I wondered at your dream," he said. "You were whimpering like a puppy. But no; you are in Milano with me, and you are safe in bed." He took his hand away and scratched at his beard as he regarded me. "You fell in a dead faint onto the floor yesterday. It was by good fortune I was able to catch you, else you might have struck your head."

"I fell into your arms?" I breathed, wanting to creep beneath the blanket and hide from shame.

"You did. I carried you up and put you in this bed, where you have been for near on a day since."

"Oh!" I lifted the blanket and held my breath as I looked down at what I was wearing. I have ne'er been so relieved to see I was still clothed in my laced bodice and kirtle. At least Angelo had not undressed me as I slept. I shivered despite the warmth of the bed; that would have been so much worse than fainting in his arms and being carried up like a babe.

But there was a greater cause for concern.

"You have let me sleep for all but a day?" He gave a small nod, which made me frown. "But Angelo, do you not see? We were perhaps a day ahead of Janet Crosse. Now we have given her enough time to catch us up."

"Nay," he said with an easy smile. "Hundreds of travellers arrive each day into the city of Milano; what is remarkable about two such persons that she might find us by inquiry? And we are in one of many hundreds of taverns within the city walls. If she were to ask in every one, she might take a week to get round them all."

I chose not to reply, for he seemed most sure of himself. But I knew that with the devil guiding her footsteps, Janet Crosse might choose this very tavern to begin her enquiries. It was perfectly possible.

But I felt I must allow him the point. "If you say," I demurred.

"I do," he said, with finality. "But you have a point, Maria. We must make our plans to continue our journey," He tapped his fingers on the hilt of his sword, as if helping him reach a decision. "I suggest you resume men's attire once more, so you can move around more easily. Now that Janet Crosse has seen you in woman's clothing, it is better you become Thomas again."

—0—

Resuming a man's jerkin and hose seemed like making the re-acquaintance of a long-lost and much missed friend. I let out a deep sigh of contentment as I adjusted my cap.

There was the agreed series of knocks at the door, so I unlocked it and let Angelo in.

He came into the chamber and stood with his hands on his hips, casting a critical eye across my attire. He nodded, as if I had passed muster. "*Benvenuto* Thomas," he said, and I noted he used the masculine form of the word. "It is good to have you back."

"I feel the same," I said, pulling the hem of my jerkin down and checking the sword at my belt.

"When you were asleep, I found the energy myself to go out and make enquiries about the safety of the road to Napoli." He paused a moment. "There was a time when the states of Napoli and Milano were at war, but now we are both under Spanish rule, we are friends."

"Then that is good, is it not?" I asked.

"Not necessarily. There are still many bands of disaffected

soldiers on the road, as well as brigands preying on travellers. So while it is good that you are again dressed in man's garb, it is better that we travel as part of a larger group. It is too dangerous to be on our own."

I could see the sense of this, but it caused me grave concern to think we had yet more dangers on the road. Now I must add the threat of disaffected soldiers to Janet and her crossbow.

"I have found a party of men setting off from here tomorrow, heading first for the Duchy of Firenze. They have said that we may join with them."

"Then that is good," I repeated, and we were agreed.

16

SCORONCONCOLO

The following morning, Angelo and I rode to the *Piazza Mercanti*, a square in the heart of the city, where he had agreed to meet our fellow travellers.

Hestia had been standing in her stall when I went to saddle her, pulling idly on the straw in her manger.

"Forgive me, old friend," I said, putting my head on her neck and giving her a conciliatory pat. "I did not give you mash." I brightened my tone. "But we have both had a day's rest, and I did find you a warm blanket." But this brightness seemed to have no effect, and she lifted her head away, giving a dismissive-sounding snort.

I ran my hand from her withers to her leg, then reached into my jerkin pocket for the apple I had secured earlier from the tavern. She eyed me as I cut it into four pieces with my knife, and gave her each one in turn. "There," I said when she had finished, "Is that not better?" I stroked her muzzle. "Friends once more?"

She paused a moment, then gave a small whinny. "There," I said. "Now, we need to continue on our journey."

I mounted up and rode into the courtyard where Angelo was already waiting.

"Come," he said, "and stay close. If we are separated, we may never find each other again."

As soon as we headed out I could see what he meant. The streets of Milano were heavily crowded with men and women on foot; noblemen, soldiers and merchants on horseback; tradesmen with handcarts, children running almost under horses' hooves, and a general flow of people. If we were not close, we would be swept away from each other. It put me in mind of bees swarming around a hive.

After many turns left and right, I was concerned that we could easily become lost among the maze of narrow streets. I asked Angelo if he was confident of the route.

"This is not my first visit to Milano," he replied. "Keep close and we will soon be there."

Shortly after, he turned off the street and took us under an arch. There was a table beneath it with a merchant standing talking to a couple of men in fine blue and yellow tunics edged with white fur. One of the men was examining a bolt of russet-coloured cloth, while the other was leaning on the table and writing a note; frequently dipping his quill into a silver ink pot as he wrote. I followed Angelo as he squeezed his mount past the table, and we emerged into a spacious square.

"*Piazza Mercanti*," Angelo called over his shoulder. "The place where merchants and guildsmen make their trades."

The bustling square was lined on all sides with archways like the one we had just come through, and each had a similar table with a merchant standing behind. There were men selling every conceivable type of merchandise; hats, swords, clothing, boots and cloth were all being traded, and those were only the ones I was closest to. Merchants were showing their wares and weighing coins in scales, although it seemed that the majority of trades were being made in exchange for written papers, like the one I had seen under the arch coming in.

I must have been frowning as I tried to understand the meaning of these. "Promissory notes," Angelo explained, leaning towards me. "The buyer makes a promise to pay the seller a set amount on a particular later date. Such notes therefore have a value in themselves, and there are banking families like the de Medicis who facilitate trade in them." He rode on a little further. "It is even said the first such note was written here in Milano, most likely in this very square, some two hundred years ago."

We reached the middle of the piazza and Angelo dismounted,

so I did the same. He led us towards a large building on the north-eastern side, which he told me was the *Palazzo della Ragione*. "It is the main *broletto*," he added, "or administrative building. Most of the life of Milano is controlled from here."

At that moment a party of four men came over, each leading a horse. Angelo held up a hand in greeting, and went up to them.

I took it that these were the ones we were to travel alongside. I smiled inwardly; as a group of men, they inspired confidence; no band of brigands or disaffected soldiers would think to attack these fellows. Each was clearly a fighting man; well-armed, with swords and knives at their belts. All four also had longbows on their backs, with a quiver of arrows at their hip.

One of the men stepped forward and Angelo approached him, then stopped and gave a small bow. The other bowed back, while sweeping off his cap. As the man straightened up, I was able to see him more clearly. He was of above average height but well-built, and had not a single hair on his head nor any on his brow or chin. The close-set eyes on either side of his prominent nose were coal black.

He turned away from Angelo and stared at me with such an intensity that I found myself wishing to run away as fast as I could. But suddenly he smiled, and it was the difference between night and day. This man's smile was so infectious and so full of charm, that I immediately warmed to him. I wanted to know more of him; a man who could appear so dark one minute, and so bright the next.

I also bowed. "*Signore* Thomas Richardson," I said.

"Michele del Tavolaccino," the man replied. "But to many I am known by a different name." I was pleased that I could grasp his meaning easily with my knowledge of the Neapolitan tongue. His smile disappeared in an instant, and he was once again full of menace. "So if we are to travel together to Firenze, *Signore* Richardson, you must call me by the name I most usually use." He paused, as if to give greater meaning to his next word. "Scoronconcolo."

17

HOW MUCH WINE IS TOO MUCH?

We gathered our little band of riders together, and I was introduced to each of the others by Scoronconcolo.

"This is Pietro," he said. One with the build of a large ox bowed from the saddle and swept off his cap, revealing a head of thick black hair that fell across the broadest pair shoulders I have ever seen on a man. As he replaced the cap, Pietro made a quick sideways glance at Scoronconcolo that seemed almost fearful, as if he would follow the man out of concern for reprisal, rather than respect for the other's leadership. For such a large bull of a man like this to give such a look, spoke to me further of Scoronconcolo's menace.

"Thomas," I replied, with a bow of my own.

"Tommaso?" he rumbled, in a voice so deep I could almost not hear it. I nodded, not wishing to correct him. The man had a neck seemingly thicker than my waist.

"And this is Giuseppe." Another rode forward to acknowledge me. "Tommaso?" he asked, and I nodded again. Giuseppe was not as well-built as Scoronconcolo and Pietro, but no less a fighting man, as attested by the red puckered scar that ran from his temple to his cheek. It put me in mind of Jacob Cruddon's similar disfigurement, except that unlike Cruddon, the wound had missed Giuseppe's eye. His were both a piercing blue-grey, and seemed most healthy as they regarded me.

The thought of Cruddon gave me a small shudder, as it reminded me once more of his murderous niece. I tried to take some comfort from the presence of the men around us, telling myself that even if Janet Crosse could find us, these fighters would afford us some protection. But the bow on Giuseppe's back

reminded me of our adversary's crossbow, and I could not dispel
the fear that she could be waiting for us on the road, her weapon
poised and ready.

"Tommaso," said a voice, cutting across my thoughts. "I am
Franco." I brought myself back to the piazza. The fourth man had
come forward, and was bowing like his comrades. I returned the
greeting as I appraised him. This one was neither as big as Pietro
nor as small as Giuseppe, but somewhere between. He appeared a
little older than the others, with some grey peppering his beard,
and lines upon his face.

With introductions completed, Scoronconcolo called us all to
order, and we followed him out of the piazza.

The streets beyond the arches were as crowded as before. I
could not help but be cross with Angelo, for he rode ahead,
chatting with Franco and waving his hands about in an animated
manner, rather than keeping close to me. I resolved to have this
out with him once we were able to talk. For the moment I must
concentrate on keeping close to the men as the crowds swirled
around us. Fortunately Scoronconcolo seemed able to part the
throng before him, while Pietro's broad back was a clear beacon to
follow. This way I was able to keep up with the group until we
came to the city gate and took the open country road towards
Firenze.

I rode up to Angelo, and hissed, "We must talk." He gave me
a small grin, which I thought might be a sign of his contrition. Or,
of course, nothing of the sort. Just his way.

We both slowed until we were riding far enough behind the
others to be unheard.

"You would leave me to become separated back there?" I
enquired in an icy tone.

"You would have me shepherd you like a dog does a weakling
sheep?" He shook his head slightly. "Act the man you pretend to
be," he said. "Lest these fellows think you might be a woman in
need of protection." He grinned again. "And yet 'tis no matter.
You were quite able to stay with us withal."

The fact he was correct did not cool my temper; if anything, it made it worse, and I felt my belly tighten up. "That is not the point," I snapped.

His grin returned. "Which is?"

But I had no answer, and he knew it. His smile got even greater, and I had to grit my teeth to stop myself punching his arm.

"Anyway, how did you come to find these men?" I said, looking to change the subject.

He glanced across and his smile faded, to be replaced by a raised eyebrow. "You sound as if you have a concern?"

"Only that they are quite fearsome," I replied. "Pietro is enormous, and their leader Scoronconcolo has a real menace to him."

"Is that not a good quality in a man who has said he will keep us safe?"

"I warrant it is," I agreed, my anger starting to cool. "But when he is not smiling, his manner seems threatening to us all."

Angelo gave a small chuckle. "But when he smiles, then all is well?"

I felt my belly tighten again. "You make light of my concerns," I hissed, and Angelo finally had the grace to look contrite.

"Nay, Mar… Thomas," he said, holding up a hand. "I trust your judgment too well for that."

"Then answer my question," I replied, taking a deep breath to steady myself. "How did you find them? And what bargain did you strike?"

We rode on in silence a few paces, then he said, "Yesterday morning I awoke at the usual time, while you carried on sleeping like a babe. So I thought I would find out about our journey to Napoli, and the state of the roads. I had heard of the brigands and ex-soldiers preying on travellers." He patted his saddlebag. "I was concerned, lest *il Fiume di Fuoco* is stolen once again. We have come this far, and I have no wish to make the whole journey for naught.

"Your mother's birthday is still some weeks away," I said. "How far are we from Pozzuoli?"

"Near enough to make it in plenty of time," he replied. "But only if we still have the jewel."

Once again, I had the picture in my mind of his mother, grieving for her husband and waiting in hope to see her son once more. Wanting to get back the jewel that secured her continued life. "You are right to remind me of the true purpose of our journey," I said, my anger quite gone. "So what did you find?"

"It was as I thought," he said. "There were tales of travellers being robbed and even killed. So I asked around for word of protection, and was passed along a chain of different recommendations until eventually I came upon Scoronconcolo and his band of men. I was told they were planning to travel to Napoli via Firenze. I introduced myself and asked if we could join them, then agreed a price for our passage."

"How much was that?" I asked.

He made his usual grin. "More than I wanted to pay, but less than he was asking."

—0—

Soon after leaving the city gate, we emerged onto the main road to Firenze. As we rode, I took the opportunity to observe the Milanese country. Field after field sloped up on both sides, all filled with regimented rows of leafy plants like lines of soldiers ready for war. Angelo rode up beside me. "Vines," he said. "Stripped bare by the harvest. The wines here are some of the best." He paused, then smiled. "Although, of course, not as good as on the mountain slopes of Napoli."

I gave him a warm laugh and waved my hand at the nearest vines. "I would try these Milanese wines," I said. "If you are willing to rate them almost as high as your Neapolitan ones, then I must put your claim to the test. Where do you recommend I start?"

"The Pollentia reds from the Nebbiolo grape are well worth it," he replied. "I would start there."

"Then I shall," I replied. "And I hope they might live up to your promise."

Shortly after, the open country came to an end, and we headed into a forest. The light turned from a clear blue to dappled browns and greens, and I looked about in wonder. These were not the types of trees I was used to, but large plants with enormous leaves, interspersed with many large chestnut trees.

Immediately Scoronconcolo broke into a fast canter, waving us all onwards as well. Hestia seemed to need no urging, for she gave a small neigh, her ears pricked up, and she leapt forward. "You have been standing and walking for some time, eh, old friend?" I said to her. "Now you can stretch out your legs!"

And that she did; picking past plants and shrubs with practiced ease, leaping across roots and fallen branches, and soaring like an elegant swan across ditches. I could only share her joy as we thundered through the echoing forest, as I realised that it must be because we were finally making good speed away from Janet Crosse. Every hoof-beat, every jump that Hestia made, made me feel as if we were just a little safer from the threat of the woman's vengeance.

But it was not possible to keep up this pace for ever, even with Hestia's enthusiasm. After maybe fifteen minutes, I could see that she was now starting to tire. Every few strides she dropped her head, and after she had made a small, uncharacteristic stumble, I knew we would soon need to give her, and presumably the other horses too, a rest. I urged her forward and she responded with a burst of speed, so that we came up alongside Scoronconcolo.

"How long must keep up this pace?" I called. He barely looked at me as he replied. "Until we are back in open country and are less likely to be attacked."

"But the horses will need to rest soon," I protested.

"We must keep them going," he snapped, glancing across.

I decided not to argue further, as the look on his face suggested I would not be successful. I dropped Hestia back and tucked her in between Giuseppe and Pietro, thinking that having horses close in front and behind would give her some encouragement.

Angelo appeared beside me. "Art well, Thomas?" he called across with his customary grin.

I gave him a smile in return and was about to respond, when Hestia suddenly dropped her head again and made another stumble. "She is most tired," I yelled. "We must stop soon. But Scoronconcolo would keep us going. I fear he will do so until the horses drop."

"I will have a word with him," Angelo said, and urged his horse forward. He drew up alongside Scoronconcolo, leaning across to talk as they rode side by side through the foliage. Scoronconcolo responded, and there were a few more exchanges, then the other man nodded. Angelo slowed and came back to me. "He will stop as soon as we are in the open, and we will seek out a stream where the horses can drink."

"That is good," I said. "What did you say to him?"

"That we must rest the horses soon, lest we are attacked and they have no speed left in them to escape."

"A good point," I agreed. He fell back behind me, and we continued for another five minutes or so, with Hestia continuing to pick her way through the greenery.

Then I gave a small cheer and patted Hestia's neck. "We will stop soon, old friend," I whispered. "Look!" She raised her head. There was a growing patch of blue sky ahead between two large trees, marking the edge of the forest.

With my spirits lifted, I pressed my heels into her flanks, and she gave me a last burst of speed.

Just as three men on horseback appeared on the path ahead with their swords drawn, blocking our way.

Immediately Scoronconcolo pulled his horse up so it reared on its back legs with a fearsome neigh. Giuseppe and Franco did the same, while Pietro pulled his up without rearing. I did not need to tell Hestia anything; she could see what was happening. She came to a quick halt by herself. I glanced round; Angelo was a few yards back.

And behind him were yet two more swordsmen.

"Look out!" I called, pointing back.

Franco looked round, and in one smooth move, drew an arrow to his bow. There was a snap in the air beside me as the shaft flew past, burying itself in one of the men's chests with a sickening thud. The man grunted, fumbling at the arrow as if he would pull it free. But this was a hopeless task. He fell forward and slid to the ground.

His companion gave a roar and rode towards us; his sword out. He came first at Angelo, who also had his sword in hand. There was a clash of blades as he rode past, then he wheeled round and swung again. Angelo parried, giving another ringing sound of steel on steel.

I drew my own sword, and urged Hestia towards Angelo and his assailant. As I reached the man, I swept my blade at his back, just as he leaned across to take the next swing at Angelo. I missed the full cut but nicked his side, causing him to yell and turn. His red face was before mine, full of anger. I tried to bring my sword round again, but now Hestia had raised her head and it was in the way. Seeing this, the man gave an evil grin. He flicked his sword back, then leaned at me, preparing to run me through.

But before he could, a blade emerged from his chest; its blood-covered tip coming straight towards me.

The man gave a cough, and his look of anger turned to surprise. A gobbet of blood bubbled up onto his lip. Then he coughed again, and more blood appeared, just as the blade withdrew as suddenly as it had appeared. The man's eyes rolled up, before he started to fall slowly sideways, as if he were a tree that had just been felled. His fall gathered speed, until he could no longer stay on his horse's back. He crashed to the ground, and was still.

The man's fall revealed Angelo, who was sitting still on his horse with the blood-covered sword in hand. He gave me a small grin. "That was close," he said. He paused. "And you have not answered my question, Thomas. Art well?"

I took a deep breath and said, "Yes. And thank you for your quick action. You saved me."

"You too," he replied. "Your sweep distracted the man so I could run him through."

A choking sound caught my attention, and I spun round.

Pietro had a man in a tight grip around the throat from behind. There was a crack and the man's head fell forward. Pietro stepped back, and let the body fall to the ground. Meanwhile Scoronconcolo was pulling his sword out of the prone body of one of the other men, and Giuseppe was wiping blood off his knife using the jerkin of the third man's body.

Scoronconcolo nodded at each of us. "In truth I would have preferred to have killed them all by my own hand, but I see you have saved me the trouble."

—0—

The sun was sinking below the western hills as we came upon a wayside tavern. "I say we stop here for the night," Scoronconcolo said, and there was a murmur of agreement from Franco and Giuseppe. There may well have been one from Pietro as well, although it was perhaps too low a sound for me to hear.

"I warrant we have earned a good drink, something to eat, and a well-deserved night's sleep," Scoronconcolo added. "I always sleep well after a good kill."

Giuseppe sniggered, and Pietro grunted, as if in agreement. I had no doubt they had heard this many times before.

But it was the mention of sleep that awoke in me a concern I had previously put to the back of my mind. But now it came back in full force. I waited until Angelo and I were alone in the stable after we had unsaddled and secured our horses for the night, then I whispered across to him, "I would not be discovered as a woman while we sleep. Keep them well away from me." The thought of men such as Scoronconcolo or Pietro—or in truth, any of them— discovering my true nature, made my blood freeze like ice over a midwinter pond. I could imagine how quickly their protection would disappear and I would become their prey instead.

"Then sleep fully clothed," Angelo whispered back. "As you have done many times before."

"But what if I cry out in my sleep, or somesuch?" I replied. "What if we are together in a dormitory of men and I make womanly sounds? You have said oft how I make small cries while I slumber."

He was silent as we emerged from the stables and made our way to the tavern. "Then perhaps you should have three or four drinks first," he suggested as we got to the door. "Then you will sleep most soundly."

"Three or four?" I asked. "I rarely have so much." My mind returned to the tavern in Den Haag, where even a sip of the beer had made my head spin. "I rarely exceed a glass or two of wine," I said.

"Then have enough to make you sleep," he said. "But no more."

"No more," I agreed. "I promise."

I could see the sense in this, so when we sat down as a group to eat, I leaned back with my legs apart and called to a serving girl for some Nebbiolo wine from Pollentia, as Angelo had suggested. She soon brought a full carafe of deep red wine, and I took a small sip when it was poured. By good fortune, this did not make my head spin, so I took another.

There was a snigger from Scoronconcolo, and I glanced across at him. He was fixing me with his black eyes. "Drink," he barked. "Not like a blushing maiden, but like a man!"

Such words startled me. Was he suspecting my true nature? Desperately, I threw back my head and gulped down the rest of the goblet. But some went down the wrong way, and I was forced to breathe deeply through my nose, lest I cough it all out again.

Scoronconcolo laughed to his men. "Tommaso is unused to strong Milanese wines," he chuckled. He filled my goblet again. "Drink on, young man," he ordered. Was there a twinkle of mischief in his eye, or was it a suspicion of my secret? "You will find it most agreeable," he added.

How could I now refuse? I picked up the goblet and swirled the wine around, as if I was savouring the possibility of more richness. Then I took a long drink, finishing it all in one go.

"Is this wise?" Angelo asked. "Thomas is young. He is not used to strong drink…"

But Scoronconcolo gave a dismissive laugh. "Then it is good for him to learn."

"What say you, Thomas?" Angelo asked, with a worried-looking frown. "Is it not enough?"

But I was not listening, for I was now more concerned with the strangest feeling that had struck me. A deliciously warm glow had begun to spread around my body. It had started at the tips of my fingers and toes, and was now working its way inwards. I glanced up, as the room now gave a small spinning shudder. I frowned. Had it been picked up and moved by a giant hand?

Scoronconcolo filled my goblet again, and this time I grabbed at it like a man dying of thirst and gulped it down. The glow in my body became hotter, but it felt so good, that I wanted more of it. A further goblet of wine followed, and by the time Scoronconcolo was calling for a new carafe, I was eager to drink as much of it as I could.

Angelo put his hand on my arm and said quietly in English, "I think this is enough now. Remember our agreement. No more. You made a promise."

I shook my head. It was quite plain now that my earlier pledge was meaningless. Silly, even.

"You recommended this wine, and I take it. The recommendation, I mean." I giggled. "And the wine, of course." My goblet seemed to have refilled itself, so I drank it down in one go, then banged it down on the table as a demand for Scoronconcolo to fill it once more.

"Enough, I say," Angelo repeated, but by this time, I had no care for his words. I liked this wine, and I wanted as much of it as

I could get. As we ate, I fear I must have lost count of how much I was drinking. I vaguely recall Angelo sitting back with folded arms, saying something about regret, but I was more interested in calling for more wine, and throwing it down my throat as if I was dying of thirst.

This must have caused my tongue to become dangerously loose. Looking back, it nearly had the very effect I was trying to avoid. In my increasingly drunken state it was as if I was becoming a shrewish scold, waving a flag above my head that said, 'I am a woman'.

I took Scoronconcolo to task about his manner.

"You have the smile of an angel," I said to him, and I vaguely recall wagging an accusing finger. "Yet without it, you are such a menace. Why so?"

Angelo kicked me hard under the table. "Ow!" I yelped, leaning down and rubbing my shin. "What did you do that for?"

Angelo remained silent, although he may have mouthed, 'Be quiet!' at me.

Scoronconcolo gave a loud laugh. "Your friend Tommaso may now drink like a man, although in truth, he is poor at holding his wine," he said. "But I will answer him." He gave a grin at his comrades and put a hand to the hilt of his knife. "In my line of work, it pays me well to have charm for those who reward me for my services." He made a short pause, staring hard at me, now with his menacing look. "And to instil fear in those who are the target of their disapproval."

"What line of work is that?" I demanded, then yelped again at Angelo's kick.

"Tommaso asks a fair question," Scoronconcolo said. He took a draught of his wine. "I solve problems." He paused. "I make difficult situations—go away."

Angelo tugged at my sleeve, a look of deep concern on his face. "Come Thomas," he said, his voice rising, "You are most tired. It is time to lay your head down."

I pulled away. "Nay," I muttered. "I want to know more of

this. Come on, Sconcon… Scoronconcolooncoll… Sconsconcolly… Whatever is your name. What are these 'difficult situations'?"

"Thomas!" Angelo barked. "To bed. Now!"

"I agree," Scoronconcolo said, his voice most quiet. "Lest he becomes a 'difficult situation' himself."

"By Heavens, Thomas," Angelo muttered, his hand going to his own hilt. "Come now, or I will march you upstairs on the point of my sword."

I may have tried to resist, but I do not recall, for the next thing I knew, I was being pushed up some stairs, through a door into a large room full of beds, then put face down onto a rough straw mattress that smelled of mould, and being turned onto my side. "In case you needs must vomit," Angelo seemed to say, his voice echoing as if from the far end of a long tunnel.

Then everything went black.

18
A QUESTION OF GENDER

In all my years, I have only ever had a few unpleasant awakenings. But I could not recall one so bad as the next morning.

I came slowly out of slumber, with immediate concerns only for my physical state. My mouth felt drier than a lakebed in summer, and no attempt to moisten it with my tongue would have any effect. Added to which, it was as if someone had placed my head on a blacksmith's anvil, and invited the smith to beat it regularly with the heaviest of hammers.

Why did I feel this way?

I coughed, and burst of stale wine came up from the back of my throat.

So that was it. I must have been drinking to excess. I had been drunk...

My eyes opened wide and I let out a deep groan. *I had been drunk*. In front of Scoronconcolo and his band of men. And Angelo.

Fleeting images now appeared before me, as if invited in by this realisation... Slouching like a coarse fellow and bawling out for wine... Pouring it down my throat... Angelo kicking me under the table...

I groaned again. Had I truly wagged a finger at Scoronconcolo?

I tried to sit up. But the room was spinning too fast and I collapsed back onto the mattress, curling on my side like a newborn babe. In that brief moment, I had seen where I was; in a dark room with just enough moonlight coming through an open window to show there were many other mattresses such as mine. Each had the shape of a man asleep upon it, and one so large it could only be Pietro.

A hand touched my shoulder, and such was my state I made no reaction. "Thomas? You sat up. Art awake?" I struggled to turn over; a move that nearly made me vomit, but after a couple of tries, I made it as far as my back. I squinted up at the dark shape of Angelo.

"Thomas?" he repeated in a whisper. "You should come outside, away from here. We need to talk."

"Leave me alone," I muttered, closing my eyes. "I would die in peace."

"No."

"I may vomit all over you."

"A risk I will take." He pulled on my arm. "Come," he hissed. "It is near dawn. We must talk before the others awaken. It is important."

"I must dress."

"You are already fully clothed." He tugged my arm again. "Come on!" He pulled me almost bodily off the mattress, then put his hands either side of my chest and lifted me upright. Once I was standing, he marched me across the room and out of the door. This led to the open air, at the top of a wooden stairway running down the side of the building.

The difference between the cold of the night and the dormitory warmed by so many bodies, was so severe that the shock made me immediately a little more sober.

Angelo led the way down the stairs to a cobbled courtyard, then across to the other side, where he sat down among some trees.

I staggered up to him, and was about to sit, when there was a rumble in my belly and a catch in my throat. I knew for certain this meant my body was about to relieve itself of all I had eaten and drunk the night before. I continued past him, then leaned against a tree and was heartily sick many times, until I was sure little of the wine remained.

Sadly the same could not be said of the banging headache, but at least now it felt a little easier to bear. Once I was sure there was nothing more to come, I stepped away from the small lake of vomit at my feet, wiped my mouth on my sleeve and made my way to where Angelo sat. I dropped down beside him.

"Feeling better now?" he enquired.

"A bit."

"And good fortune that you did it out here, and not as you slept."

"What do we need to talk about?" I asked, hoping a show of innocence might cause him to be more understanding. But I knew the answer full well; I was about to be given a stern lecture on the evils of drink and on the consequences of a loose tongue. I was not disappointed.

"Have you any idea how close you came to having Scoronconcolo's knife in your guts?" he said, his eyes wide in the moonlight. "The man told us with near certainty that he is a paid killer; an assassin. Such a one as him thinks nothing of dispatching a person who shows disrespect."

I dropped my head into my hands. "And I wagged a finger in his face," I groaned. "And told him to be less menacing."

"Indeed so."

I turned to stare at him. "Then why do I still live?"

"Because I spoke for you, and said you were but a callow youth, unused to drink."

"Thank you, Angelo," I whispered.

He paused, as if choosing his words with care. "But we had an agreement," he said.

"Scoronconcolo pushed me to drink," I replied, hoping he could see I was not fully to blame.

"Yet you could have stopped, especially when I cautioned you."

For a moment I felt once again the warm glow of the wine. "I liked it," I said. "I wanted more."

He regarded me silently a while. "And that you did." He nodded, almost to himself. "At least it made Scoronconcolo reveal what he truly is. We must be most wary of him as we travel together to Firenze."

I gasped in surprise. "You would have us stay with him?" I tried to stand, but thought better of it. "We must slip away now, before they awake."

"And go where?"

"We press on to Napoli."

"And have them behind us, riding hard to catch us up?"

I could see his point, so I gave it some thought. "We could head back towards Milano," I suggested, "then circle round when it is safe?"

"And run into Janet Crosse?" His tone was curt. I was silent, as the prospect of meeting her again did not appeal to me either. "No," he said with a shake of his head, "we must stay with them, but act as if nothing is out of the ordinary."

"Why?"

"There are two reasons." He held up a finger. "The first; because we are still in danger from brigands like the ones we fought yesterday. Alone, we would be an easy target, and I am not prepared to risk *il Fiume di Fuoco*. Scoronconcolo and his men may be dangerous assassins, and yes, I might have chosen travelling companions more wisely, but right now, we need their protection." He gave me a stern look in the moonlight, as if to reinforce the point.

"And the second?"

"Scoronconcolo has told us exactly who he is and what he does. I have no doubt there is a reward for handing such a man to the authorities. If we run now, it could look as if we want to turn him in. For sure, he would suspect this as our motive. He would hunt us down." He paused, then added, "And I warrant they would catch us much more easily than would Janet Crosse."

—0—

An hour after dawn broke, we mounted our horses and joined Scoronconcolo, Pietro, Franco and Giovanni in the courtyard. Scoronconcolo was in a jovial mood, enquiring after my health with his charming smile, as if he really cared about how I fared.

"I am well, thank you," I replied, hoping my face did not show how I truly felt. "And," I added quickly, "I must apologise for anything I might have said while my tongue was loosened by the drink."

He waved a dismissive hand. "Nothing to apologise for, Tommaso," he said. "I recognise it was the wine speaking." The matter seemed closed, and he became once again the commander of our group. Wheeling his horse round, he faced us. "For all it was a pleasant diversion to dispatch those five men yesterday, I would rather we ride to Firenze today and arrive in the evening without being attacked once more." His horse skittered sideways, and he paused to control it. "So we ride close together," he continued, once he had his horse still again. "We try as much as possible to stay in the open, and we keep a close eye out for brigands. Agreed?"

There were nods and grunts of approval. Scoronconcolo gave a decisive wave of his hand, then led us out of the courtyard in tight formation, and onto the path.

Our journey began in open country, surrounded as before by vineyard slopes on either side. I found it difficult to look at them, for even the sight of the plants reminded me of the night before. And if that was not reminder enough, I must deal with the headache that continued to pound on my temples, as well as the churning that still stirred up my guts. I had not wanted any food to break fast earlier, for the thought of eating nearly made me vomit once more. It had been hard to make conversation with the men in the tavern, even with my newly learned Neapolitan tongue, when all I wanted to do was crawl back into bed and sleep for a week. The best I had managed was half a cup of small beer, and even that felt as if it may not be inside me for very long. Although thankfully it had stayed put. So far, at least.

I slumped in the saddle, letting Hestia walk me onwards. Why is it, I wondered, that men have need of strong drink? How could they consume so much wine on a regular basis and not suffer as I did this morning? My stepfather for one, would down a couple of bottles in one sitting, and show not the slightest ill effect from it; almost as if he had had nothing at all. Although now I thought on it, his foul temper when sober was little improved when drunk. If anything it made him somewhat more unpleasant, were such a thing possible.

A thought hit me and I grasped the reins tighter as I tried to understand it. If I would pass as a man more effectively, must I now learn to drink like a man? Must I have more evenings like the one I had yesterday, and more mornings like this to follow?

What might be the alternative? Women did not drink like men—at least none of my acquaintance. Or maybe I should avoid the sickness of drinking by doing as I had thought before; surrendering to my nature and becoming a woman again.

I glanced across at Angelo, who was riding close beside me. Here was a man who said he accepted me as I am, and would not force me to be more womanly. Yet surely he would be happier if I chose to live as Mary rather than Thomas?

He must have sensed I was looking at him, and gave me a smile. I smiled back, and was about to lean across and pat him on the leg, when I stopped myself. Mary might do that, but Thomas most assuredly would not. And for now, I was Thomas.

Angelo's smile seemed reassuring, as if he had forgiven me for my behaviour the previous night. That made me feel strangely— what? Comfortable? As if having his approval once again made me a whole person; one who was completed by his love.

I gave a small gasp and sat up straighter. His… *love*? Had I just thought that, and without any qualm? Angelo himself had never mentioned again the words he had said back in Yarmouth—'*mio amore, Maria*'—but I had caught the occasional sideways glance at me; the soft smile when he thought I was not looking, or even a touch on my arm in a way that was slightly more than just companionable. And, of course, his reaction when I let slip about him wooing me—thankfully now seemingly forgotten.

But… was I having feelings for him as well?

Should I tell him? What would be his response? If he truly saw me as his '*amore*', then surely it would be positive?

I glanced at him again, and got the same smile back. Once more, it gave me a feeling of comfort, as if I was a child secure in the arms of her parent. Which meant I did have feelings for him, of that I was sure.

I took a deep breath, and my head seemed to clear itself of the headache. This was surely a sign that I had reached a decision; that I must one day soon cast off my manly disguise! Yes, for being Thomas was no longer working for me. It was forcing me to drink to excess, making me attract the unwanted attention of devious girls like Adriana de Vries, and causing me to live in perpetual fear of discovery. The time had come to step away from Thomas Richardson, and become Mary Fox once more.

I gave a small gasp as a further thought hit me. Or maybe I would become Maria di Luca?

Maria di Luca? I said it to myself a few times. It felt good.

But that would only happen—could only happen—if I confessed my feelings to Angelo. I glanced across once more, and got an even broader smile in return.

I would do it.

My decision made, I relaxed in the saddle. I would tell Angelo as soon as we arrived in Firenze.

—0—

After a few hours, we found a wayside inn and Scoronconcolo said we should stop to eat. As Angelo and I dismounted by the horse stalls, he turned towards me and asked, "How do you feel now, Thomas?"

I wanted so much to put my hand in his as I replied, "Much better, thank you."

He gave me a small grin; the one he would often make when he wanted to show he was amused, yet also full of understanding. Now my wish to hold his hand disappeared; instead I wanted to reach up and put my own hand behind his head, then pull his mouth to mine and crush my lips on his. If I did, how would his tongue feel on mine? I wanted so badly to find out.

Firenze could not come soon enough.

He untied the leather pouch with its curious markings containing his mother's ruby necklace, and fastened it to his belt. It was something he always did; the pouch was tied securely to the saddle when we rode, so he could see it easily at all times, and to his waist once he was dismounted. When he had it fixed to his belt, he gave it a reassuring touch. I also made sure my own purse of coins was secured to my belt, as we turned away from the horses to make for the inn.

We both stopped sharply. Scoronconcolo was standing there, having come up behind us without a sound. His dark eyes narrowed as he stared directly at the pouch on Angelo's belt.

"You have a concern, *Signore*?" Angelo asked, a sight chill to his voice.

Scoronconcolo looked up. "Nay," he replied. He glanced down at the pouch again, then back up at Angelo. "None at all," he said smoothly. "Shall we go inside?"

We followed him in, and I noted that Angelo kept his hand firmly on the pouch.

It was dark inside the inn, and it took a moment for my eyes to adjust. Gradually, I made out Giovanni and Franco on one side of a small bench-seat table, with the massive bulk of Pietro on the other. There seemed little room for the rest of us, although there was some space beside Giovanni on one side, and Pietro on the other. I squeezed in beside Giovanni, while Angelo encouraged Pietro to move along the bench seat so he could sit. Scoronconcolo then placed himself on Angelo's other side, effectively pinning him between them.

An elderly man who I took to be the innkeeper came up and asked what we wanted. As I now felt very hungry, I asked for one of the local baked flatbreads topped with cheese, ham and pomodoro, and the others all echoed my order. I resisted asking for wine as well, although the others did so.

As the innkeeper hurried away, Scoronconcolo turned to Angelo and said, "You keep that bag close by, *Signore* di Luca. I have now noted over the last two days how much it clearly means to you. Might I ask what it contains?" His voice was conversational, but there was an edge to it that caused me concern.

Immediately the easy companionship that had marked our group since Milano disappeared, to be replaced by a distinctly uneasy silence.

Angelo looked either side of him; at Pietro's bulk blocking him on one side, then at Scoronconcolo, pushed up on the other. "That is my own business, Scoronconcolo," he replied, with the same level of calmness. But I could see he was holding himself ready to defend his precious belonging if necessary.

"It must contain something of value," Scoronconcolo insisted. "For you hold it by you at all times."

"As I say, it is none of your concern," Angelo repeated.

There was a long silence, as we all waited for Scoronconcolo to respond. Eventually he gave a thin smile and said, "Then it is of no matter. Please forgive my idle curiosity."

I let out the breath I must have been holding, and Angelo nodded slowly, as if he understood what was going on here. Scoronconcolo was clearly not idly curious. He was fully intrigued. And for such a dangerous thieving assassin, that was not a comfortable place for me and Angelo to be. I wanted to go to his side; to be prepared to fight for him if needed. But, while I was on the end of the seat and could get up, he was truly trapped. My hand went over to the hilt of my sword and gripped it tight. Angelo caught my eye, and it was as if he knew what I was thinking. *Be ready*, he seemed to be saying. *I am*, I shot back.

"But then again," Scoronconcolo said, "my interest is pricked. I am now keen to know its content." He nodded at Giovanni, and suddenly a knife appeared in the hand of the man beside me. There was a sharp pain and I winced as he pressed it into my side.

"Unhand your hilt," Giovanni hissed in my ear, "lest I go

further still." I did as he demanded.

Scoronconcolo continued, "Now, I am sure Tommaso is a man who is used to a little pain, just as he is unused to strong drink." He paused. "But I warrant, like any man, he would not want that pain to become, let us say, any stronger." He nodded at Giovanni, and I tried not to shout as the knife was pushed in further.

Angelo's eyes widened, and I could see he was trying to calculate which meant more to him; my life or the necklace? My wellbeing, or potentially that of his mother?

Angelo di Luca chose me.

"Very well," he snapped. "I will show you. Just leave her alone." Then his face became ashen white, as he realised what he had just said.

There was a long silence, as the word echoed over and over in my head.

"Her?" Scoronconcolo whispered. "Her? Tommaso is really a woman?" He made his trademark smile—only this time it was not one of charm; it was even more menacing than his usual expression. "Now *that* is much more interesting."

19

THE ASSASSIN'S MOVE

Scoronconcolo frowned, his hard, dark eyes studying me without blinking. Then he shook his head, and said, "I did have my doubts, when you first supped your wine like a maiden." He paused, then continued, "But when you drank to excess, and took me to task, I was reassured." He nodded to Giovanni. "It seems on this occasion I was wrong." He made another nod, this time to me. "I commend you, my dear, for fooling us all." He held his hand up at Giovanni, "Take your blade away, Gio. We do not threaten women in such a way. We hold her, though." The knife was withdrawn, and I winced again, as Giovanni took hold of my wrist with a grip of iron. I reached across and put my finger to the cut in my jerkin and it came away glistening with blood.

"No, we have other uses for one such as her, do we not, boys?" There was a sickening grunt of agreement from his men, as he turned to Angelo beside him. "Which we will attend to in due course. Meanwhile, I would know what is in that bag, di Luca."

"And if I refuse?"

I admired Angelo's courage, if somewhat misplaced in the current circumstances.

"Then we will take this woman out behind the inn and each of my men will use her for his pleasure, while you are forced to have a full view of the proceedings." He made a small grimace. "I imagine one so slight will cope with Gio and Franco atop her, but perhaps the mighty Pietro here might prove a little too heavy. I warrant he will crush her to death, either before, or perhaps even after, he has reached his satisfaction."

Angelo stared at me, his eyes wide. *I cannot allow that*, he mouthed in English as he shook his head. Then he reached to his

157

belt, untied the pouch, and put it down in front of him.

"Open it," Scoronconcolo ordered.

With a small sigh, Angelo undid the ties and shook the necklace out onto the wooden tabletop. Even in the dim light, the rubies glittered like red suns in their silver mount. It was many days since I had last seen *il Fiume di Fuoco*, and I had forgotten just how beautiful it was. Scoronconcolo leaned over and scooped it up, holding it to the candle and turning it this way and that, as he whistled through his teeth.

"Truly a fine jewel. I have no wonder that you have kept it close." He slipped it back into the pouch. "I will do the same," he added, and seemed to be about to add more, when he stopped.

This was because the innkeeper had appeared, carrying a large tray. It was loaded with trenchers of flatbreads and a couple of flagons of wine. In a moment that would have been funny if it had not been so dangerous, Scoronconcolo paused with the bag in his hand, while the innkeeper handed round the trenchers, then poured the wine, and finally, with seeming insensitivity to our situation, he nodded at each of us and withdrew.

"You will not take it," Angelo growled, once the innkeeper was far enough away. "It has been in my family for generations."

Scoronconcolo tied the pouch to his own belt. "I have no care for such sentiment," he said in a matter-of-fact manner. "Although be assured it will be in my family only for as long as it takes to sell it."

"No, you evil monster!" Angelo yelled, and made a grab for it.

Scoronconcolo turned to face him, and suddenly there was a knife in his hand. With an almost casual flick of the wrist, he swept it across Angelo's throat.

As I watched in frozen horror, a thin red line appeared under Angelo's beard.

At first it seemed as if it was painted there with the finest quill. But in seconds it grew thicker and thicker, then deep red blood started to bubble out. Angelo's mouth fell open and he tried to take a breath, but it was clear he could no longer manage this. His hand went to his throat; his eyes wide as they fixed on mine, and I could see the fear and confusion as he seemed to struggle to understand what had happened. Then he coughed, and suddenly the blood gushed out thick and fast between his fingers, spraying across the flatbreads on the table, soaking into the pomodoro as if it was but another red sauce.

Angelo gave me one last look, and I mouthed, '*I love you.*'

He made the smallest nod, but it was enough.

He knew.

He would carry that knowledge to Heaven.

Then his eyes rolled up; he fell forward onto the table, and was still.

—0—

I wished I could have taken him in my arms and rocked him, while keening and wailing and rending my clothing in my grief.

I wished I could have sat with his body for as long as I needed, stroking his cheek and recalling the fun and the adventures we had shared, as well as the tender moments we had lived through in the weeks we had come to know and love each other.

I wished I could have had him securely embalmed and prepared; a fine mass said for his soul, before he was lowered into a well-dug grave topped with a fine headstone; one that declared my love and my pain and my grief at the loss of such a good and kind man.

A man who had once told me I could run him through with my sword if he ever played me false.

I wished I could call up to Heaven, and demand that his soul be returned to me, because it was not ready to join with the Lord; because it was too soon; because he was too young; too beautiful.

But I knew I could do none of these things, because unless I moved now, right now, just as his head hit the table, I would soon be joining him in Heaven.

And while I could see the joy that might bring, it would be too soon for me as well.

Instead I needed to save myself from this cold-blooded killer, so I could scheme and plan and find a way get back Angelo's precious jewel. So I could return it to Angelo's mother, and we could hold each other tight. So we could cry together for the son she had longed to see again and for the man I had decided I would stay with for the rest of my life. For the man who had never asked me to become Mary again, but who I am certain would have valued it. For the man who would never see it now.

So I did none of the things I wanted to do. Instead I used Giovanni, Franco and Pietro's immediate moment of surprise to pull away from Giovanni's grip, leap up and be out of the door before they could react.

I ran across the courtyard to Hestia's stall, untied her, grabbed her saddle and bridle, threw the saddle across her back and scrambled up without securing it.

Holding tight with my legs and clutching at Hestia's mane, I just about managed to stay on her as we thundered out of the courtyard and galloped onto the Firenze road.

20
LEONARDO DE GINORI

A body once known by the name of Mary Fox rode hard on a horse called Hestia for many hours towards Firenze that day. But there was nothing of any substance inside this body. It was stripped bare; hollowed out like a crab shell after the flesh has been scraped away. It was incapable of thought; mindlessly riding away from Scoronconcolo and his fellow killers. Riding away the from the earthly remains of a good man; from the life of love and happiness that the killer had taken away with such a casual flick of his knife.

There must have been brief stops; for water, maybe food, and to fix Hestia's saddle and bridle. For by the time the pair trotted through the high arched city gate into Firenze—and Mary Fox had begun to inhabit the body once more—the saddle seemed to have become securely fixed and she was guiding Hestia with correctly fitted reins.

I finally came fully to myself as we progressed into the city. Two things then became the focus of my thoughts; two tasks that were quite contradictory to each other—for I could not do one without failing at the other.

The first task was how to keep away from Scoronconcolo and his men, for I had little doubt they would want to deal me the same fate as Angelo, even if they did not carry out the killer's original threat and use me for their pleasure first. The thought of any of those men defiling me—and particularly the monstrous Pietro crushing me under his weight—made my belly heave once more. But I could see how difficult it would be to stay away from Scoronconcolo, and I must assume he would be searching for me. I had no knowledge of this city, while doubtless he knew it well, and had many contacts who could act as his eyes and ears.

Which brought me to the second task—which I could only achieve if I failed in the first. This was to get close enough to Scoronconcolo to steal back *il Fiume di Fuoco* before he sold it on—which I assumed he would do in Firenze. Which meant I would need to stay in this city for as long as it took to find him and get the jewel back.

On this thought, I found a meagre room for the night and collapsed into a dreamless, empty sleep.

—0—

My first thought as I awoke the next morning, was to go to Angelo and discuss our plan for the day. And for the smallest part of the smallest moment, a warm glow filled me at the thought.

But then the awful, crushing realisation swept it away, and suddenly I found myself sobbing like a babe; wailing with tortured grief for him, as I writhed about on the hard bed, unable to find any comfort.

I had planned to declare my love for him in Firenze.

But he was with the Lord now, not me. Never again with me.

I watched again as my beloved clasped his hand to his neck, his eyes on mine.

I love you.

He had nodded. Then he had died.

I cried until there were no more tears left. Until I could do no more than lie on my back and stare blankly at the ceiling, thinking of a hundred different ways I would make Scoronconcolo pay if I ever had the chance.

The sound of men calling their trades in the street outside reminded me that I still had a life to live.

That I still had a jewel to recover, and a mother in Pozzuoli who must have it before her fiftieth birthday.

I had planned to resume my female person for Angelo—but I now realised that such action was no longer advisable. Better to stay a man, and perhaps merge into the city as a Fiorentino. My

162

ability to speak fluently the Neapolitan tongue—thanks to Angelo's patient tutelage—would surely serve me well here.

"Come now, Mary Fox," I muttered to myself, "live your life. You owe it to Angelo to keep going. It is what he would have wanted."

I could almost hear him say it; *Come on Maria. Pull yourself together and stop weeping like a babe.*

I will, Angelo.

That is my girl.

I found a merchants' piazza like the one in Milano, filled with men who sold all manner of goods, including clothing. I bought a finely tailored dark brown tunic with a wide leather belt, black full-cut velvet sleeves, red and black two-tone hose and a broad-brimmed woollen hat. At another stall I chose a fur-trimmed overgown for warmth in the winter cold.

The high quality of the whole outfit made me feel like a Fiorentino man of some substance. I admired myself in the merchant's highly polished mirror. It shocked me just how thin and hollow-eyed I now appeared.

After thanking and paying the man, I walked on through the city, which was a thing of rare beauty. The streets made me want to stare around in amazement, for every building was more magnificent, more colourful, more beautifully decorated than the last.

It seemed that my new clothing made me fit in without comment as I made my way through the streets. Every man who passed me got a careful assessment from under my pulled-down hat, and I was pleased that not a single second glance came my way. I was particularly looking for Scoronconcolo and his men, but I was also studying the faces in case any looked like Janet Crosse, in either her male or female guise. I had little doubt that she would still be on my trail, and that she could well have followed it all the way to Firenze. Tales of a young man becoming sickeningly drunk outside Milano, or of one who ran away following a foul murder in a wayside inn, would readily allow her to identify me. I must be careful lest she found me here in Firenze before I could retrieve the precious necklace and make good my escape to Pozzuoli—which I had discovered was around two weeks' ride away, according to the landlord of the inn.

Which meant I had no more than three weeks before I must leave for Pozzuoli.

But for now, I must gather my wits about me. Should I see Scoronconcolo or one of his men, I would turn and follow, to see where they were staying. After that I could plan how to get in unseen, find the jewel, and be away.

Such a plan was thin, that was obvious, but it was the best I could think of as I walked the streets for an hour or more. There were many questions left unanswered. How would I get access to their rooms? And once inside, how would I find *il Fiume di Fuoco*? How would I get away, without feeling the sweep of Scoronconcolo's knife across my own throat and dying in agony like my poor Angelo?

I swear I growled as I walked on. Scoronconcolo was an evil, casual murderer; one who deserved to face justice. If not in this life, then for sure in the next. Which brought up the final question; could I resist plunging my own knife into his back, if the opportunity presented itself? Could I break my vow never to kill in cold blood?

On this thought, I looked up—and stopped immediately. Rising above the tiled roofs as if it were a giant surrounded by small children, was possibly the most magnificent building of all. It seemed to be a church—but I had never before seen one as large and as dominating as this. There was a fine square tower, rising up to the winter-grey sky as if it would touch the Heavens themselves. Beside it was a dome—but 'dome' was too small a word to describe this enormous structure. It was made of red bricks, interspersed with white stone beams running up from the base to meet at an ornate cupola standing at the very peak. Below this roof was a series of large round windows, as if they were eyes looking out across the city.

I wanted to see more, so I kept walking round until I came to a space between two buildings, opening up onto the area where the dome stood. I walked in and stopped, my hands on my waist as I took in the size and beauty of the full structure.

"*Santa Maria del Fiore*," said a voice beside me. "Completed a hundred years ago. *Il Duomo* is a magnificent structure, is it not? It seems supported by the hand of God alone." I turned to find a tall elderly man dressed in black, with grey hair flowing out from under his cap, and a grey-flecked red beard reaching halfway down his chest. He was regarding me with a quizzical smile, looking me up and down. "I saw you gazing in wonder, young fellow," he explained. "*Il Duomo* has that effect the first time it is seen." He paused, then asked, "This is your first time?"

I decided to respond in kind, for the man had an air of authority that demanded respect. "Yes," I replied. "And it is truly a wonder to behold," I looked across at the three magnificent doors set in the western entrance; a large one in the centre and a smaller one set either side. "Might it be possible to see inside at some time?" I could only wonder how it might be within, given the beauty of its outside structure.

"Of course," he replied. "In four days it will be the service of the Feast of the Nativity. I suggest you come for that."

"I thank you," I said, and turned to go.

He put a hand on my arm. "You have a strange accent," he said. "I am curious. Where are you from?"

I searched his eyes, but could see none of the caution I might expect if he was planning to play me false. I decided to accept him as a possible friend, for I knew no man in this city, and it might be useful to make his acquaintance. "I am from the town of Pozzuoli," I said, offering up a quick prayer that he knew it not. "It is in the Bay of Napoli."

He frowned and moved his hand away. "I think I have heard of it," he said slowly, "but have never visited."

I breathed a small sigh of relief. "It is a fine place," I said. "I am sure you would like it."

He seemed to take this as a call for introductions. He gave a small bow, took off his cap, and announced, "Leonardo de Ginori."

"Tommaso di Luca," I replied, sweeping off my own cap with a bow of my own.

He regarded me thoughtfully a moment, then said, "I would you come and share some wine with me, Tommaso. You are not from Firenze, so it will be my pleasure to tell you more of our fine city."

"A small wine only," I replied quickly, "As I do not drink that much." But I was eager to learn some useful information in case it might help me if—or when—I found Scoronconcolo. Meanwhile, there could be little harm in joining with this pleasant Fiorentino for a drink and a discussion.

21

CATERINA SODERINI

Leonardo and I walked away from the magnificent church and back out onto the street, which was bustling with Fiorentinos. They were mainly men, but there were some women also, walking with their husbands or fathers. Although their dress was not dissimilar to English women's, if maybe more elaborate, fewer had any form of head covering. Even some of the women walking with men who were clearly their husbands, had either small hoods with loose hair beneath, or none at all. I said nothing to Leonardo, but it did surprise me.

Leonardo led me to a small side street taverna close by the church. It was not particularly crowded, so I was able to make a quick check of every face to ensure none of my enemies were inside, before taking my seat.

Once we had wine before us, Leonardo raised his cup and said, "I must welcome you, young Tommaso of Pozzuoli, to our city. I trust your time here will be most fruitful." I raised mine, and made some comment about being full of gratitude for his hospitality. I then sipped very carefully at the wine, trusting that this man, who seemed as refined as Scoronconcolo was coarse, would think no less of me if I did not throw it back. Thankfully he appeared not to notice.

"Tell me," he began. "What brings you here?"

I had expected this question, and had used the walk from the church to consider how I would answer. I said, "I was in Milano seeing my brother, and now I return to our mother in Pozzuoli." This seemed close enough to the truth to sound plausible.

"I see." He gave a wise-looking nod. "And how long will you stay here in Firenze?"

I told him I planned to stay a week or two, then set off on my return to Pozzuoli. He asked me some more questions about my family, which I answered as best I could with the information Angelo had originally given me. I also repeated each of my answers to myself a few times, so they were well-enough fixed in my head that I may remember later what lies I had used.

He ordered more wine, and again, I sipped it with care, as he started to tell me of Firenze. "We have a duke who rules the city and the Tuscan state around it," he told me. "His name is Duke Alessandro di Medici, a member of the banking family who have had a strong influence in the region for many years now."

"And he lives here in Firenze?" I asked.

"He does indeed, in the *Palazzo della Signoria*. He is a young man, known as *il Moro* for his dark complexion. He has a firm hold over Firenze." He paused, then added, "Although it is well-known that he often breaks the sixth of God's holy commandments."

I quickly ran down the list in my mind. "He commits adultery?" I asked.

For a moment his face clouded over. "So it is said," he muttered.

I sat back and took another sip of wine; rich and fruity. I put it down carefully. I had no wish to prove my manliness again.

"And where do you stay?" Leonardo asked, breaking into my thoughts. I named the inn where I had spent the night, and where Hestia was stabled. He raised an eyebrow. "That is not a safe place," he said. "You are dressed well, young man, and will most certainly be robbed in such a place." As I stared in disbelief, he nodded, with a small frown. "Or worse. A man was killed in a fight there only a week ago." He shrugged. "It is your choice, of course, but I know this city, and would not advise you to stay there."

"Then where do you suggest?" I asked, deciding that if there was even a chance he was telling the truth, then I should seek somewhere else.

"You will struggle to find a better place," Leonardo said. "With

the Feast of the Nativity the city is most full, and will be until after
the festivities end after the Twelfth Night."

He looked away a moment, then back at me, as if he had made
a decision. "You could stay with me if you wish. I can guarantee
you a warm bed, good food and the safety of my humble home
while you visit our fine city."

Perhaps it was because he had such an authoritative manner,
but like a blind fool, I said, "Yes. That is most kind, *Signore* de
Ginori."

—0—

I walked back to the inn. Looking around with caution and keeping
my hand on the hilt of my knife, I ran up the stairs to the room
and collected the saddlebag in which I kept my meagre
possessions. Thankfully seeing no other man, I found the landlord
and gave him a coin from the purse on my belt. Then I collected
Hestia and led her out onto the street where Leonardo was waiting.

He was standing easily, talking to a smaller man he clearly
knew well. Leonardo was nodding as they talked, his beard waving
like a flag in the breeze. He looked up and smiled at me, clapped
the man on the arm as a farewell, and walked over.

"Come, Tommaso," he said. "Let us go to my house."

Our journey through the streets was marked by more men who
were known to Leonardo stopping to talk, so it took us much
longer than expected to walk the short distance.

"You are well known," I observed, after Leonardo had
finished conversing with a couple of finely dressed merchants.

"I have a position here in Firenze," he replied, as we started to
walk again. "Like many from the older families I have a role to play
in the city's governance. I also contribute to the cultural and artistic
life of the city." He looked down at me. "Have you heard of a man
by the name of Michelangelo?" I shook my head; the name was
new to me. "He is an architect and artist, and was working recently
on the *Sagrestia Nuova* in San Lorenzo. It is a burial chapel for the

Medici family. He made the architecture and was commissioned for the sculptures. I worked on behalf of the Medicis to oversee the project."

While I was considering this we turned another corner, stopping outside a tall building with three high arches at the street level. Each had a merchant underneath selling their wares; one seemed to be selling female clothing as there were a number of women leaning over his table and picking at cloths, while the other two sold foods including breads and meats.

Leonardo waved a hand at the building. "My home," he said.

I took a sharp breath; this was anything but humble. Above us were two further floors, each with several arched windows, and carvings featuring gargoyle heads above.

He led me and Hestia round to the side and a groom came out to take her to the stables. I was ushered in through a side door, and we went down a short corridor. We emerged into an arched gallery that ran round all four sides of a central open courtyard. A small fountain on a carved plinth splashed into a pool at the centre. I looked up; the afternoon winter sky gave a bright, clear light to the space, reflecting off the marble and the stone, as well as the leaves of large plants in pots. They reminded me of the ones we had seen in the forest outside Milano. Laburnum trees were trained across a decorative archway, and although their leaves and flowers were gone for the winter, they looked as if they would be glorious come the spring.

I would have loved to stop and relax in this courtyard. It was a place with a sense of peace, and for a moment I was reminded of how different it was to the dark and forbidding house of my birth and upbringing. How much better to have been raised here, instead of by my hateful stepfather in Marchington.

But I was not able to stop, as Leonardo waved me towards a door. "Come," he said. We went inside, up some stairs to the first floor, and emerged into what was surely the main hall.

If the courtyard was peaceful, this room was magnificent. A high ceiling was crossed by heavy looking squared beams, each as thick as the mast of a ship. Running the length of the room was a long table with three large silver candelabras, surrounded by chairs. A sideboard stood to one side with a wine carafe and some glass goblets. The walls were painted with a repeating device of trees on alternating blue and yellow panels, while the hangings below them were woven in a diamond pattern in the same colours. A fireplace with a large stone hood sat in the middle of one wall, decorated with a blue shield crossed with a yellow stripe featuring three stars.

"My family arms," Leonardo said.

As I moved closer to the fire to gain some warmth, a well-built manservant came in and spoke quietly to Leonardo. He nodded, then said, "Paolo will show you to your room, then we will eat back in here."

The servant Paolo led me along several passageways and up a stair, until we came to a chamber. It was a large panelled room, with a bed in the centre of one wall and a lit fire in the grate opposite.

He took a black doublet and a white shirt from a chest, and held them out. I thanked him and took both items. "You may wait outside," I said, not wishing to reveal my bound chest while I changed.

A short while later, Paolo led me back through the maze of corridors to the main hall, where Leonardo was waiting.

Another servant came in with some platters containing a roast fowl, vegetables and fruits and set these down at the table, while a third went over to the carafe and poured two glasses of deep red wine.

We sat opposite each other at one end of the table, and I noted that there were only the two places laid.

"Is there not a *Signora* Ginori?" I enquired. "Is she at home?"

Leonardo hesitated, and for a brief moment I saw the smallest flash of fear in his eye. Then he seemed to recover, and said, "My wife, Caterina Soderini de Ginori, has gone to stay with her family for a few days. They are in Sienna. They came recently and she went with them to tend to her sick brother. He relies on her, you see, for she understands him better than any other in her family."

I shrugged slightly, wondering why he needed to tell me in such detail. Then I put it from my mind, as he said, "You must be hungry, *Signore*. Some food?" and I nodded. It was a while since he and I had eaten at the taverna, and now my belly was telling me just how empty it was.

Leonardo gestured to Paolo, who served us both. Then Paolo went over to the door and stood with his arms behind his back.

The meat and vegetables were delicious, and I had to restrain myself from wolfing them down. The wine was also very fine; rich and with the aroma of ripe berries, but I allowed myself only a few small sips.

I soon cleared my plate, and the meal progressed to the fruits. Leonardo was a good conversationalist, telling me of his work with this man Michaelangelo. It seemed the master craftsman rejected the company of other men, rarely washed or changed his clothing, and ate only for sustenance, not pleasure.

Then Leonardo went on to talk of the politics of Firenze. Their complexity meant that you had to consider carefully which families were ascendant, and make sure you were correctly aligned at all times. You also had to ensure that you kept on the side of Duke Alessandro di Medici, who, despite his relative youth and marital infidelities, was proving to be a firm ruler. "Maintaining my position is a full-time occupation," Leonardo observed, as Paolo cleared the plates

As Paolo came back to fill my glass, I put my hand over the top and gave the servant a small smile. "Enough, thank you," I said, trying to keep my voice firm. He made no response, but moved away.

Leonardo raised an eyebrow. "You are not liking my wine?" he asked. "I have only the finest from the vineyards around Firenze."

"It is very good," I said, "but I prefer to keep my head clear."

"Very wise, young man," Leonardo observed. "But you must drink something as you eat. We still have some almond *Biscotti di*

Prato to come. In Firenze, we serve these with a sweet *Vin Santo*."

He gestured to Paolo, who nodded, and came to the table with plates of small *biscotti*, then followed these with a glass of white wine. I took a small sip of mine, and it seemed less than sweet; rather there was a slightly bitter edge. But Leonardo was looking at me with an expectant smile, so I drank it all, and ate one of the *biscotti*, which had a taste a little like marchpane.

As the conversation continued, I felt pleasantly relaxed. The wine had been good, and the food sat well in my belly. But within a few minutes I became concerned that something was wrong. Why could I not fix my gaze on Leonardo at the far end of the table? I tried to concentrate, but it was as if he was moving further away; as if the table were becoming longer. Had I drunk too much wine? No, I had been most careful.

I frowned. Now he seemed to have gained a halo of light, as if fireflies were swarming around his head and shoulders. I shook my head to try and clear it, but if anything, this made the fireflies become more frantic. Then Leonardo spoke; his voice sounding as if he were inside an echoing cathedral.

He was staring hard at me, and I knew what I wanted to answer him, but could not seem to find the words. Instead, a strange blackness started closing in from either side of my sight. For a moment I tried to fight it; to make it go away.

But I knew I had no option other than to accept it.

Then all went dark.

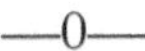

I awoke to a feeling that I was lying on a cold floor, with my head resting against a wall and my neck so stiff I could scarcely move it.

I winced with pain as I struggled lift myself further up the wall. Eventually I managed to get my shoulders to it. Now my neck could move a little more freely. The movement made my belly heave and I thought I would vomit. But thankfully not this time.

My neck cracked as I eased it slowly to the right and stared through part-closed eyes. There was a single barred window letting morning light in through thick diamond-paned glass. My neck cracked again as I looked over to the left. There was nothing there, apart from what looked like a pile of rags in a dark corner, next to a small, bare table. The only other thing in the room were three storage chests lined up against the wall. I was in a storeroom of some kind.

Surely I should be in the fine bed chamber Paolo had shown me to, before we sat for supper? How had I got here?

I forced myself to try and remember the previous evening. Had I become drunk again? But I had been careful to limit my drinking. The last thing I could remember was sipping the white wine and eating the *biscotti*. Then nothing.

The wine had had a bitter taste.

Had I been given a sleeping draught?

If so, why?

I managed to get to my feet and looked down. I was a wearing a loose night shirt, with bare legs and no shoes. I gave a shocked gasp.

That could only mean one thing.

Someone had undressed me.

What if it had been Paolo? What if he had seen something that showed that I was not the man Tommaso, but a woman with binding around her chest? I gave a small cry. What if he had seen another part of me; one that showed without doubt that I was a woman?

The thought was so dreadful that I tried to put it from my mind.

There was a door over to the left, opposite the pile of rags. I went over and tried the latch handle, but unsurprisingly, the door was locked. I decided not to beat on it and shout—for whoever had put me here had clearly planned this.

I had been trapped.

I looked over to the window. The bars were too close together to get through. I was never going to get out that way.

Perhaps there was something I could use in the chests? I tried each one, but there was nothing but women's gowns that had a slightly musty smell.

I went to the rags. As I got close I noticed a slightly sickly odour. It reminded me of something at Marchington Manor when I was small. I frowned and drew in a breath. I had it! It was like when I found a dead fox in one of the outbuildings.

With a sense of dread, I moved closer. In the dim light from the window, it seemed that the bundle had a vaguely human shape. I moved the table to the side so it easier to see the rags. There was a roundness at the top, under a dark piece of cloth. Could that be a head? I cautiously pulled back the covering.

And stepped back in horror.

The white face of a woman stared back; her eyes fixed open. But the strangest thing was that she was entirely bald.

She was also entirely dead—of that there was no doubt.

There was the sound of a bolt being pulled back.

Before I could turn, a hand grasped my shoulder. I looked round.

"I see you have met my wife," said Leonardo de Ginori.

22

A HANGING PROMISE

Leonardo put the candle he was carrying on the table, then pulled the cloth back over his wife's head. It was a relief not to have her eyes staring at me; but in truth, that was small comfort.

Paolo came in and stood like a statue by the door with arms folded.

"I do not suggest you consider trying to escape," Leonardo said, indicating Paolo with a brief movement of his head. "He is most accomplished with a knife, and has no issue using it on a woman."

For the briefest moment I thought he was just saying this as a form of speech, but then I saw the look in his eye in the candlelight. It was the triumphant look of a man who knew a secret. My secret.

"Yes, Tommaso, or whatever is your name," Leonardo continued. "You have been fooling us into thinking you were a man. When in truth you are nothing of the sort." Then he added, "Eh, *Signorina*?"

I glanced at Paolo, who had a sickly smile on his usually expressionless face. Then holding my eye, he slowly looked down at the top of his hose, then looked back up and smiled more broadly.

I felt my belly heave. It was as bad as I had feared. The man had seen more than just my bound chest; he had seen...

I stumbled over to the window, and was violently sick.

I leaned against the wall as the liquid splashed against the wooden floor, until eventually I could do no more than dry retch.

I stepped away from the foul-smelling puddle, watched by Leonardo. "Paolo has told me what he found when he unclothed you and put you in here," he said, his almost conversational tone

177

at odds with the dreadful nature of his words. "And he was surprised by what he saw." He stopped and regarded me with a raised eyebrow. "And I am sure you are wondering if he, shall we say, took further advantage of the situation?"

I had no words to answer this.

"Well, you will be pleased to know that he did not, and has sworn on Our Blessed Lady that this is the honest truth."

I found a small whisper. "That is…" I swallowed hard. "That is… good."

"But, *signorina*, do not think this means we are finished with you."

"What do you want with me?" I whispered.

Leonardo scratched his beard. "What indeed?" he said. "You have now seen the corpse we previously left in here. And as I said, it is the body of my wife."

"You killed her," I said, my voice flat and without expression.

"No, no," he replied quickly. Then he nodded. "Well, actually, yes I did." He put his fingertips together. "It was not something I wanted to do, but it was necessary."

"Why?" I had no knowledge of the woman, so I could not understand his motives, but I was now seeing the kind of man this Leonardo de Ginori truly was. And he was bringing to mind Sir Reginald de Courtney, a vile bully that my stepfather tried to force me to marry; a man who told me how he would have taken great pleasure in causing me pain. De Courtney could also be charming if it so pleased him, just as Leonardo had been when he first lured me into his trap; just as a spider captures a fly. For there was now no doubt in my mind that I had been trapped.

"I had to kill her, for she was unfaithful to me," he said, giving an intense stare. It was as if his casual nature had changed, and he suddenly had need for me to believe in him.

Although it would not be me assessing him on the Day of Judgment.

All I could believe was that his poor wife must have sought solace in another man's arms as a refuge from her scheming husband. But this was not something that would be politic to point out. "How did you know?" was all I could think of saying.

"I heard it from the man himself. The one who cuckolded me."

I raised an enquiring eyebrow. "Then he must have been most confident you would not take revenge on him."

"Indeed so. Much as I would if I could." He made a hateful grimace. "But this is a man holding the ultimate position of authority in this state."

My jaw dropped. "The Duke?" I whispered.

He nodded. "Yes. I believe I told you how the man is a godless adulterer. He made no secret that he admired my wife, and would oft remark on her beauty. At first I took it as a compliment, and even thanked him. Then two weeks ago, he invited her to his *palazzo* and made it clear she was to come alone."

"You could have refused to let her go," I suggested.

"Against the wishes of *il Moro*?" He gave a thin laugh. "You do not do that, not if you want to keep a position of power and influence in Firenze."

"You agreed?"

"I did." He nodded, almost to himself, as he stared over to the window. "When she returned the following day. I asked what had happened, and she answered that it was nothing untoward. They had done naught but drink wine and talk."

"But you did not believe her?" I asked.

He looked back at me and made a small nod. "No. She had a smile such as I had not seen before, and she would scarcely hold my eye as I asked. So the following day I challenged that devil who calls himself the Duke of Firenze, de Medici himself, and he had no shame at all. He readily agreed that she had lain with him, not once, but twice." He swallowed hard, then took a deep breath before continuing. "He said... He said the second time was at her insistence." He took another breath. "He seemed to take pleasure in telling me this. To him it was just another conquest; one like any other."

For a moment I almost felt sympathy for this old man. But then, I recalled how he had trapped me into coming to his house with lies about the danger of the inn where I was staying; how he had given me a sleeping draught, and was now keeping me a prisoner.

"I assume that you had some purpose when you first spoke to me?" I asked. "Because you are not otherwise in the habit of taking unknown young men to a taverna and offering them a room in your house?"

He looked mildly impressed. "You are correct, *Signorina*," he said. "I did have a reason for bringing you here."

"And I am guessing it has something to do with… her?" I gestured at the covered body.

"When I met you at the *Duomo*," he said, "I was seeking just such a person, someone from outside the city. So when you told me you came from near Napoli, it was as if the Blessed Lady herself had sent you."

"How good of her," I observed with bitterness.

"At first I thought you were simply a callow youth, too young for a beard on his chin," he said, appearing to ignore my tone. "But then I saw something in you. Something I had seen before in other young men in my capacity as a magistrate. Godless sinners. I know now that what I was seeing was in truth the woman behind your deception, but at the time I thought it something else."

Then he did something truly awful. He walked behind me and put his hands on my shoulders. He gave my cheek a pat, nearly making me retch again. "You," he whispered in my ear, "had the look of a lad who commits the sin of fornication with other men. It meant my soul was at peace with my plan."

"Your plan?" I asked. I did not want to think of him standing behind me; touching me. So instead, I tried to focus all my attention on the candle on the table. A small drip of wax was running down the side. Perhaps if I could maintain my attention on this drip, I could avoid thinking of him behind me.

"Yes," he said. "I will have you arraigned for the murder in my place." I tried to turn my head round so I could look at him, but his hands on my shoulders restricted this. "I am a prominent man here in Firenze," he continued. "In time it would be noted that my wife is no longer seen by my side. Questions would be asked; questions I would rather not have to answer. Questions that kept me awake at night, lest I must address them, and endanger my position. This meant I needed someone to be arraigned for the killing in my place. Someone guaranteed to be found guilty and hanged. Then the matter would be closed, and I could sleep easy."

The casual way he was telling me this robbed me of the ability to respond. He clearly had no problem with me knowing the plan; which meant he was going to carry it through.

Must I die just so he could sleep at night?

"You were given a strong sleeping draught," he went on. "You could then be put in this room with the body. This is where you will stay until I have a couple of *Birra* constables brought here, to have you discovered with your murder victim. They will bring you before the *Otto di Guardia e Balìa*; the Duke's court of magistrates. As one of them myself, it will be a formality to have you found guilty of killing my wife."

"And by what reason will you say I did such a thing?" I asked, my voice flattened further by the enormity of his scheme.

The drip was slowing down as it neared the cooler base of the candle.

"I have said I thought you had the look of an unnatural lover of men," he replied. "Such a one might form an attachment to a husband." He gave my shoulders a squeeze, and this time I did have to swallow down the bile that rose in my throat. "One who seeks an assignation with the husband, sets off in a state of undress to find him; but when the wife tries to stop his evil intent, he kills her."

He let go and walked round in front of me. I took a few deep breaths to settle my gut, then gave a sigh of relief that he was no longer touching me. Not that it made any difference to my predicament.

"And now I know you are not a boy at all, but in truth a girl masquerading…" he faltered to a stop, frowning, then shook his head as if to clear an unwelcome thought. "The story might change a little, but I am sure the *Otto* will find you guilty even more easily."

I lifted my chin. "I will tell the court who I am in truth, and accuse you of the murder," I said.

He laughed. "Then I wish you good fortune, *Signorina*," he chuckled. As I say, the *Otto* will be even less likely to believe an unnatural woman who masquerades… as…" Again, he paused with a small frown, and I did wonder what kept making him stumble over this word. "…Who masquerades as a boy." He paused a moment, then said, "My case is made stronger; as a woman it is even more likely that you are minded to kill the wife. After taking a strong liking to the husband."

"You flatter yourself, *Signore* de Ginori," I growled.

He shrugged. "It is not what I believe that matters."

"Then I will argue that your wife has clearly been dead for many days, and must therefore have been killed before I came to this house," I said, trying to keep my voice steady. "Which will be clear to any man who sees the body."

"I think not. It will make little difference to the *Otto's* decision. They will take my direction on this, and will have no interest in seeing my wife's remains. No, *Signorina*," he gestured to Paolo to come over. "You are the perfect killer; a woman disguised as a man, and from outside the state of Firenze. The *Otto di Guardia e Balia* will find you guilty and you will hang for the foul murder you so clearly committed."

Paolo pushed me down, so I was again lying on the floor.

"Lock her in," said Leonardo. "Then find a couple of *Birra* constables, and bring them here."

23
A CHANGE OF PLAN

In all my years I think I have spent more than my fair share of time unjustly imprisoned by others.

Pieter de Vries held me in his cellar for a night and a day. My hated stepfather kept me locked in a room at Marchington Manor for many months. If I point out that these incarcerations were never through fault of my own, you will think me too full of self-pity. But I swear it is the truth; I have never done anything myself that justifies such treatment.

Other than being too trusting. And sometimes being seriously lacking in judgment.

And so it was with Leonardo de Ginori. When Paolo pushed me to the floor and threw the bolt on the door, I could take some small comfort from the thought that once again, I was not the main cause of my own misfortune. But by Heavens, I should accept some of the blame, for the grave sin of being a stupid trusting fool.

As I sat with my back to the wall, I cursed myself. How could I have possibly believed Leonardo would be genuine when he came up to me at the *Duomo*?

Even if I was not being held through fault of my own, I resolved I must never trust a man again.

Not Leonardo de Ginori. Not Pieter de Vries. Not Scoronconcolo. Definitely not Scoronconcolo.

Except for one. Angelo di Luca.

This thought brought back the overwhelming feeling of grief. It was followed immediately by an even stronger one of guilt. How could I have forgotten Angelo, even for a single minute? There had been times since coming to Firenze and meeting Leonardo, when

Angelo, and his death at the hand of the evil Scoronconcolo, had not been at the front of my mind.

This thought of death reminded me of Caterina de Ginori. I got up and moved as far away as I could from her body, then sat again. I pulled my legs up to my chest and clasped my arms around my knees, as stared up at the window.

Of all the men I had known, I had trusted Angelo. Because he was the only one I had fallen in love with. Even though at first he had sought to have me punished by Joan Cruddon, he had then proved himself worthy of my trust—and eventually, worthy of my love. I had even been prepared to surrender my identity as Thomas, and become Mary Fox again for him.

Or *Maria di Luca.*

I clasped my knees tighter and rocked against the wall.

I cursed the fortune that had brought me to this point. If only I could find Scoronconcolo and recover Angelo's precious jewel, and return it to his mother in time, I could redeem myself from the stupidity that had led me here. But there was little chance of that; I could expect nothing more than being arraigned before this *Otto* court and brought swiftly to the end of the hangman's rope.

The thought of being led to the gibbet and having the noose put about my neck, then the stool being pushed away, left me in a cold sweat. Would death come with swiftness and mercy, or would it be slow and filled with pain as I must fight for breath? I felt the blackness of my fate closing in on me. I prayed hard to the Virgin, that She would save me from this dreadful fate. Or at least, show me the kindness of a quick end.

Such dark thoughts filled my head over the next few hours, with no chance of even a minute's sleep. I knew I dare not allow myself such a luxury, lest the hour of my trial and execution come even more swiftly. As I contemplated my imminent fate, the light from the window faded and eventually grew black.

—0—

The bolt slammed back and the door swung open.

Leonardo came in first, his features made gaunt by the strong light of the candle he held before him. Another man came in behind, with his own candle.

Was this a *Birra* constable come to arrest me?

There was a movement in the shadows beyond them as a third man moved into the doorway. I took it from his bulk and folded arms that it was Paolo.

"I trust you had a comfortable time, *Signorina,*?" Leonardo asked, as I stood up.

I had neither the voice, nor the inclination, to give him an answer.

Leonardo's companion stepped forward and held a candle to my face, studying me intently. His features were impossible to make out behind the brightness of the flame, but he was of the shortest stature. I tried to maintain my calm, although it was not easy with a burning candle in my face and this man looking up as he examined me.

He stepped back and turned to Leonardo. "She will do. With one of your wife's hairpieces and rouge on her face, she will look as near as necessary."

"Then let it be so." Leonardo said. He put his hand on the short man's shoulder. "Come, let us be away." He moved to the door. "Paolo, take her to Sophia, who I have now called back. She will make the girl ready."

I found my voice. "What are you going to do with me?" I cleared my throat. "Is this not a constable? Am I not to be taken to the *Otto* court?"

Leonardo turned back. "Our plan has changed, *Signorina,*" he said. "We have found a new use for you."

185

"Which is?" I asked, unsure whether to be relieved or apprehensive.

The short man stepped forward. "We have need of Caterina Soderini de Ginori, wife of Leonardo, and as it happens, also my sister. But, as I believe you are aware, her body lies just there. Thus, it is necessary for our purpose that someone plays her part."

"It occurred to me that you are one who masquerades," Leonardo said. "Which gave me the idea. You will be taken to Sophia, my wife's maid. I have recalled her back to the house to resume the duties she had when my wife was alive. She will clothe you, and school you in Caterina's manner. Then you will be instructed on the task we need you to complete." He turned to go, but I still had a question.

"And if I refuse?"

Leonardo stopped by Paolo and raised an eyebrow. "Then we will continue as originally planned," he said in a matter-of-fact manner. "You will be taken to the *Otto*, found guilty and hanged for murder."

There was a heavy silence. "And if I agree; will you let me go?" I asked.

He paused a moment, as if this question had taken him by surprise. Then he said, "Yes, I suppose so. If you do as we need, and the plan proceeds as we expect, then I will release you. You will be free to resume your male garb and be on your way."

"But why should I believe you on this?" I snapped. "You have lied to me before."

He shrugged. "It is up to you."

I tapped my foot. If I succeeded in masquerading as his wife, then there would be a chance he would keep his word. If I were to refuse, then I would most certainly die. I sighed inwardly; it was no choice

"Then I will do it."

"That is the right decision," Leonardo said. "I am pleased that you have seen sense." The two candles moved past Paolo and out of the door, leaving me in total darkness once again. There was the sound of a movement towards me and a hand took my arm. I was pulled almost off my feet, then made to stumble out of the room.

24

BECOMING CATERINA

Paolo pushed me into a well-decorated chamber lit by a few candles, then left without a word. A bird-like woman of maybe twice my age came up and observed me with her head on one side.

"What is your name?" she asked. I gave a small start; Leonardo had only ever called me *'Signorina'* and had clearly been quite uninterested in discovering anything more of my true identity.

"Maria," I replied.

"Well, Maria," she said, "From this moment on, you will be Caterina. You understand?"

I nodded.

Like Leonardo's companion, Sophia moved closer and examined me intensely, her dark eyes unblinking as she walked all round, giving me the feeling of being a prize cow at the market. I almost expected her to pinch my side to see if I was well-enough covered in flesh. Eventually she stood back, put her hands on her hips and said, "You are perhaps thinner and slightly shorter than the mistress, but she wore slippers with no heel, so we will find some that have one." She stood back, her eyes flicking up and down my body. "We will need to teach you her ways," she continued. "Although not her temper; she would oft show great anger at even the smallest transgression." She nodded, as if to herself. "I cannot say I was too upset when the master told me she had been slain." She gave a cold smile. "Other than it cost me my position here. But enough of that. Have you any experience of such learning?"

I did not reply immediately. Should I admit that I had previously spent three years taking the part of a young boy called Prince Henry Fitzroy, even on occasion for his father King Henry? And that I had been schooled extensively in how the prince walked, held himself, and even how he spoke? For all it proved beyond doubt that I had the capacity to take on a new person's character, my experience of learning the ways of a boy might raise too many new questions. I simply shook my head and said, "No, but I am willing to learn."

"Good." She bade me sit on a stool, then went to a chest and pulled out something that had the look of a long switch of black hair. "We shall start with this." She walked up behind me and said, "put your hand up above your eyes, with the fingers forward." I did as she asked, then it felt as if a leather cap had been pushed onto the back of my head, then over the tips of my fingers. "Pull it forward and down," she said. I did so, and the cap fitted tightly onto my head. It was as if a pair of black curtains had been placed on either side of my vision. "This is one of her best pieces," Sophia observed as she adjusted it, then stood back, viewing it with a critical eye. "Real human hair. She had several made after she caught a high fever and lost her own."

Fighting down my revulsion at wearing a dead woman's wig, I said nothing. She came forward and made a few further adjustments, before standing back again and nodding. "Now some rouge." She busied herself with several brushes and pots, applying their contents across my face, as well as some tinted wax to my lips, which gave a strange, slightly honeyed taste. She would continually pause as she worked, regarding me with her head on one side, before darting forward and applying something more. Eventually she seemed satisfied.

She hunted around in a chest and found a gown; a deep brown bodice with full skirts and a fitted waist. She then produced a pair of embroidered sleeves, linen stockings and heeled slippers. She whistled tunelessly between her teeth as she had me cast off my nightshirt, then she forced me into the gown. She pulled the lacing tight, causing me to gasp as the breath was expelled from my chest. She pulled the skirts into place, then had me hold out my feet so she could put on the stockings and shoes. Finally she added the sleeves. "You are the true vision of the mistress," she muttered. She came up with a polished hand mirror. "See for yourself."

I looked at my reflection, and felt my knees start to shake. If I had not been seated, for sure I would have fallen to the floor.

The woman who looked back at me was one I could not begin to recognise. Her black hair was parted in the middle and held back with red ribbons. As with other women I had seen in Florence, she wore no hood. While this would have been unthinkable for a married woman in England, it seemed perfectly acceptable here. This bare-headed woman's lips were a deep crimson, her eyes enlarged with kohl and her cheeks a glowing red.

Her coloured lips were parted in a look of deep shock, and her darkened eyebrows were raised.

I searched hard, but could see no sign of the Mary Fox that I knew from polished mirrors in the past. And certainly none of the young man calling himself Tommaso di Luca who had arrived at this house a while earlier. He was quite gone, as if he had never existed.

A lump rose in my throat as I stared at this person. Would that Angelo had seen such a vision of womanly elegance; it would have pleased him greatly, of that I had no doubt. I could just imagine his amused smile, and a comment such as '*Santa Maria Madre di Dio*, I could not have believed it possible!"

Was he looking down on me from Heaven above? Was he seeing this vision? Did he approve? I glanced up and let out a long breath; my words to him drifting silently upwards. *I am doing this to stay alive, Angelo. So I can find the necklace and return it to your mother in time.*

Was it the wind outside the window, or was there an answering whisper? *Do as you can, mio amore Maria. Do as you can. I trust you to do your best.*

I gave the mirror back and stood, smoothing my hands down the skirts. "So tell me," I said with the strongest voice I could manage. "How does Caterina walk? How does she speak?"

—0—

As the dawn broke and the winter sun rose outside the window, I was shown the way to become Caterina Soderini de Ginori. Sophia taught me how Caterina had held herself; how her mistress had moved, how she talked, and even how she would put her hand on her chin and nod to show she agreed with what another person was saying. But if she found them uninteresting, or if they were of a lower class, then she would keep her hands by her side. Another of her traits was a hard edge to her voice. This I found easy, as it made use of the way I had deepened my tone to pass as a man. She also would give a small toss of her head to add weight to her words, and this I practiced throughout the day, until I had it to Sophia's satisfaction.

I paid particular attention to these characteristics, for if you get such details right, people will overlook the more obvious differences, such as height, or look. Or, in the case of Prince Henry Fitzroy, the fact that I was a not even a boy. He had a custom of looking slightly to one side of a person as he conversed with them, and I am sure this had helped me carry off the deception. It had even become a habit of my own, and I found myself wondering if any of Caterina's ways would become mine once this was over.

Always assuming it would be over at some time.

Leonardo and the small man would surely not have me play the role for more than a few days? And what would happen when their task was completed? Could I become Tommaso again and slip into the shadows, so I could then start my search for Scoronconcolo and the stolen jewel? Or would they revert to their original plan, and have me tried and hanged for murder? For I would then be something of an inconvenience to them.

No, I must use this opportunity of becoming Caterina to make my escape. I would do whatever they demanded of me, but find my moment and get away. And this must be done before the middle part of the next month, if I was to have any chance of returning the jewel in time.

If I could even find it.

"The mistress did not stare into the distance like an idiot child," Sophia snapped, bringing me back to the task in hand. "Now, let us work again on her voice."

As she spoke, I felt a sudden heaviness in my bones, spreading from the tips of my toes to the ends of my fingers. Then a deep yawn forced its way out of my mouth.

Sophia gave a frown. "This learning bores you?" she asked. "I can assure you, it is necessary, and you will thank me for it in time."

"Not at all," I replied. "But I have had little sleep these last two nights, and I can take no more of this learning for now."

She tapped her foot as she considered me, her head on one side, and I thought for a moment she was going to insist we continue. But she said, "I accept. You have made good progress; we will carry on tomorrow."

But before I could cast Caterina off and go to my bed, the door opened and Leonardo came in, followed by the short man.

They both stopped short at the sight of me. *"Buon Dio!"* Leonardo whispered, coming up and staring wide-eyed. "It cannot be true!" He walked from my left to my right, never once taking his eyes off me, as if I was once again a prize cow. "Lorenzino," he said over his shoulder, "can you believe this? It is as if Caterina has arisen from the dead!"

The one called Lorenzino came up as well, his face even whiter than his brother-in-law's. "Say something," he whispered to me. "As Caterina."

I considered the way Sophia had instructed me, then put my hand to my chin. "My name is Caterina Soderini de Ginori," I said, holding my gaze on Lorenzino. "I am the wife of Leonardo de Ginori of Firenze, and," I added a Caterina toss of the head, "I am most tired, so I would you allow me to go to bed this instant."

Lorenzino let this pass. "Quite remarkable." He glanced back at Sophia. "You are to be congratulated," he said. "Both in look and in manner, she is Caterina."

"I believe I might also take some credit?" I enquired, dropping my hand to my side. "I have followed her instructions with the greatest of care."

"Yes, yes," Leonardo said, with a dismissive wave, as if swatting away a fly. "As you say."

"She is ready to be seen," Lorenzino said, as if I had not spoken. "It is important to stop any questions on the real Caterina's disappearance."

"Tomorrow is the Feast of the Nativity," Leonardo said directly to me, as if he finally acknowledged that I was a real person. "We will be expected to attend the procession through the city, then Mass at the Cathedral. It is the perfect opportunity for you—or should I say, Caterina—to be seen by all of Firenze." He turned to Sophia. "Have her get some sleep, and make sure she is ready in good time tomorrow. We will set off at sundown."

25

A CHANCE MEETING

Sophia came to wake me the next morning, and must have had to shake me for quite some time, judging by the look of annoyance on her thin face.

I struggled to sit up, and for a moment, this awakening was like all the others since Angelo's killing—that all was well, and we would continue our journey together… then I gave a small groan as once again, the truth of the situation came flooding back.

I rubbed my eyes and looked out of the window. The sun was just rising above the orange roofs of Firenze, casting a rich warm glow across the city.

"If it were not for the small mewling noises you were making in your sleep, I would have thought you dead," Sophia observed, her brow furrowed. "You were indeed weary."

"As I told you," I replied. "And I could have slept two more days and nights."

"Well, that is not going to happen," she said. "We have much to do if we are to have you ready for the procession, then Mass at the Cathedral tonight." She tapped her foot regarding me in her usual way; with her head to one side. Then her frown seemed to melt away, and quite unexpectedly she gave me a small smile. "I know nothing about you, except what I am told; that you are from somewhere near to Napoli, and were clothed as a man." She stared at me a moment, her dark eyes holding mine. "But what I see for myself, is someone who works hard, and has a talent for learning. That is good enough for me."

Feeling strangely pleased with myself for gaining her approval, I followed Sophia back to the chamber where we had spent so much time the previous day.

"You are the wife of one of the city's foremost men," she said, once I was seated before her. "Which means you will be wearing your finest clothes. It was my honour to dress the real Caterina, and I will do the same for you."

"Thank you," I replied.

"That alone is more gratitude than she ever showed," Sophia muttered, as she brought the wig over and secured it on my head. She then proceeded to braid the hair and pin it up, before adding a thin veil attached to an embroidered band. I was tempted to ask why so many women went out with their heads uncovered, but stopped myself; this was something Maria di Luca of Pozzuoli should know, even if Mary Fox of England did not.

The pots of rouge and powder were next, which she applied with patience and care, continually standing back to check the progress of her work. Once she had added the tinted wax to my lips, she nodded. "There. It is as if the mistress herself sits before me once again."

She went to a chest and handed me what looked like a linen shift, except that the collar and cuffs were finished in a soft pale blue. They were embroidered with golden flowers intertwined with fine silver leaves. I held it a moment, turning it over and admiring the fineness of the stitching.

"The decoration on this *camicia* is as nothing compared to the gown," Sophia observed, as she pulled me to my feet and lifted my nightdress off. Then she had me keep my arms raised as she gathered the *camicia* up, before sliding it over my head and letting it open up down my body. While I was admiring the cuffs at my wrists, she returned to the chest, then came back with a short partlet made of the finest lace. This went over my chest, so that my neck was decorated with the lace pattern over the *camicia*.

"I said the gown would be more sumptuous," she said, coming over with a heavy garment in the richest deep blue. It too was embroidered with silver and gold thread, and featured a squared neckline, with a stiffened bodice that held my belly in tight and pushed my chest upwards. "You are perhaps a little slighter than the mistress," she said. "But by good fortune, there is some space at your back that can be made smaller with the laces." As she fastened them, I ran my hands down the skirts. These flowed outwards from the waist, then on down to the floor. Sophia added full light blue sleeves that matched the embroidered cuffs, then a thin waistband in a fine tanned hide.

"Now," she said, standing back and looking me up and down, "some jewels to set off the gown." She went to another chest and took out a box made of polished cedar, inlaid with ivory and gold. "Here," she said, and took out a pair of golden earrings. She clipped them on me, then searched again in the box and brought out a beautiful gold chain with small rubies set into the pendant. As she fitted it round my neck, I could not help but think of *Il Fiume di Fuoco*. Would Scoronconcolo have already disposed of it? Or was he keeping it for longer before finding the right buyer?

Either way, I knew I could not let him benefit from the appalling murder of my love. I must get the necklace back, however it might be, so as to avenge Angelo and to help his mother. The thought of that vile killer sickened me, and if I could find a way to have my revenge for Angelo, then I would not lose the chance.

Sophia came over and put some gold and silver bracelets on me, plus a few rings. Then she went back to the jewellery box and returned with a pomander. She waved it before my nose and I caught the scent of rose petals and cloves, as well as something spicier which I could not identify. She clipped it to my waistband.

Finally, she fetched a pair of plain honey-coloured velvet slippers with a wooden heel and pointed toes. She bade me sit and hold out my feet. A pair of fine stockings went on first, followed by the shoes, which by good fortune fitted me quite well. I stood and took a few steps towards the end of the chamber. The gown flowed around me, and it was only by holding my hands clasped before my waist, that I was able to walk with any sense of feminine grace.

"You have too long dressed as a man," Sophia said, as I turned at the wall and made my way back. "But I warrant you will soon find yourself as a woman again." She was holding a grey fur-lined mantle, which she draped across my shoulders, then came round and fastened it with a gold and enamelled brooch. "There," she said, standing back with a satisfied-looking smile. "You are ready."

I stepped carefully as she led me down to the main hall. I was trying hard not to stand on the hem of the gown, for I had no wish to fall on my face. Each movement was an effort in the heavy clothing, and it reminded me with some force why I preferred the lightness and simplicity of men's garb.

Leonardo and Lorenzino were waiting by the fire, both with their own cloaks and boots on. They were talking in quiet voices as we came in, and stopped as soon as I was announced. They both seemed to have an almost guilty look as they fell silent, causing me to wonder just what they had been discussing.

Leonardo recovered first, and offered me his arm. "Caterina, my dear," he said, his voice sickeningly smooth, "you look as elegant as ever. Does she not, Lorenzino?"

The small man nodded, and gave me a bow. "Indeed, she is quite glorious this evening. All of Firenze will marvel at her beauty as she steps out on the parade through the city."

They seemed to have decided to treat me fully as Caterina, and I noted that they were doing so without a trace of irony or amusement. I wanted to shout at them, to remind them that this was only a piece of play-acting; that I was performing the part against my will and under the greatest of sufferance.

Leonardo took my arm and drew me to one side, "Today you will meet *Il Moro*—Duke Alessandro de Medici," he said. "It is most important that you do as I say."

The arrogance of his tone annoyed me, and I bit back a sharp retort. I took a small breath, then enquired, "And what might that be?"

He seemed unaware of my coldness, and answered, "First, you must remember that he has already bedded you." He swallowed hard, and added, "and that by my understanding, you were a willing partner."

"As you have told me already," I replied. "What would you have me do?"

He stared at me a moment, then said, "I want you to make him think that you would be willing to repeat the encounter."

I pulled my arm out from his and stepped away, my hands on my hips. I could feel my anger rising like a burning coal in my chest, and now I struggled to control it. "Are you trading your own wife like a common prostitute?" I demanded. "Are you trading *me* that way?"

"*Santa Maria*, woman," he snapped. "Still your voice!" His cheeks reddened to the colour of his beard. "I would remind you that your position here hangs by a thread."

"A most unfortunate phrase," I snapped back.

"And a reminder of what will happen to you if you do not go along with our wishes." He took several deep breaths, then said in a calmer voice, "It is not our plan that you actually lie with him, but that he thinks you will." He scratched his beard. "Do you understand?"

I caught his meaning very clearly. "I understand that you are setting me as bait in a trap," I replied. Then a thought occurred to me. "But it cannot work. If he has been intimate with Caterina already, then for sure, he will know I am not her. He will expose me as an impostor."

Lorenzino came up and joined the conversation. "Not at all," he said. "Be assured; you look close enough to her in form and face, that he will not question you at all."

—0—

The household of Leonardo and Caterina de Ginori must have made a most impressive sight as they stepped out that evening to join the procession around the city of Firenze. Leonardo and I were at the head with Paolo and Sophia just behind, then perhaps another twenty servants and retainers after these two. These all carried lit braziers, casting a bright flickering light all around us.

Lorenzino had left to join with Duke Alessandro, as apparently he was a close friend and confidant of Firenze's ruler, and was expected to be at the man's side. This revelation surprised me, for it seemed clear that the plot, whatever it might be, was intended to bring harm to the Duke. I had tried to find out more before we set off, but all I could glean from Leonardo was that 'I would be told what to do when the time came.'

So for now, I must concentrate on walking in the heavy gown, not stepping on the hem, and breathing in the tightly laced bodice.

I took it that Caterina would be conscious of her position as the wife of one of the city's foremost men, and gave her an arrogant lift of the chin. This not only helped give the impression I was seeking, but also meant I need not have the chance to catch the eye of anyone in the cheering throng who lined the streets as we passed.

Leonardo kept hold of my arm, and occasionally looked across with a reassuring smile. At least, I believe he thought it so; for me it had the sickly feel of a captor checking that his victim was content with her lot.

Was I content? Not at all. Just as I had been fearful of discovery when I played the part of the Tudor Prince, I had a horror of some worthy fellow pointing at me and shouting 'That is not *Signora* de Ginori; 'tis an impostor!' Would I then be dragged before the *Otto* to be arraigned for the murder of the woman I was attempting to replace, and summarily led to the gallows?

Now I felt as if I would need to stop and empty my churning belly.

Did they use tumbrils here in Firenze? Or would I be dragged on foot, bound and filthy, through these same streets as a condemned prisoner to the place of execution? Would I be hooded, the rope put about my neck, before the sickening drop into… into what? Would I continue down into the pit of hell, to suffer eternal torment for my apparent crimes? Or would I be blessed, as someone who had always tried to do the best by others? At least then I might join with Angelo in a better place.

"Have a care, Caterina," Leonardo hissed at me, his smile like a grimace. "You have the face of one who has bitten into a bad apple." He squeezed my arm. "Come now, this is a joyous occasion. These people have come to admire their betters. Show some grace, lower your head, and look as if you are pleased to be part of this important event."

I kept silent, but did as he said, starting to smile weakly at the people lining the streets on either side, their faces glowing in the light of our servants' braziers, as well as those burning on every building. They were gathered several deep; cheering and waving as we passed. The men were generally dressed in well-cut jerkins, and the woman in colourful dresses. I took it that they were wearing their finest clothing to celebrate the Nativity and view the parade; no doubt they would all be off to celebrate Midnight Mass at their own church, while we did the same at the Cathedral.

A small boy who had climbed onto a column for a better view gave me a cheery wave, and I smiled back. If Leonardo wanted me to show grace, then I would do so. Although not for his sake, but for my own. These people had made such an effort to come out, that I must reward them with some form of recognition for their efforts.

Leonardo leaned across again. "That is better, Caterina," he said. "We are near to the *Duomo* now; just a few more streets." I continued to smile at the crowds; the very model of a gracious noblewoman bestowing her favour on the common folk. They waved back, no doubt pleased to have recognition from the great Caterina Soderini de Ginori of Firenze. Little knowing she was in truth, plain Mary Fox of Marchington Manor in the county of Essex, England.

I caught the eye of a buxom woman in a red laced bodice; reminding me of the same style of garment I had worn in the Netherlands. Perhaps she was a Dutch woman, who had travelled here as well? I gave her a cheery smile and she nodded in recognition, dipping her head slightly as if she was making a curtsey.

It seemed that I was being foolish. How could I think I was in danger of being called out? I was Caterina, and she was me. Why should any person think differently? If I must play this part, then I may as well get some enjoyment from it. I stepped forward with more purpose. I would make the most of this.

We turned a corner, and here the crowds were a little thinner, making it even easier to see individual faces. Once again I bestowed my most gracious smile on each person I saw. A beardless young man with a large cap over half his face and a dark jerkin caught my eye, and I inclined my head to show I acknowledged him. His own eye flicked onto mine then looked quickly away, as if he had no time for such frivolity from the noble classes. A rabble-rouser, perhaps? One who would try to change the natural order? I let my gaze move past him to the next person—then took it back again.

Something about him had seemed familiar. Something that made my breath catch in my throat.

As I studied him, I must have frowned, for his own eye narrowed in return.

Then it widened in seeming recognition. Now his look changed. It became one of shock, before moving to ill-concealed anger.

Then it changed again—to one of triumph. He removed his cap so I could see him in full.

My blood ran cold.

Those eyes were well known; I should have seen it before. I knew exactly who 'he' was.

It was Janet Crosse.

26

A BOLT FROM THE BLUE

In truth, I do not remember much of what happened for the rest of that night.

I vaguely recall how we filed into the Cathedral and sat at the front of the quire. I must have taken in the magnificence of the building with its paintings, statues, golden decorations and above all, the glorious dome, but if you had asked me to describe it the following day, I would have struggled to do so.

Thankfully, the Midnight Mass was a familiar Latin service; I had attended such worship more times than I could count, so I went through it almost as if I was asleep; making the words and movements with little or no conscious thought.

I also made sure to keep apart from the other noble wives, lest any who knew Caterina well were to call me out.

Even the meeting with the Duke afterwards passed without incident. I know I made the required coquettish behaviour, giving this tall, dark man with his unpleasant lewd grin a sideways smile of my own, and being congratulated by Leonardo for having fooled the Duke that I truly was his wife, after we had moved on.

But my mind was far from this task.

Janet Crosse!

Not only had she found me, but now she knew exactly who I was. It would not be difficult for her to identify the Ginori residence, and shoot her crossbow at me. Or even take aim at me in the street.

We set off back to the house after Mass, and I kept so close to Leonardo that at one point he stopped and pushed me away, as if he wanted to see me better.

"What ails you, Caterina?" he asked, with a raised eyebrow.

"You cling to me like a nervous kitten, and look about you with the widest eyes. If you were a deer at the hunt, I would think you less worried." He paused. "What is it?"

"Nay, 'tis nothing," I muttered. "I am tired and would go to bed. And," I added, "all these people make me concerned. I would be home as soon as possible.

He glanced at the nearly empty streets. "What people? Most have gone."

"Well, I do not like them. Stay close, please." I looked round for Paolo. "And him, too. Keep me safe, both of you."

He shrugged. "If you wish." He gestured to Paolo, who came up beside me. With his bulk on one side, and Leonardo on the other, I felt a little more reassured.

Thankfully, we made it back to the house without encountering Janet or one of her bolts, and I excused myself and went straight to my chamber, taking care to close the shutters before lighting a candle, lest I could be seen from the street below.

Sophia soon joined me, helping me take Caterina's clothing and wig off so I was once again Maria in a plain nightdress. She talked as she worked, with comments about how well I had performed as her mistress, and how nobody could have seen the difference.

She could not be more wrong; one person *had* seen through my disguise.

At all times the picture of Janet Crosse kept forcing its way before my eyes; Janet Crosse looking shocked. Looking angry. Looking triumphant.

I thought I would be sick.

How could I concentrate on finding Scoronconcolo and recovering the necklace, if I must also keep one step ahead of that evil woman?

"I will stay inside now," I said to Sophia. "I have no desire to venture out again, until I must for Leonardo and Lorenzino. I will keep to the house, and you may give me more instruction in the art of being Caterina."

Sophia raised an eyebrow. "I think perhaps you have already had enough," she observed. "For you have just given an order worthy of the mistress herself."

I pulled open the bed hangings and climbed under the covers. "Nevertheless, I wish for more." I slid down and rested my head on the bolster. "Thank you Sophia. I will see you in the morning."

She gave a small laugh. "I am dismissed?" she asked.

"Yes, indeed," I replied.

She regarded me thoughtfully, her head on one side. "I see I have created a new mistress," she said. "Good night, and sleep well." She closed the hanging, and I heard the door open, then close behind her.

Sleep was, of course, out of the question. I lay on my back and put my hands behind my head.

There had been no sound of a bolt being drawn. I chewed my lip; perhaps she now trusted me enough to think I would not try to escape? Should I dress once again as Tommaso, and slip away into the night?

To what?

To make my way to the stables and saddle Hestia. It was an appealing thought; to ride out of Firenze and head down to Pozzuoli as fast as Hestia could take me; presumably to the safety of Angelo's mother.

But how could I take the risk of Janet Crosse watching the stables, ready to shoot her infernal bow? Or to chase me out of the city, then take her shot.

And what of Scoronconcolo? Would I be abandoning my chance to recover the necklace and revenge myself for Angelo?

No, for now my safest option was to keep behind the walls of this house. Of course, that meant I would have to go through with whatever infernal scheme Leonardo and his brother-in-law had planned for me. But at least I would be safe until then. Maybe I could find a way to recover the jewel and escape after that…

On that thought I must have drifted off to sleep.

—0—

The next three days were spent with Sophia, being coached even further on Caterina's manner. We spent the time in Caterina's chamber, working in even greater detail on the woman's walk, her speech, and the way she would both sit and stand. In time I found I was even thinking of myself as Caterina, and struggling to cast her off when I retired each night to my own bed.

But in truth only half my mind was on this task; the other half was much concerned with Janet Crosse. Every moment of every day I imagined that I was being watched. Was she on the street below, or perhaps at the window of a house opposite? Was she staring down the length of her crossbow, picking a window and hoping I would appear so she could take her shot?

Thankfully all the glazed casements were being kept firmly shut against the midwinter chill, but I was taking no chances. Even when Sophia bade me walk across the chamber in Caterina's distinctive gait, I made sure to slow just before the window, then rush past as if my life depended upon it. Which, of course, it did.

"The mistress would keep a more constant pace," Sophia observed on the afternoon of the third day. "Not start and stop like a soft-headed child."

"I must practice her walk in each possible way," I muttered, moving further away from the window. "Both fast and slow."

"For sure," she answered, her foot tapping ominously. "But not both within a single journey."

I hurried back, keeping to a single fast pace.

Sophia's foot stopped its movement. She gave a deep sigh and held up a hand. "Enough, Mistress," she said. "Enough. I think there is nothing more I can teach you. If you are able to walk slow then fast then slow again, and still have me believe I am looking at the *Signora*, then your instruction is complete. I will advise the

master that you are fully prepared and have nothing more to learn."
She went out of the room.

Left alone, I stood still for a moment. I was pleased once again to have Sophia's approval; pleased to have shown that I could learn to play a part that was both a woman and a foreigner. Pleased also that the intense teaching by Angelo, and his insistence on me speaking Neapolitan as we had travelled had left me able to converse with these people so well in their own tongue, that they thought me a Neapolitan by birth.

Angelo's kindness and his patience had borne such fruit. I looked upwards and whispered, *Your teaching has done me so well, my love.*

That is good came back the answer. *But I would you stay safe from that woman with the crossbow, Maria. And have revenge on Scoronconcolo for me.*

I will. I whispered back.

But... I shook my head. Was Janet Crosse really out there?

Perhaps she was, or perhaps not. Better to be safe, as Angelo wanted. I moved a little further away from the window.

But then... my curiosity got the better of me.

The window seemed to pull me towards itself. It was as if a line was hooked to my chest, and I was but a fish on the end. 'Take a look,' the window seemed to say, as it glowed brightly. 'Just a quick one, Mary Fox. Reassure yourself that she's not there. Then you can rest easy.'

I stood beside the casement frame and took a deep breath.

This is madness, I thought. *I am imagining this danger, when there is little chance it is real.*

I peered slowly round, with no more than half my head visible. I glanced down to the street.

The merchant tables below were all gone. People were moving around in groups and there were faint sounds of shouts and laughter coming up. No doubt they were still celebrating the Nativity, with another nine days until the revelries would end on the Twelfth Night, and merchant trading would start again.

A small movement in the house opposite caught my eye. There was a window open, despite the chill. A face was visible. For the briefest moment, I glanced at it in curiosity.

Then I realised what I was looking at.

I snapped my head back, just as the glass where it had been shattered into a thousand sharp fragments with the noise of a lightning crack.

With a scream I scrabbled away, then slid down the wall to the floor.

The cursed woman had been there all along, just as I had feared.

Janet Crosse!

Beside me there were shards of glass all across the tiles; each like a knife blade glinting in the candlelight. I looked up. The flights of a crossbow bolt quivered in the panel on the wall opposite. It had passed through the glass before embedding itself. I thought I would be sick. What would it have done to me if I had not moved aside in that instant?

A sharp pain made me put my hand to my cheek, and it came away red with blood.

I was just examining my reddened fingers when the door was thrown open and Leonardo strode in, followed by Paolo. Sophia was just behind.

"*Madre di Dio!*" Leonardo exclaimed. "I heard such a sound. What has happened here?"

Paolo crossed to the bolt and wrenched it free. He gave it to Leonardo. "Caterina?" Leonardo demanded, holding it up to me. "What is the meaning of this?" His face was twisted in rage, and he grasped the bolt as if it were a dagger ready to strike. For a moment I realised I was looking at a man who had truly killed his wife, and I resolved to show him no fear.

Sophia bent down; frowning as she looked over my cheek and forehead. "*Signora* de Ginori is hurt," she snapped. "Save your questions until I have checked her." With a grunt, Leonardo lowered the bolt and moved back.

I winced as she examined the cut, then gave a small cry as she pressed her fingers into the wound.

"Shh, Mistress," she whispered. "There is a buried shard. I will need to get it out." I clenched my teeth as she squeezed again, then she said, "There. I have it," and held up a sliver of glass for me to see. It was red with my blood.

She resumed her examination with a look of concentration and withdrew another shard. I tried not to cry in pain as she dealt with several more on my face and neck.

Sophia flicked a lace kerchief from her sleeve and dabbed at my face. "Each is a small wound in itself," she said with a nod. "And in time they will all heal without a scar. But," she added, looking up at Leonardo, "there are so many that she will show a general swelling and redness first."

She ran her eye down to my clothing. "There may be some here as well. Let me see…" She studied carefully, then gave a sharp breath and eased something out that was stuck in the side of my bodice, before holding it up for me to see. It was a wickedly pointed shard of glass, like the thinnest *stiletto* blade, and perhaps the length of my smallest finger. "Good," she observed. "There is no blood on its tip." She tossed it aside. "You were lucky."

"Lucky?" Leonardo said, bending down. He waved the bolt at me again, and I had to stop myself from flinching. "What luck is it to be targeted by a crossbow? Lorenzino and I need you for our plan and it is to happen tomorrow night."

Sophia gave him a sharp look. "I think not, *Signore*. She is not in any state for that now. You must change your plan."

Leonardo stormed over to the door, then stopped and turned back. "I will discuss this with Lorenzino," he snapped. "But for now, you will stay in your chamber." He made to go, then stopped again. "Paolo, you take her there. And make sure she stays away from the casement." He gave me another scowl. "And when you get her there, Paolo, close the shutters."

27
THE ASSASSIN

I saw nothing of Leonardo for the next few days. As he had ordered, I kept to my chamber with the shutters closed day and night, and I mostly stayed in bed. Sophia and Paolo were my only companions, bringing food, fresh candles and changing my chamber pot three times each day. Sophia tended to my wounds, washing them carefully until the scars formed, then inspecting them on each visit.

"These are clean," she observed one morning, as she held a candle up and ran her fingertips lightly across my cheek. She stood back and nodded. "And the redness all over is almost gone. Apart from some slight swelling to one side of your face, I warrant there will be little else to see in time. Which is good, for *Signore* de Ginori has said he will need you to play your part in his scheme in three days' time, on the evening of the Twelfth Night. It will be when the streets are most full of the common people celebrating. T *Signore* de Ginori says this will give the best chance of getting you to the place they want without your assailant aiming a crossbow at you again."

"Where is this place?" I asked.

She perched on the side of the bed. "In truth I know not. They do not share their plans with the likes of me." She paused a moment, regarding me without expression. "But tell me, Maria," she continued, "you have not explained why some person is trying to end your life. Why is this?"

I had long been expecting this question, so I gave the answer I had prepared.

"A man tried to rob me as I crossed the mountains of Switzerland," I said. "But I fought him off and managed to escape.

He swore to get his vengeance, so I believe this is him seeking it now. I saw him on the night of the procession, and knew at once he had recognised me. There was little secret made of who *Signore* de Ginori was, so this man could easily discover where to find me." There was enough truth in it to make it seem credible.

Her eyes held mine as she considered my words. She made a frown, as if she was not sure if she should believe me, then she gave a small nod. "As you say." She got up and walked to the fire, then added some fresh wood so it blazed. "Paolo went over to the house of the Carino family opposite, the day after you were wounded," she turned back to me. "*Signore* de Ginori sent him, wanting to find out more about your would-be killer." She came back to the bed and sat once again. "*Signore* and *Signora* Carino are kindly souls; much given to Christian charity. It seems that when they had attended Mass a few days earlier, a young foreigner had come to sit beside them."

I pushed myself up in bed, keen to hear more of how Janet Crosse had schemed her way into these good people's favour. "Although he had none of their tongue," Sophia continued, "he was able to make them understand that he had been robbed of all his coins, and was unable to afford a room to stay." She came to a stop, then said, "Perhaps the good Lord has sought to punish him for trying to steal from you? He has himself been robbed."

"I warrant that was just another one of his lies," I observed.

She shrugged. "For all that, they say he was a pleasant enough fellow, and had such an honest face, that they took pity and immediately offered him shelter under their roof."

"Then he is clearly a better liar than even I thought."

"Maybe so. They say he was most attentive, offering to help as best he could."

"Did he give a name?" I asked.

"It seems he did," she replied. "He said his name was Jacob."

I stifled a laugh. *Jacob!* Janet must have known that if she failed to kill me, I would hear of this. She was sending me a message that she was still seeking revenge for the death of Jacob Cruddon. "And what of this man after he made to kill me?" I said.

She observed me in silence a moment, her face sharply shadowed in the candlelight. "They say he packed his bag and disappeared immediately after."

"I could believe so."

"But the strangest thing," she continued, "was that once he was gone, *Signora* Carino discovered one of her gowns was missing from a chest, as well as a pair of shoes, some jewellery and pots of rouge." Sophia paused a moment. "I suppose this Jacob fellow thought he could sell them to gain some coins."

"Perhaps," I said. I sat back. It was more likely that Janet Crosse was securing yet another disguise. If she had women's clothing, she would be even more difficult to identify. I took a deep breath. I would need to be truly vigilant when I finally left the Ginori house, for if there were many people out celebrating the Twelfth Night, any one of them, male or female, could be Janet Crosse trying to kill me.

—0—

Three days later in the morning—as far as I could tell from the meagre shafts of sunlight filtering through the shutters—the door was unbolted, and Leonardo strode in. His look was slightly less angered than the last time we were together, but not greatly.

"Your face is not fully healed, Caterina," he snapped, holding up a candle for better light and giving me a hard stare. "And there is still some swelling. I would prefer it has gone down fully, so you are more like my Caterina, but we must proceed now, or we will lose our opportunity."

"With some powder and rouge, the marks will be quite concealed, *Signore,*" Sophia said, coming in behind him. "And the swelling is nowhere near as bad as it was."

"Very well," Leonardo conceded. "Have her ready. We will set off at sundown." He went out, leaving me alone with Sophia.

"We must see to your dress," she said. "You can leave this

211

chamber now and return to the *Signora's*."

With some reluctance I followed her out of my room and down the many passages to Caterina's chamber. She opened the door and stood back so I could enter, but I paused. I had been dreading the return to the scene of my near-murder, and now I was here my heart was beating like a blacksmith's hammer at the thought of once again being in that room. Sophia said nothing, and I could see she understood.

Then I swear I heard Angelo's voice from above. *Come now Maria*, he whispered. *Where is the courage you showed so many times on our journey? When you fought the widow in the graveyard? Or the brigand in the forest outside Milano? I need you to be strong, Maria, for my sake and for my mother.*

I took a deep breath, put my shoulders back, then walked inside.

The first thing I noticed was that the broken glass had been replaced, as if the bolt had never passed through. I raised my fingers to my cheek, and ran them across the raised marks left by the shattering windowpane. The panels opposite had also been repaired. However close I looked, there was no sign of the hole made by the bolt.

"The *Signore* wanted no trace of the incident to remain," Sophia said, as she closed the door. "And Paolo is standing in the street below, keeping watch for the man Jacob." She made a small smile. "So you can be assured you will not be targeted again," then added, "even if this Jacob fellow is still in the city."

I did not respond, even though I had little doubt that 'Jacob', or whatever name his female counterpart was using, was definitely still in the city.

"Come," Sophia said. "Let us get started making you into Caterina de Ginori."

I held up a hand. "I can do much of this myself," I said. "I would you let me alone a while and I will call you when I need your help."

She regarded me with her head to one side. I thought for a

moment she was going to insist on dressing me herself. But then she nodded, and said, "As you wish."

She went to a chest and took out a deep red gown, a set of red and grey sleeves, and a *camicia* with embroidered cuffs finished in black with gold stitching. A pair of stockings joined them on the bed, as well as some heeled shoes. "I have found these," she said, "with a wood and leather sole. It is not often we get snow here, but this season, God has seen fit to let it fall. There has been much coming down while you have been recovering." Now I glanced out of the window, I could see there was indeed a white blanket across the cobblestones outside. Sophia gave me the shoes. "These will allow you to stop your feet from freezing, while keeping the grace and elegance the mistress favoured." I turned one of the shoes in my hand. The sole was thick and the heel sturdy, if not too high. "But walk with care," she added as I put it back on the bed. "For they will afford you little grip in the cold." She pointed to a bell on the table in the corner. "I will need to tighten your lacing. Use this to let me know when you are ready." Then she left me alone in the room.

When she returned, I was just stepping into the shoes. Sophia walked all round me, and gave a satisfied-seeming nod. "Excellent, *Signora.*" She pulled the lacing at the back of the gown tight, and secured it. "Although I warrant that you have even gained a little weight since we last dressed you."

I said nothing, as she then bade me sit so she could attend to my hair and face. Once again she applied the wig and powders, taking extra care as she covered over the side that had been damaged. Eventually she stood back with a satisfied-looking nod, and said, "Good. *Signore* de Ginori should be well pleased. I will get him."

I stood up once she had gone out, and tried to manage my breath. After enjoying the freedom of a loose nightdress for many days, it was difficult being laced into the bodice again, and as Sophia had said, it was even tighter than before. I took the opportunity to accustom myself back into it.

Leonardo came in, followed by the small man Lorenzino and Sophia.

"She looks well," my supposed husband said. "It suits my purpose."

"Which is?" I asked, putting a touch of frost in my voice. "I have done all you have asked, and will do whatever you require this evening. I think it is right that you not only tell me what this is about, but also," and here I added an even sterner tone, "you give me your assurance that once this thing is over, you will let me go."

Leonardo ran his hands through his beard as he stared into my eyes. "Very well," he said. "You are to come with me and Lorenzino to his house, where you are to await the arrival of Duke Alessandro de Medici. When he arrives, you are to invite him to lie with you."

"You wish for me to give myself to him?" I said, my voice rising.

"Nay, I have said earlier that we do not," said Leonardo. "You will have some wine for him, which will contain a powerful sleeping draught. He will readily accept it, as he is a degenerate that drinks to excess."

I felt the mention of the sleeping draught deserved some comment, given he had tested it on me. But he seemed either to have forgotten, or thought it of little matter. At least I knew it would work, and within a short time.

"You will tease him, that is all, while you wait for the draught to do its task," Leonardo continued. "Then, when he is asleep, you will return here, where you will be given back your men's clothing. You are then free to go wherever you wish."

What I wished, was that I could believe he would keep his word. But given how unlikely this seemed, I must prepare accordingly.

"And what will you do to the sleeping duke?" I asked, although I fancy from the stern look on their faces, I already knew the answer. I was correct.

"We are going to kill him," Leonardo said, "and rid the city of the pestilence and debauchery of *il Moro*."

Lorenzino spoke, and even in the candlelight I could see his face was a twisted mask of hate. "The man is an ignorant bastard, a stupid, half-caste usurper who makes a false claim to the Medici name; an honour that he defiles with every woman he screws, every goblet of wine he downs, and every self-serving decision he makes as ruler."

Leonardo said nothing; it was clear that these grievances were well-known to him.

"And do you know the final thing?" Lorenzino growled. I shook my head; there would be no stopping him in this hateful rant. "The final thing; the last god-forsaken thing this evil man has done, was to have my cousin, my own cousin, Cardinal Ippolito de' Medici, poisoned! A good and god-fearing man; a true Medici, and one whose boots *Il Moro* was unworthy even to lick!" He stood back a step, and took a deep breath, as if to regain his temper. "So we will rid ourselves, and our glorious city, of this monster. Then there will be a different Medici ready to take his place." His voice rose again. "An honest and just ruler of Firenze; a true Medici, not a darkened half-breed!"

"You?" I asked, despite myself.

"Oh yes!" He nodded. "I will step forward and take my rightful place, once that man is dead. A man who belittles me at every turn!" He wiped some spittle from the corner of his mouth. "Then there will be justice and peace in Firenze once more."

"You will be the one to kill him?" I asked, looking at this small man, and thinking of the taller, well-built duke I had met briefly at Mass.

He gave a short hollow laugh. "I will have help. A professional killer will do the final act."

"Who will join us shortly," Leonardo added.

As if on cue, the door opened and Paolo came in, then stood to one side.

There was a movement behind him, and I shivered, as if all the warmth was being drawn out of the room. A dark shape in the shadows resolved itself into a man in a black cloak, who walked past Paolo and came in. The man moved into the candlelight, so I could now see he was hook-nosed with close-set eyes. He bowed to me, then removed his cap to reveal a head with not a single hair upon it.

"*Signora* de Ginori," he said in a gravelly voice. Then he straightened up and my breath caught as I recognised him.

Scoronconcolo.

28

AN APPOINTMENT WITH DEATH

I kept my voice quiet as I acknowledged Scoronconcolo.

"*Signore,*" I whispered. He straightened up and replaced his cap, giving me only the briefest glance.

"She knows her part?" he asked Lorenzino, almost as if I were not present.

He does not recognise me, I thought. *And why should he?* He last saw me as Tommaso, and although he knew I was in truth a woman, he had never seen me dressed as such. Now here I was, clothed in the finery of Caterina, with a dark wig, powder and rouge. Why would he even question that I was her? He might recognise the shape of my nose, my brow or even my eyes—were he to look at them—but my whole face was different; still somewhat swollen on one side after my brush with Janet Crosse's evil bolt. *I must use this to my own advantage.* I thought. *But how? Help me here, Angelo. This could be my chance to get the necklace back. But he is not likely to have it on his person.*

Why not? came the answer. *If he has not yet disposed of it, then surely the safest place to keep it would be on him?*

But he has had days to dispose of it, I replied.

The merchant tables are all gone, as there is no trading during the Nativity celebrations. You saw this from the window a few days earlier.

I drew a quick breath. *So he would have had no opportunity to sell it until after the Twelfth Night celebrations are over on the morrow, when the merchants will return?*

Exactly, Maria. So you might still have a chance.

Scoronconcolo was talking to Lorenzino and Leonardo, and I gave him a surreptitious look. He was wearing a black doublet with dark hose and boots. I could just make out a tan hide belt under his black cloak, with a purse secured to it. This would no doubt be the one that held his coins. But maybe he had the distinctive leather pouch on the other side?

I leaned across to Sophia. "Perhaps the *Signore's* cloak is damp after being outside," I whispered. "Should he be relieved of it, lest he catch a chill?"

Her eyes narrowed and she gave me a quizzical frown, as if wondering why I should have such excessive concern for the wellbeing of a stranger—and an acknowledged killer at that—but she nodded, and went over to him. "May I take your cloak, *Signore?*" she asked.

Without appearing to give any thought, he turned towards her, then unclasped and slipped it from his shoulders. Sophia took it and hung it on the finial of one of the sconces.

Although he was now facing more towards me, I could not see far enough around him to catch sight of his other hip.

I took a few steps to one side to get a better view; just as he moved back.

I took a few further steps into the shadows by the wall. The three men were talking among themselves, and did not seem to notice, but Sophia gave me another frown. I shook my head to tell her to let it be, and her frown deepened, but she said nothing.

Now I had a better view.

There was something tan-coloured close to his knife, but I could not see it clearly.

Then he moved into a patch of light, and the shape became well-defined.

The leather pouch with the Saxon markings!

You see, Angelo whispered, his voice coming to my head like a feather on the breeze. *Trust to your judgment, mio amore, Maria.* There was a pause. *Now you must plan how you will get it back.*

—0—

Lorenzino, Scoronconcolo and I set off for Lorenzino's house a

218

while later, once all the plans were agreed. Leonardo wished us good fortune as we left, and even put a hand on my arm so I stayed in the doorway after the other two men went into the snowy street.

"Play your part, Caterina," he whispered, "and it will go well for you, as I have said."

I nodded, as he walked back into the house. Sophia, who had also come to see us off, reached up and adjusted the cloak about my shoulders.

"There, *Signora*," she said, pulling the hood up over my head. "Your face will be in shadow, but keep looking down and you will not be recognised." She gave me a frown. "I know not what that was all about back there, but whatever it was, put it from your mind." She peered past me into the street, which was filled with thronging crowds of revellers. Some were in small, fast-paced groups of two or three, while others were part of larger, slower gatherings of eight, ten or more. They were laughing and shouting as they went, sounding for all the world like raucous flocks of geese. "Your attacker will scarce attempt anything with so many of these people around." Sophia had a look of mild distaste on her face as she said 'people'. I took it she had no time for such wantonness.

I wished I had her confidence, for my attacker was nothing if not resourceful. It had occurred to me before, that the people celebrating in the streets could be as much to Janet Crosse's advantage as mine. Just as I could use them to protect myself against her loosing off a crossbow bolt, she could use them as cover to get close enough to slip a knife into my back. The thought made me shudder as if I had a sudden ague, and in my imagination I could feel the agonising pain of a blade piecing my skin, then being pushed deep inside me.

"Come Caterina," Lorenzino said, standing a few yards away. He was stepping to one side or the other as revellers ebbed and swayed past him, "we must be there soon." He seemed to be taking care not to slip on the icy snow.

"Haste, woman," snapped Scoronconcolo, who was standing

by Lorenzino and making a better job of ignoring the revellers. "Do not tarry."

I forced myself to see sense. *Come Mary Fox*, I thought. *Surprising as it may be, Scoronconcolo will protect you. He does not know who you are in truth, and he needs 'Caterina' to reach Lorenzino's house unharmed. That vengeful Janet Crosse will hardly try to attack you while such a man is close by.*

"I said haste, woman!" Scoronconcolo repeated, his voice raised against the shouts of the crowd. He emphasised his point by tapping impatiently on the handle of the knife at his belt. That small movement made me hesitate a moment more, although I tried hard to keep my face impassive as I returned his stare. That hand—that tapping hand—was the same one that had held the same knife—that had swept so casually across Angelo's throat.

Once again I saw the line of blood appear on my love's neck; saw the look of shock and confusion on his face, and the smallest nod when I mouthed *I love you.*

I will get the jewel back, Angelo, I told him, *and I will avenge your murder.*

I squared my shoulders and walked carefully over to the two men.

Lorenzino held his arm out for me to take, and we set off through the crowds. Scoronconcolo came up and took his place slightly behind me and to one side. I glanced back and caught his eye, getting an unpleasant stare in return. From his expression, he seemed to consider me no better than dirt beneath his heel. I lowered my head as if chastened by him, but in truth, I was checking his belt. The distinctive pouch was still there, swinging in and out of view from behind his cloak as he walked.

How to get it off him? I gave a small shrug as I turned back towards Lorenzino. I would find a way. I must.

After pushing through the crowds, we finally stopped outside a grand-looking house, similar in size to the Ginori residence. Lorenzino took us round to the side, and let us in through a nondescript door. He took us through several passages until we came into a small parlour that had a fire burning merrily in the grate, with several lit candles on a table. "You remain here," he instructed Scoronconcolo. As the assassin cast off his cloak and took a seat near the fire, Lorenzino beckoned me over. "Caterina," he said, "I will show you where you are to await *Il Moro*."

I followed him back out into the empty passageway. "Where are the servants?" I asked. I assumed they would know their master's sister, and I had no wish for any of them to call me out as an impostor.

He glanced back over his shoulder. "They are all given leave to go out and celebrate the Twelfth Night," he said. "I had no wish for them to bear witness to what will happen here shortly."

In truth, nor did I. But I was committed to this dreadful enterprise; in part so I could take leave of my captor Leonardo, but mainly so I could stay close to Scoronconcolo and retrieve the precious necklace. If it took being part of a murderous plan, then I must take it as an opportunity to achieve my own aims.

Even if my part led directly to the death of another?

While I had no reason to wish harm on this Duke Alessandro, Lorenzino and Leonardo clearly wanted him gone, with Lorenzino planning to take his place as ruler. It seemed that such assassinations were well-known among the city states of this land, even as far back as ancient Rome. Angelo had once told me of a ruler named Julius Caesar who had been stabbed many times by a group of his men, led by a so-called friend, Brutus. Perhaps this was even the model for Lorenzino's plan?

As Lorenzino led me up some stairs, I struggled to remember the conversation with Angelo. Did Brutus assume the leadership of Rome after the murder? I did not recall Angelo saying this, but I thought not. But for sure, the killer would forever have carried the guilt of causing his friend's death.

And what of my own guilt now? Must I also carry this forever? I paused a moment on the stair, and shook my head. My part in this was naught but the bait on the hook of Lorenzino's line. This murder would happen even if some other woman was used as a lure—so why should I carry guilt?

I hurried on after Lorenzino. My task was to retrieve the necklace, and make my escape. That was all.

—0—

Lorenzino ushered me into the bed chamber, then came behind me and slipped the cloak off my shoulders.

There were a few candles giving light, along with the roaring fire. The room was well-appointed, with an ornate bed in the middle; its gilded posts resplendent with heavy red velvet drapes. On one wall was a richly polished table, on which were two goblets and a silver *foglietta* of wine. The walls were decorated with silken hangings, as well as several fine portraits of stern-looking Fiorentinos staring down their long noses. I tried to ignore them; it would not help me do Lorenzino's bidding if I was concerned by their disapproving glares.

"Place yourself on the bed," he said, pulling back the drapes. "We have been teasing *Il Moro* for some days that my sister Caterina is now keen to have another assignation. He is like a dog scenting a bitch."

I chose to ignore the comparison.

He went to the table. "The wine is not yet laced with the sleeping draught," he said, indicating the *foglietta*. He took a small twist of paper from his purse. "This is it," he said, handing it over. "There is enough in here to fell a horse. Pour glasses for you both first, so he does not suspect poison, then add it to his glass when he does not see."

"Do I give it all in one?" I asked, turning it in my hand. The paper was tightly twisted, and the contents seemed a fine powder that gave a little when I pinched it.

"Yes. He will be asleep within minutes." This I knew.

"And he will not suspect the taste?"

"No. He will already be drunk. The strong Barolo will mask the bitterness of the draught." This I also knew; although for me

222

the powder had been in a sweet *Vin Santo*. Lorenzino pursed his lips and nodded. "As soon as he is asleep, ring this bell. We will come."

"And commit murder," I observed.

Lorenzino looked back as he went to the door. "It is not a murder," he said. "But a way to put Firenze out of her misery."

"If you say," I replied, trying to keep the disdain from my voice.

"I do. And if you play your part, you will be remembered as the saviour of the city." With that, he left and closed the door behind him.

Caterina may be so remembered, I thought as I eased myself onto the bed. *But never Mary Fox. History will not even record her name.*

A few minutes later the door opened again, and a richly dressed dark-skinned man with short curled hair slipped in. He threw off his cloak and adjusted the knife at his belt as he came towards me.

Duke Alessandro de Medici. Come to meet his death.

29
DUKE ALESSANDRO DE MEDICI

"Caterina de Ginori," the Duke said with a lop-sided grin.

I gave him a half smile, and a coquettish nod. "I am," I said. "It is good to see you again, Duke Alessandro."

"I recall our last encounter," he said. "And your willingness to repeat it. I have looked forward to this moment."

He advanced into the room, his eyes running up and down my body. Even without the aid of daylight I could see his eyes were glazed, and he made a small stumble as he advanced to the bed. As Lorenzino had said, the man was already drunk.

"You are as lovely as I remember," he said, but then he frowned as he studied my face. "You have some swelling on your cheek? It changes your look."

"A small accident, my lord," I said.

"As may be," he said with a dismissive flick of his hand. "I would have had you again in the *Duomo* at Mass if there were not people about. And your old lump of a husband." While the brazenness of this shocked me, I did breathe a small sigh of relief that he truly thought me to be Caterina. He came closer. "We are now alone. I am told you would once again entertain your duke."

"Then you were misinformed, my lord," I replied, keeping my voice as low and sultry as possible. "I am a woman of the highest virtue." I had decided I would play him for as long as possible, so I could make sure of the opportunity to slip him the sleeping draught before he could seduce me.

"Hmm. As you say." He leaned over me, and I caught the smell of wine on his breath. "Your beauty fascinates me," he murmured, breaking into the same lewd grin that I recalled from our brief meeting in the *Duomo*. Then he stepped away from the

225

bed, still observing me with his dark eyes. "A woman of virtue. I like that," he said. "It is no fun if they are too easy." He started to unbutton his doublet. "Will you resist me now, Caterina de Ginori?" he asked. "So I must use force to get my satisfaction?"

I kept my smile with some difficulty. "What would please you most, my lord?" I asked, between gritted teeth.

He paused, his doublet half unbuttoned. "For you to resist, woman," he replied. "Resist all you can; scream and cry rape. I like that the best." Then, before I could stop him, he marched to the table and poured himself a full glass of wine. As I watched in horror, he downed it all in a single gulp. "Hmm," he said, refilling the glass. "Barolo." He poured another, and drank it as well. "A fresh wine is this." A third glass followed the first two.

I felt my blood run cold. How could I slip him the sleeping draught if he was helping himself to all the wine before I could get to it? I frowned. Lorenzino had not thought of that possibility. Even if the Duke left enough for me to use, he now knew the taste. I started to slide off the bed, with the twist of paper clutched in my hand. If I could get to him, perhaps I could find a way to add my powder to whatever wine remained.

He put the empty glass down and came over, then pushed me hard so I fell back onto the bolster. "Oh no," he snarled, "you stay where you are." Then he leaned over and put his full weight onto my body. His head came down and his lips crushed onto mine. I was forced by his probing tongue to open my mouth, and endure the disgusting push of it deep into my throat. I nearly gagged at the taste of the wine he had just drunk, and raised my hands to his shoulders, trying to push him off. There was a satisfied-sounding grunt as he pressed harder, so I must now try beating at him with my fists. This drew another such sound from him, and I realised he was taking satisfaction from my struggles.

Something hard was pressing into my thigh, and for a moment I thought it was the knife at his belt, but then I realised this had been on the other hip. I almost retched as I realised what the hard thing must be.

A hand crept under my skirts, starting to feel its way up my stockinged leg.

I used my fists again, but as before this only seemed to encourage him.

He moved his other hand onto my wrist, so now I only had one to punch at his shoulder.

As the pawing reached my knee, he broke away from my mouth. "That is good," he growled. "You want me to stop?"

"Yes!" I exclaimed. "Stop!"

"Ha!" His mouth twisted into a sneering grin. "But of course, I will not." His hand reached the top of my stocking. "It is what you want—like last time!"

Then he suddenly withdrew his hand and stood up. "But what I want now is more wine. Then we will take this further."

I tried to stand. "Let me, my lord," I said, trying to smile. "I will pour for you."

He pushed me back down again. "I may be the Duke, but I am perfectly capable of serving myself with wine." He walked over to the table and while I was still sprawled across the bedding, he poured more wine into his glass. I sat up and winced as he shook the last drip from the *foglietta* over his glass. "Finished," he muttered, then turned to me. "I am assured we are alone in this house," he added, "Or I would call for more. Too bad; I will need to make this my last."

I started to get off the bed, desperate to find a way to add my powder, when he came towards me, glass in hand.

"You stay there!" he ordered, then used his free hand to push me back once more. As I stared up at him, my mouth open in horror, he emptied the last of the wine down his throat.

"Oh no," I yelped, but I do not think he heard me. I pushed the twist of paper deep under the bolster. What use did I have for it now?

"Where were we?" he said. He threw the empty glass into the fire, where it shattered with a loud report.

I used this opportunity to try and slither away across the

bedding, and almost made it halfway across, but he grasped my ankle and pulled me back. I yelped with the pain in my joints, but stopped as the breath was forced from my chest when he fell on me again.

Once more he crushed his mouth onto mine, and forced his foul tongue inside me. Once more the hand started feeling its way up my leg. Once more he held one wrist in a tight, painful grip. And once more I tried to batter his head with the other.

The hand reached the top of my stocking, and continued with probing fingers onto my thigh.

It stopped.

He pulled away and looked down at me with a frown. "You are wearing hose?" he asked, his voice in a whisper. I said nothing as he reached down and lifted my skirts up, to expose my full leg. Then he pulled my stocking down and stared at what I had been wearing under it.

"Why are you in men's hose?" he asked. I moved back and raised myself, so I was sitting up against the bolster. "Why?" he repeated, swinging out his legs so he was seated on the side of the bed.

I said nothing, but instead I balled my hand to a fist. As he stared at me in his drunken confusion, I took my chance.

I swung my fist at him with all my strength, hitting him in the jaw. His head snapped round as he took the full force of the blow, but he remained seated, and turned back with a deep frown.

Ignoring the excruciating pain that had erupted in my hand, I swung back and hit him again, this time with even greater force.

Duke Alessandro de Medici's eyes rolled up into his head. He swayed slowly a moment, then slid off the bed and fell into a crumpled heap on the floor.

A fine blow, Maria. I could scarce have done better.

Shh, Angelo. Now is not the time.

I slipped off the bed and crouched by the Duke. He was still breathing, so I had not done Lorenzino and Scoronconcolo's work for them. But at least I had achieved their aim for me, and had put the Duke to sleep. I ran to the bell, then came back to the sleeping man. Hooking my hands under his arms, I managed, with much grunting and cursing, to lift his weight onto the bed. I then arranged his limbs so he was lying on his back, although his head was lolling to one side.

I withdrew the knife from his belt and retreated into the shadows on the opposite side of the room to the fire. For a moment there was quiet, with no sound but the crackling of the flames. The man on the bed was still.

This peaceful tableau was interrupted by the sound of footsteps in the passageway. The door burst open and Lorenzino and Scoronconcolo ran in. Without even looking for me, they headed straight to the bed, their knives out.

Lorenzino shook the Duke's shoulder. "Are you asleep?" he asked. He looked up at Scoronconcolo who had positioned himself on the other side of the bed, and it seemed as if they were agreed to commit the act. Just as they raised their knives, there was a groan from the Duke.

They paused, frozen like two statues in the candlelight.

There was another groan, and the Duke rolled slightly towards Lorenzino. Immediately Lorenzino put his hands on Alessandro's shoulder to hold him still. Scoronconcolo stepped round the bed to stand next to his fellow assassin, and again raised his knife.

"Do it," Lorenzino snapped.

As I watched in sick horror, Scoronconcolo's knife flashed up and down, plunging into the Duke's body with the sound of a butcher at work.

Alessandro started to fight back. He screamed.

It was a sound that chilled my blood; the sound of a wounded beast as the huntsman finishes it off.

Lorenzino put his hand into the Duke's mouth as if to try and rip out the tongue. But then he let out a yell as loud as the victim's, and seemed to be trying to pull his hand away. Blood appeared around the Duke's mouth.

As Lorenzino and the Duke struggled against each other,

Scoronconcolo shifted his hold on his knife, and plunged it into Duke Alessandro's neck.

There was a sickening bubbling, choking sound like water boiling over, as he twisted the knife.

Lorenzino's hand came free, and I could see the white bone beneath his blooded fingers where the Duke had bitten through.

I saw my chance.

As Scoronconcolo was bent over the still writhing body, I grasped the Duke's knife and came up behind the assassin. In one move, I grasped the leather pouch at his waist and ran the blade across the fastening. It came away in my hand.

For the briefest moment, I considered pushing my knife into Scoronconcolo's back, and having my revenge for the murder of Angelo.

Nay, Maria, you must be away this instant, lest Lorenzino turns on you. You have the jewel, now get away!

I will…

"Yes, I will," I muttered aloud, running to the door and ripping the wig off as I went. As I ran into the passageway beyond, I put the blade to the lacing at my back, and ripped through as many strands as I could. It was enough to loosen the gown. Pulling off the sleeves and using one to wipe my face clean of Caterina's powder and rouge, I shrugged out of the heavy garment and let it fall to the floor behind me. I adjusted the doublet I had been wearing underneath, and ran on. Caterina's heeled shoes would not only cause much comment being seen on a man, but would be impossible to run in, so I cast them off. It was not far to Leonardo's house; my stockinged feet would get me there before the cold of the snow could cause harm.

I was free! And I had the necklace!

With a small yell of triumph, I slipped the Duke's knife into my belt and ran into the crowded street, planning my route back. The cold of the snow and icy cobbles did numb my feet almost immediately, but I pressed on regardless. I would slip in through the side door, retrieve my boots and the rest of my belongings, then run to the stables, where I would leap onto Hestia' back and ride as fast as possible out of this accursed city.

Would Leonardo have kept his word and let me go? I could not take the risk. Not now the necklace was mine!

A large crowd of drunken men were in my way, so I slowed to push my way through them. One of them said, "Hail fellow! Happy Epiphany!"

I smiled back as I forced my way through them. "And to you." I replied.

Several men jostled against me, but I grasped the leather pouch firmly and kept pushing on. Freedom beckoned on the other side of the group.

I pushed past the final two men, and was clear. The street opened up before me.

The numbness was turning to pain in my stockinged feet, but again, I tried to ignore it. I would soon be pulling on my own boots.

I was just preparing to run again, when a hand grasped my shoulder, pulling me to a halt.

A sharp pain in my side made me gasp.

"Stop there, Mary Fox," a woman's voice whispered in English into my ear. "Or I will stick you with this knife like the pig that you are."

30
JUST KEEP WALKING

"Janet Crosse?" I asked, trying to keep my voice steady. She remained silent, while the blade nicked into my side. I could feel a wet trickle of blood start to run down towards my hip.

"What do you want of me?" I asked. The English words felt unfamiliar on my tongue after weeks of speaking Neapolitan.

"Hold your peace" she hissed. "Keep walking."

I maintained the same pace, putting one foot before the other on the icy cold ground as she pushed up behind me. The pain in my frozen feet was becoming unbearable as we walked agonisingly slowly on the snowy cobbles.

But that was of little consequence, compared to being captured by this woman. How could I have been so careless?

"You were dressed as the wife of Ginori when you went into that house," Janet said. Her tone was accusing, as if it was only her that I was trying to deceive. "But now you are back in your man's clothing." There was a pause. "It was not hard to recognise you again. Particularly as your head is uncovered."

That was true. I could have brought my cap, but the man's clothing I had dressed in when Sophia had left me alone was already so bulky beneath my gown that I had decided against pushing my cap under the doublet as well. Sophia thought I had grown fat enough as it was. So I had left it in my bag, along with my boots and other possessions, ready to be snatched from Leonardo's house before mounting Hestia and fleeing.

I decision I might live to regret.

If I was to live at all.

"Where are we going?" I asked.

"Hold your tongue!" she snapped. "I am fully prepared to finish you off as you deserve, right here."

"There are too many people," I said, as we rounded a corner, and more groups of men came towards us. "You would not get away."

"Maybe not, but you will be mortally wounded," she hissed. "It could be hours or even days of agony before you finally succumb, but you will take your rightful place before Satan soon enough."

"They will arraign you for murder at the *Otto* court," I said, as two men wearing the livery of the *Birri* constabulary walked towards us on the other side of the street. "You will die as well."

"I will take my chance," she replied. "Belike if I explain the woman I killed was masquerading as the wife of a prominent Florentine…" There was a pause. "Did you kill her, too, to take her place?"

I remained silent. There was little doubt that Leonardo de Ginori would lay the blame for Caterina's death on me if he was challenged. So if Janet claimed she was simply delivering justice herself, then perhaps the court might indeed let her go free.

The two constables were closer now. They were laughing and shouting to others, as if they were enjoying the revelries as much as everyone else. I took a breath, ready to call out to them, when Janet growled in my ear, "Hold your tongue, Fox, or I will fell you right now."

The knife blade pressed a little harder and I increased my pace, almost as if I could outrun it. Janet kept close behind me, her body pushed onto mine and her free hand on my shoulder. The constables looked over at us from the other side of the street as they drew level.

"Had too much wine, eh?" one called over to me. "So your friend here must keep you from falling over?" He elbowed his colleague and pointed at us, as if to share the joke. Then he must have seen the fearful look of denial on my face, and stopped with a frown. "Are you well, young sir?" he asked.

"What did he say?" Janet whispered.

"He wanted to know if I am well," I replied out of the side of my mouth. My heart gave a small jump. Janet Crosse still spoke only English, and had no word of the local tongue. It was as the people opposite Leonardo's house had said.

"Tell him all is good," she ordered, "or this knife will go in up to the hilt and I will run."

I called back to the constable, "Very well, thank you." Then I continued in the same reassuring conversational tone, "This person is an attacker, with a knife to my back." I even added a small laugh.

Janet pulled my shoulder, and I winced at the press of the blade.

"What did you say?" she demanded.

"I told him we have been celebrating, but are now heading home."

"Very well," the constable replied with a nod, as if he had nothing further to ask, and the two of them walked on.

I gave an inward groan, as hope died. He must have believed from the lightness of my tone that I was not truly in danger. He must have thought I was a drunk being taken home by a concerned friend, and I was just making a jest.

"Keep walking." Janet said. "There is a small passageway on the left. We will head into it."

I looked over, and saw where she meant. It was a thin black space between a pair of tall buildings, scarcely wider than two men walking abreast. I had little doubt this was where she had been heading all along. It would be the ideal place to commit her murder undisturbed. She could knife me and be away down the far end of the passage long before I would be discovered. The only question was; whether she would do me the courtesy of a swift end or carry out her threat of a mortal wound only, so I must die in agony over some hours? I would most likely remain undiscovered, at least until the daylight eventually broke in the midwinter morning.

Could I try and run before we reached the dark maw of the passageway?

As I had the thought, Janet's grip on my shoulder tightened, and I winced as she pushed the knife in a little harder. The trickle of blood increased, and I could feel the material of my jerkin become sodden.

If I did not try to run, she would kill me anyway. So what did I have to lose?

I made a twist away from the blade, while dropping my shoulder from under her hand. The suddenness of the move so close to the entrance to the passage seemed to catch her by surprise.

In an instant, I was free.

Like a startled hare, I broke into a run; my stockinged feet scrabbling for purchase on the icy cobbles.

If I had been wearing shoes, I might have got away. But there was such little feeling in my frozen feet, that it seemed like I was wading through a thick bank of mud.

I had not gone more than a few paces when my arm was grasped, and I was pulled round. It felt as if my shoulder was being separated from my body and I screamed out.

"Oh no, Fox!" Janet snarled. "You do not escape me that easily." I was pushed forward into the passageway, scraping my shoulder against the side as the blackness closed around me like a cold, dark fog.

A hand in my back gave me a hard shove. My feet failed to find purchase, and with a scream I fell forward, crashing face first onto the cold stones. The breath was knocked from my body, and I was unable to move. There was the sound of her foot behind me.

"I have longed for this moment, Mary Fox!" she exclaimed. "This is for all the family you have stolen from me" There was a pause, then she added, "And for Rutger, the true love I had only just found."

I waited for the knife to plunge into my back; expecting it at any moment. I took my final breath and held it for the end.

Nothing happened.

There was the sound of feet, and an immediate gasp from Janet. I rolled over and looked up.

Silhouetted against the night sky were two men beside my attacker. One was holding her arms against her sides from behind. The other stepped round them, grabbed her wrist and shook it, so the knife fell to the ground with a metal clatter. Then he held a hand out to me and pulled me to my feet.

"It seems we were just in time," the *Birri* constable said.

31
COLD FEET OVER A PROMISE

Leonardo and Sophia were waiting for me as I stumbled into the house. Leonardo was standing with folded arms, his eyebrows raised with a look that I took to be one of hope.

"The deed, it is done?" he asked. "We are free of that degenerate?"

"I believe so," I replied. Then I recalled the sound the Duke had made as the knife was twisted in his neck, and I nodded. "Yes, it is done." No man could have survived such a wound.

I took a step and nearly fell, as my unfeeling feet struggled to take purchase on the smooth tiled floor. Sophia caught me, holding me up as my legs finally gave way.

"*Madre di Dio!*" she exclaimed, "you have no shoes! Did you walk the streets like that?"

I nodded. "Yes. I thought to run back here quickly, but I was… er… held up a while."

Sophia whispered in my ear, "I see you have dressed again as a man. We will talk of this later."

Leonardo seemed so preoccupied with the assassination that he appeared not to notice my garb. He asked, "Was it Lorenzino who gave the fatal blow?"

"It was the assassin," I began, but Sophia turned on him.

"Shush with your questions! The girl is frozen near to death!"

With a strength that surprised me, she started to walk me towards a door, with my feet dragging behind. I called over my shoulder to Leonardo, "Lorenzino was bitten by the Duke. His fingers were badly injured."

"Badly injured?" he repeated.

"I saw the bone."

Sophia clucked like a mother hen, and moved me on. "You can tell him all later," she exclaimed. "For now we must get some warmth into those feet!"

Leonardo took a step towards me, and I could see he wanted more information, but Sophia was determined, pushing me towards the door. We went through to a passageway lit with several braziers.

"Can you walk at all?" she asked.

"I think not," I muttered.

"Very well." She continued to support me as we made our slow and painful way down the passage; Sophia taking small steps to match my ungainly shuffling.

"How on earth did you manage to walk all the way back to the house?" she asked after we had managed around ten or twelve such paces.

"Because I had to," I said.

Nothing more was said, before she pushed me into the kitchens.

The great heat of the fires was a welcome change after the cold outside, and I realised it was not just my feet that were frozen, but my whole body. I began to shiver, as Sophia led me to a stool, close by one of the hearths.

Even at the late hour, there were several servants busying themselves at the long tables. One was chopping vegetables, while another was using a pestle and mortar to crush some green leaves. Others were scrubbing pots or carrying cauldrons.

Sophia harried them all out, so we were alone in the room, then used her toe to move the stool further away from the hearth.

"Not too near the fire," she said, "you need to warm up slowly." She lowered me down, and I winced as she pulled my legs out in front of me. Now, let us get your hose off, and see what we are dealing with here."

She unlaced my hose at the waist, then eased the garment down and pulled each leg off. She gave a gasp as she stared at my feet.

I looked down, and also recoiled in shock. Both feet were completely white, as if they had turned into the same marble as the statues in the Cathedral.

"*Madre di Dio!*" Sophia said again, then went over to one of the hearths and collected a large earthenware pot. She emptied a small amount of hot water into it from a pan suspended over the fire, and added more from a jug. She put her finger in, then added again. When she was satisfied, she placed the pot on the floor in front of my stool, and the pan back on the fire.

She carefully lifted each foot and lowered it into the water.

"Is that warm enough?" she asked.

"I know not," I replied. "There is no feeling at all."

She looked up, and I could see the moment when concern turned to exasperation. "Were I your mother, I would chide you for being so foolish," she exclaimed. "To run through the streets without shoes in this weather. What were you thinking?" I did not answer, so she continued, "And let us discuss your change to man's clothing." She shook her head with a frown. "Did you think to run away?"

She seemed to take my silence for assent, so she said, "Stupid girl! What must I do with you? You have warmth and safety here, yet you seek to run. You are fortunate that the master did not remark on it."

"He was more concerned by the outcome of the assassination," I replied.

Sophia poured some more water from the pan into the pot on the floor. She looked down at my feet. "Perhaps a little more colour," she observed, then added a few drops of hot water. "We will warm them in small steps."

"I have a little feeling," I said, as a slow throbbing began.

"Good." She glanced up with a concerned-looking frown. "Soon you will start to feel pain, and it will be intense," she paused, her eyes holding mine. "It is God's way of punishing you for being such a foolish girl."

Sophia was right; as she kept warming the water, the feeling came back, and with it such pain that I must hold myself from crying out in front of her. Instead I gripped her hand hard; harder than I feel I had the right to do, but she made no complaint.

As the pain ebbed and flowed like waves crashing on the sands, she held me, making soothing noises that a parent might make to calm a child. Was this what it was like to have a mother? To have a person give care and love without condition? The pain of my feet seemed almost to fade away like a dying ember, to be replaced by a greater pain in my heart. As a motherless child, I had never felt such love. Yet here was a woman I had known but a couple of weeks, treating me as her daughter. Caring for me as I suffered. Suffering with me.

"There, now," she whispered, as I cried out in my agony.

—0—

I should have known that Leonardo would not keep his promise.

As we sat at our meal the following eve, he shook his head when I raised the subject. "Nay," he said, "you sought to betray me. I cannot forgive this."

"Betray you?" I exclaimed. "I did as you asked. I went with Lorenzino and the assassin, made the Duke unconscious, and let them in to do their foul deed. How is that a betrayal?"

"You dressed as Tomasso under your gown, and would have ridden off on your horse as soon as you had crept in like a thief and taken your bag."

I made a petulant scowl. "You said I could go, so that is exactly what I was doing."

"I did not mean in that way."

I gave a derisive snort and folded my arms. This was just like arguments with my stepfather—and just as fruitless. "So what did you mean?"

"That I would decide when to release you. My decision, not yours." He took a mouthful of meat and chewed, staring at me with undisguised dislike. "It was only because you stupidly decided not to keep your shoes on, that you are still under my control."

I frowned. Once again, it was a decision I was bitterly regretting. "I thought that to try and run through the streets dressed as a man, but with inappropriate women's shoes on my feet, might cause comment." I explained, as if to a child.

"It might indeed," he replied. "But you were delayed somehow?"

I saw no point in holding back on the real reason, and welcomed the chance to change the subject. "I was attacked by the same, er... man... who shot at me with the crossbow. He walked me to a dark passageway with a knife to my back, and sought to kill me." I touched the wound in my side, that had, by God's grace, finally stopped bleeding and was starting to heal over.

"But you escaped?" Sophia asked from beside me.

"Two constables of the *Birri* came to my aid before the man could strike, and arrested him," I explained. "They let me go when they saw I was unharmed."

In truth, the constable had shown little concern for my welfare, noting only than I could stand, and was apparently able to walk. He had asked where I lived and I had named the street, but no more.

"And the man?" Sophia asked.

"They told me that he would be taken before the *Otto* and charged with the attempt on my life," I said. I did not add that Janet Crosse had screamed high-pitched obscenities at me in English as they held her, until the other constable had pulled out a length of cloth and gagged her. "I warrant your attacker is a woman masquerading as a man," he had said with a raised eyebrow, as Janet had struggled against the gag. "Which is an unnatural offense against God. That will not help her case." I had nodded, and kept my mouth shut, while Janet had given me such a look of burning anger and hate that I thanked God she had been screaming in English.

After they had marched her away, I had stood a while to catch my breath, although this was where I had lost almost all feeling in my feet. I had resisted sitting down to relieve the cold on them, lest I was unable to get up again, but had set off slowly, holding onto each wall and column as I went, until I had finally stumbled into the house.

"I will ensure your attacker is punished by the *Otto*," Leonardo observed. "Not particularly for the attack last evening, but for loosing off a crossbow at my house and causing me great expense by breaking my window."

This was welcome news, for I had no wish to worry further about Janet Crosse when I eventually set off on my mission to Pozzuoli.

"So, when can I take my leave?" I asked.

He observed me silently as he took another mouthful, chewed with agonising slowness, then swallowed. "When I said 'no' to that, I meant it," he said. "We have now disposed of the previous Caterina's body, but it suits me to have her available to me, and you have shown you can play her part extremely well."

As I stared at him in horror, Leonardo continued, "So you can remain as my wife." He took a sip of wine and observed me over his glass. "I can assure you it is in name only. I have reached an age where I no longer have interest in my conjugal rights. But I do need to have Caterina seen in public." He put the glass down. "And this is an arrangement that does not need to end any time soon."

I glanced at Sophia for support, but she seemed almost pleased, as if she welcomed the opportunity to keep me close.

Leonardo cleared his throat.

"Or ever."

32

NOT HEARING MASS

At the age of seventeen, my stepfather had promised me in matrimony to a truly vile older man. Naturally, this was not something I was prepared to accept with any form of grace. Which is why I did what no woman in my situation would have been expected to do; I ran away.

And now, three years on, it was clear that I must run away again.

For here was another older man, just as unpleasant as the one my stepfather chose, forcing me to be his wife. And even if this was not ordained in the eyes of God, it seemed Leonardo would have it validated before all of Firenze.

I learned more on this the following day, while Sophia was selecting something of Caterina's for me to wear. "You are to accompany the Master to hear Mass," she announced as she held up a green velvet gown. "At *Il Duomo*, the Cathedral of Santa Maria del Fiore." She paused a moment. "You will be seen once more as Caterina by all of the *Nobili Fiorentini*."

"But what if someone who knows Caterina talks to me?" I asked. "It was by good fortune this did not happen at the Nativity Mass. Maybe it will this time? For sure I will say or do something that Caterina would not." This had been on my mind ever since Leonardo's treacherous announcement the evening before.

"We taught you well," Sophia replied with a dismissive wave of her hand. "But if you are concerned, then change the subject to something you do know."

Unconvinced, I stepped into the gown. "There," she said as she went behind and pulled at the lacing. "You fit once again into the *Signora's* things with ease. No more wearing men's garb underneath, eh?" I made no reply, as I had no wish to give her the satisfaction of the bitter reply that hovered on my tongue. She came round to my front, and applied a little rouge to my cheeks. "The swelling is all but gone," she observed. "That is good." Then she gave me a stern-looking frown. "But your actions that night were not good. Casting away the mistress's clothes and shoes, so I must have Paolo steal in like a thief to recover them from *Signore* de Medici's house? What were you thinking?" She applied a little more rouge, then stood back, eying me critically. "But I suppose the less we say on that matter, the better. I shall let it pass."

Again I said nothing, pleased that she was at least prepared to overlook that particular transgression. But then she added with another stern look, "And I have removed those dreadful men's things you were wearing." She paused. "Finely made, I warrant, but in truth, you no longer have need of them." My heart sank. I did have need of them if I was ever to escape, for if I did, I had no wish to ride to Pozzuoli as a woman, and certainly not in all of Caterina's finery.

And what was more, time was running alarmingly short. Angelo's mother had her birthday on the twenty-eighth of the month, and that was but three weeks hence. With a two-week journey to Pozzuoli, I had very few days remaining.

I forced a small smile. "The clothes are well-made and cost me greatly. It would be a shame if they were destroyed."

"Oh, I would not do such a thing. But they are kept safe, I can assure you." Her hand went slightly towards her waist, and I noticed a key that hung on a ribbon. I wondered if she had meant for me to see that, or if she was even aware of what she had done. "I might have them sold—they will fetch good money."

"My money," I observed with small bitterness in my voice.

"But you will benefit," she said with a smile, her head on one side. "I have such plans now I am fully returned to my rightful position as your maid. I will secure you the finest gowns and jewels, so you will truly be the grandest lady in all Firenze." Then a frown clouded her face. "Unlike that ungrateful shrew who came before you." The smile returned, as if it had never gone. "There," Sophia stood back and surveyed her work. "We will make the master so proud, will we not?"

She led me down the stairs, to where Leonardo was waiting, together with the ever-present Paolo. Looking at this old grey man dressed in his customary dull black doublet and hose, I could see no reason why I should wish to make him proud.

"Come, Caterina," Leonardo said. "Let us attend Mass."

He said little as we walked to the Cathedral, followed close behind by the silent figure of Paolo. Leonardo's conversation covered only such things as the weather, and a disinterested-sounding enquiry as to how I had slept. Perhaps in his mind, it was as if I was truly Caterina, and she had never been killed.

Under this perverse reality, we made our way through the streets. At one point I stumbled slightly on a raised cobblestone, and felt Paolo's large hand seize my arm. To anyone overseeing this, it would have seemed like a concerned servant having a care for his mistress. But I caught Paolo's eye as I steadied myself, and knew without doubt that he was making sure I had not been trying to escape.

We arrived at the western entrance of the Cathedral, and Leonardo instructed Paolo to remain outside amongst the crowds while we attended Mass. Leonardo led me through the main door and into the magnificence of the high-arched nave.

We had scarcely entered, when we were surrounded by a throng of white-faced men, all clamouring for Leonardo's attention. He caught my eye briefly, and mouthed *'wait,'* so I stood aside while he discussed what I assumed was the burning topic; the assassination. There seemed to be much nodding, leaning in and imparting of what I assumed was salacious tattle, as each man sought information or gave his view.

How little they know, I thought, flinching at the memory of Scoronconcolo's knife twisting in the Duke's neck. But I kept this thought to myself as Leonardo attempted to manage all the different conversations at once.

But then I realised—his attention was not on me…

Was this my chance?

I looked back at the entrance. There were the three doors, and we had come in by the largest one in the centre. If I slipped out of the furthest one, could I avoid Paolo seeing me in the crowds?

It was a chance I must take.

I took a breath, and started towards the door. If I could just get outside, away from Leonardo, I could find a way to reach Pozzuoli and return *il Fiume di Fuoco*...

But then I stopped with a groan. The jewel was not on my person; it was still hidden in my chamber. I could hardly go back into the house to retrieve it...

With a muttered curse against my lack of forethought, I turned back to Leonardo and the crowd around him. Just after I resumed my position, he broke away and came over.

"Now Caterina," he said, offering me his arm, "let us take our seats. I have learned some interesting information on the aftermath of the assassination." He led me up the nave, still inwardly bemoaning my missed opportunity.

The nave was filled with the glorious coloured patterns of light cast by the arched stained-glass windows. Leonardo stopped at two chairs on their own near to the high altar, directly under the massive dome that rose majestically above us. Even in my dark mood, I could not help but look up and gaze in wonder at its magnificence. Leonardo hissed, "Do not stare as if you have never before seen this."

"It was dark when we came for the Nativity," I replied. "It seems even better in the daylight."

"As may be," he whispered with an angry frown. "But Caterina has seen it in the daylight many times. Lower your head woman, lest someone remarks on it."

I dropped into my seat and folded my arms. How could this man treat me like a child being admonished by her father?

A bell rang, and I had to stand again, as the smell of incense heralded the Procession coming up the nave. But I had little care to follow the service. After a short prayer to Our Blessed Lady to forgive my inattention, my thoughts were all on how I might get away. As the service progressed, I must have given the required Latin responses by force of habit, but my mind was not with the mystery of the Mass.

It was coming up with escape ideas. And rejecting each one as being unworkable.

By the time the service was ending, I confess I was beginning to despair. How could I remain in Firenze, if I would miss Angelo's mother's birthday?

Just as I was losing all hope, a new idea suddenly came to me.

I considered it carefully. This one might just work...

But it would need to be put into action soon; there was little time to lose.

With excitement growing, I waited for the final prayer, so I could get home and see if I could make it work.

—0—

"The news of Duke Alessandro's death was on everyone's lips," Leonardo said later, as we were being served our evening meal. He waited until all the servants were dismissed, leaving only the two of us and Paolo, who now ate at a little table by the door.

Nothing had been said of this, but I was certain he was there for one reason only; to stop me if I tried to run.

"Such shock and disbelief," Leonardo continued with apparent satisfaction. "The body was only discovered when his guards, who had been left outside while he went in for his assignation with you, became suspicious."

He continued recounting the tale as we ate. It seemed that the guards had tried to gain entry, but Lorenzino and Scoronconcolo had locked the house when they left. It was the following morning before the body was finally discovered, wrapped in a blanket. Lorenzino had pinned a note to it, with some message about glory and conquest. "He wanted to be seen as the liberator of Firenze, and the natural successor to his younger cousin," Leonardo explained.

On the night of the murder, Lorenzino and Scoronconcolo had ridden away, with Lorenzino seen nursing his wounded hand as they galloped through the streets. "They are said to have made for Venezia, and are awaiting the call back to Firenze." Leonardo added. "As the eldest Medici, Lorenzino fully expects to be invited to become the new duke. Perhaps he will, although I have heard mutterings that it is Cosimo who is better favoured."

I let out a sigh of relief to learn that Scoronconcolo was safely away in Venezia, for I had no wish to meet him again. Unless, of course, I could have my revenge for Angelo's murder.

Later that night, as I lay in bed, I consoled myself with the thought that I might one day find Scoronconcolo, and exact justice in my love's name. I even imagined some scenarios where I came upon the killer, challenged him to a duel and dispatched him to meet Satan in Hell. Or maybe it would be from behind, so I could plunge a knife in his back, just as I might have done the night he murdered the Duke. I have never wanted to kill any person; but as God was my witness, I wanted to be the one to end that man's life.

I will avenge you one day, my love, I told Angelo. *I swear it.*

If that can be, then do it, he replied. *Just so long as you save my mother first.*

I do have a plan, I said, and explained it to him.

That could work, he said. *But have a care, Maria. It carries great risks. My mother's life depends on you, and on you alone.*

Over the next five days, I went through each step necessary to put my plan into action. *Will it work?* Angelo asked, as I lay down to sleep on the fifth night.

I do hope so, I replied. *I have tried to think of all that might happen.*

You cannot do more, mio amore.

And if I fail? If I cannot return the necklace in time?

You will. I know it. Then he made a small chuckle. *Or you will have to accept being Caterina for the rest of your days.*

<h1 style="text-align:center">33</h1>

A BID FOR FREEDOM

The following morning Sophia came into my chamber. She was alone, as she had been these past few days; no Paolo to stand guard at the door with his arms folded.

I had already been awake for some time when the sound of the door being unlocked alerted me. I eased the bed hangings open slightly, and quickly glanced out to check that Sophia was alone. She had the key in hand—presumably to lock the door again from the inside, given Paolo's absence.

I fell back onto the bed and let out a loud groan.

As I hoped, she came straight over, without locking the door. I was covered to my neck in the blanket, and turned my head as her face peered in. I gave her a look of the deepest pain.

"What ails?" she asked, with a frown of concern.

"I have such a gripe in my belly," I moaned.

Her frown deepened. "Paolo has had the same these past few days," she said. "And now you are suffering."

I groaned again. "Belike it was something we ate?" I whispered, before adding another long, low sound of anguish.

"Belike," she agreed. "But the Master and I are both quite well."

Sophia put her hand—the one not holding the key—to the top of my blanket.

I tensed myself, ready to make my move.

"Is your belly sore?" she asked. "Let me see." She pulled the blanket down, then recoiled with a shocked gasp, her eyes widening at the sight of my fully clothed body. I was wearing my man's cloak, jerkin, hose and riding boots. I knew not whether her shock was seeing me clothed in bed, or that I had retrieved the man's garb she had previously removed from my chamber.

Before she could make any further reaction, I snatched the key from her grasp, then swung past her out of the bed. I spun round and pushed her so hard that she fell through the hangings and collapsed onto the mattress with a shriek. Running to the door, I grabbed the saddle bag that I had previously placed there, ready for my escape. It contained my few meagre possessions, but most importantly, *il Fiume di Fuoco* and my purse.

As I locked the door behind me, there was another yell from Sophia, followed by the thud of footsteps and the sound of banging on the panels. I ignored her. There was no time for any last words with the woman, however much she might have cared for me. In truth, she was as much my captor as Leonardo.

Praying I would not meet anyone, least of all him, I hurried along the passage towards the main stair. My aim was to get to the side door; the one leading directly out to the stable yard.

Then Hestia and freedom!

I ran down the stair, trying as best I could to tread silently. But then I decided speed was more important than being cautious, so I leapt down the last few steps. Collecting myself on landing, I ignored the front door ahead. The one I wanted was to the left.

I scrabbled round and ran towards it. By God's good grace, I had not seen a soul since leaving my chamber, and I began to believe that my plans had worked. I was going to escape, just in time to ride to Pozzuoli.

But that grace was about to run out.

As I reached the door, there was a shout from behind.

I looked back, and gave a scream of frustration. It was Leonardo. He was running across the hallway, his long beard swaying as he came towards me, his face as red as a demon from the depths of hell.

"Getting away? *Da Dio!*" he shouted.

Desperately I scrabbled at the door handle, but it would not open. I punched at the empty keyhole in my anger. Why was it locked and the key not there? With another yell I pushed myself away, and made for the front door instead. I must get out of this house by any means.

Leonardo saw what I was doing, and changed course to cut me off. We met just before the door, and he grabbed my arm.

"Oh no, you little shit!" he yelled, using my own momentum to swing me round. "You do not get away that easily!"

"Let me go," I shouted back. "You cannot keep me here!"

He tightened his grip, causing me real pain. "Fine," he snapped. "Then I will send you to Satan's arms instead."

"Let me go!" I repeated. "You are hurting me!"

"I will do more than that," he replied.

Just then there was another shout from the top of the stair. It was Sophia. Somehow she must have escaped. She appeared above us, her face white. "Oh mistress!" she gasped. "You tricked me! After all I had done for you!"

For a moment Leonardo was distracted. As he looked up, I turned towards him and put my free hand on his shoulder. Then I raised my knee with all my strength, and drove it hard into his groin. With nothing but his thin hose to protect him, his manhood must have been crushed by the force of my blow.

"That was for the true Caterina," I whispered, as he doubled up. A thin scream escaped him, like steam from a kettle. I leaned in and added, "and for me, too."

With a shriek Sophia started down the stair. I left Leonardo to fall to the ground and ran to the main door. God's grace was on my part this time, as the key was on the inside. I unlocked it, slipped out, and locked it again from the other side.

I needed to go through the streets to get around the house to the stables, but by now I was beyond care. I ran, swift as a falcon in flight, pushing past and sidestepping the worthy Fiorentinos in my path. I prayed no *Birri* constables would happen to be passing.

Thankfully I made it to the stables without being stopped.

Hestia looked up from her manger as I ran in. She gave me a welcoming whinny.

"Hello old girl," I gasped, as I pulled her saddle from the post, threw it across her back. I attached my bag, then tightened the girth. I grabbed her bridle, but did not put it on her—no time for that. It could wait until we were clear of the city walls. I untied her, then leapt up onto her back and took hold of her mane. With a squeeze of my heels, we left the stable and clattered into the courtyard.

As Hestia's hooves scrabbled for purchase on the stones, the side door—that I had so desperately wanted to reach—opened.

Leonardo hobbled out, followed by Sophia. His face was no longer red, but was now even whiter than hers.

They started towards me, but they were no match for Hestia's speed.

"Come on," I urged, pulling her round and heading for the archway that led onto the street.

I crouched low, driving her forward as we increased speed. We quickly reached the open gates and burst through like an arrow shot from a bow onto the street beyond.

I allowed myself a quick glance back. Leonardo and Sophia were standing in the courtyard, shaking their fists and yelling. That was the last I saw of them, before Hestia rounded the corner and we made for the city gate—and the road to Pozzuoli.

34

PLANNED STEPS

Hestia seemed as keen as I was to run free. As we cleared the city gate and emerged into the glorious open country, still wearing its blanket of winter snow, she lifted her head and tossed her mane; her breath sending clouds of steam into the clear cold air. After being given only exercise walks in the three weeks since we had arrived in Firenze, she must have been desperate to have a run.

Once we were far enough from the gate, I pulled her to a stop and put on her bridle. As I re-mounted, patting the saddlebag with the necklace safely inside, I gave a small prayer of thanks that my plan—in all its elements—had worked.

It was the laburnum tree in the courtyard that had given me the initial idea. Its bark can cause a serious pain in the belly. I wondered, as I sat in the Cathedral not hearing Mass, could this be a way to get rid of my silent guardsman Paolo? For no plan to escape could possibly succeed while he was around. He had been my constant shadow, following me everywhere from the moment my chamber was first unlocked, to the final turn of the key at night. Every morning he had come in with Sophia, then would stand by the door with his arms folded and a knowing look on his large face. It was as if he knew I would try to escape, and was keenly anticipating just how strongly he would stop me.

On returning from the Mass that day, I had suggested to Leonardo that I might take the air in the courtyard, and he agreed—although as ever, Paolo kept watch. But once there, it was easy to stop by the laburnum arch and take some bark scrapings with my knife while out of his immediate sight. Once back in my chamber, I chopped them down to the finest powder. Then at supper that evening, I managed to pass by Paolo's little table. While

255

he was serving wine to Leonardo, I managed to spread some of my powder onto his food. By good fortune he must have eaten enough to make himself unwell, and had taken to his bed the following day.

—0—

Without Paolo standing guard, I was able to execute the next step in my plan; to retrieve my man's garb.

I assumed that Sophia had hidden it in a clothes chest; that seemed most likely. But where? She could have used any room in the house. But I did know of one storeroom; the locked one that contained three chests, and had, until recently, contained the body of the true Caterina. Would she have known that I was aware of this room? That I could even retrace my steps and find it again? I thought not, for I had been taken to her only after being released from that captivity. And if she thought I had no knowledge of the room, then it was all the more likely she had chosen it as the hiding place.

Then there was her hand going to the key at her waist when she mentioned keeping the clothes secure. That was a clue I could not ignore; it was almost certainly the key to the room.

But how to get the key from her? And how to get to the storeroom and back without her knowledge?

My best chance, I decided, was when we would have a few hours in the parlour each afternoon doing embroidery. Unlike Paolo, who I suspected never slept at all, Sophia would oft drift off, putting aside her tambour frame and needle, then closing her eyes. Sometimes this was for half an hour at a time.

An opportunity I must take.

It was the afternoon of two days before. Sophia and I were in the parlour as usual. As we stitched, I watched her as a hawk watches a mouse. Would this be the one time she stayed awake? It seemed so; as her eyes stayed resolutely open, while her hand made deft movements with the needle. I kept silent, lest any chatter might keep her engaged.

Time went on, and still she sewed. Just as I was beginning to lose hope, she gave a sigh and a yawn, then laid her frame on the nearby table. Another yawn, then her eyelids started to drop.

I waited a little longer, then crept to her side. The end of the key was nestled in the folds of her skirts. With frequent glances up to check her eyes and breathing, I eased it into view, with moves that were as slow and gentle as I could manage. Eventually, I could see the whole key—and the knot that secured it. Holding my breath to still my nerve, I picked at the knot. By good fortune the ribbon moved easily, and with a few soft pulls, it came undone.

As I slid the key down her skirt, she moved her leg with a small grunt, making the key push into her. I froze in fear. She grunted again, and moved her leg back. Her eyelids fluttered. This looked like an awakening, so I prepared to jump up and resume my sewing.

But again my fortune seemed good. She did not awaken, and after a moment, she gave another grunt, then settled into her chair. I then lifted the key away.

Now I had little time to waste. I slipped out of the door, and ran to the storeroom, thankfully now without Paolo following. With my heart in my mouth, I tried the key in the lock. It turned. With a small cry of triumph, I let myself in.

The three chests were still in place. The first two I tried had the same old gowns as before—but in the third I struck lucky. My clothes were all on top. Grinning to myself, I gathered them up, and ran back to the parlour.

By God's grace, Sophia was still asleep; her head dropped to one side, her mouth open and a small line of drool on her cheek. I tied the key back, then pushed my clothes deep under the wardrobe, where they nestled against my saddlebag containing *il Fiume di Fuoco*.

By the time Sophia woke, I was again bent over my needlework.

—0—

The final piece of the plan was to ensure Hestia was fed, watered and ready to ride out, with her saddle and bridle close at hand.

Early in my captivity, I had insisted to Leonardo that I must see her each day, and at the very least walk her round the stable yard. He had agreed—reluctantly—but only if I were accompanied by Paolo at all times. This had been arranged, with Paolo always ensuring that the yard gates were closed before allowing me to come out.

Since the Mass I had been down each day, until Paolo was taken ill, and my visits were stopped. But in that time I had laid my plan—which involved the young stable lad who tended to Hestia. He was little more than sixteen years, and perfect for my needs.

On the first day, he had been cleaning Hestia's bridle as I came in. "I am pleased you are taking good care of my horse," I said, keeping my voice low, lest Paulo overhear.

"She is a fine animal, *Signora*."

"Her name is Hestia," I said, bestowing on him my most radiant smile, and his face seemed to glow with a sudden redness.

"Hestia?" he repeated, and she gave a small snort and pawed a hoof at the sound of her name.

"My husband, I trust he pays you well?" I asked.

He looked down. "I am apprenticed, *Signora* de Ginori." He raised his head. "I do not get paid."

I gave him a surprised glance, although in truth I was aware of this system. "But you look so well to her care," I exclaimed, running my hand over Hestia's coat. "I must give you a *mancia* as a thank you." I reached into my purse and withdrew five silver *soldi* coins. "There," I said as I handed them over, "keep giving her your care, and make sure she is kept well fed and watered."

He nodded, and slipped the coins in his jerkin pocket. "I will, *Signora* de Ginori," he said.

"And keep her saddle and bridle in readiness, lest I want to ride her out." I was trusting he would accept this as an order from his lady, and not question why I had never ridden out before. Again he nodded. "That I will, *Signora* de Ginori."

I turned to go, then stopped and looked back with my most heart-warming smile. "Oh, and one more thing," I said. "I would not want to bother you or any of the stable hands if I do decide to ride out. Why not ensure the gates are kept open for me each morning?"

—0—

The lad had been as good as his word—Hestia had been ready and he had left the gates open.

Here we were, together on the road to Pozzuoli.

I encouraged her up to a steady canter; necessary to ensure we could keep ahead of any possible pursuit, and took the road south.

For the next few hours we cantered through the green autumn fields south of Firenze. We went past small villages of white houses with orange tiled roofs; through valleys with vineyards on the south facing slopes; their vines standing in the brown earth in regimented rows.

As darkness fell, we found a small inn. After rubbing Hestia down and giving her food and water, I greatly enjoyed my first night free of Caterina. I slept soundly on the little cot and awoke at dawn, pleased not to have the sight of Paolo and his arms crossed, standing guard.

After breaking fast, we set off again to Pozzuoli.

And on the morning of January 28th, we arrived.

35
SHARED GRIEF

I found Angelo's mother.

After securing a room at an inn and a stable for Hestia, I made enquiries of passers-by in the centre of the town. I was directed to a modest white-walled house in a street off the church square. As I walked to the door, I must admit my heart was in my mouth. It had taken me until the very day of her fiftieth birthday to get to her; more than four months since I had first met Angelo in Bishop's Lynn. More than four months since he had told me of the legend of the River of Fire.

How would this woman respond to the news of her son?

How would she feel as I gave her the necklace?

I patted my bag with the precious jewel inside, then lifted the knocker and brought it down twice on the simple red door. The wait thereafter did little to calm my nerve.

Eventually, I heard a step beyond, and the door swung open. An elderly white-haired man in a black jerkin looked down his nose at me.

"Yes?" he said.

"Is this the di Luca house?" I asked.

"Yes," he repeated. Clearly a man of few words.

"I wish to see *Signora* di Luca," I said.

"She is indisposed," he replied, as if that were the most he could manage. Then he added with seeming reluctance, "*Signora* di Luca is not receiving visitors." He started to close the door, but I got a hand to it just before it was fully shut.

"I have not come this far to be turned away," I snapped, my patience suddenly wearing thin. "Particularly on her fiftieth birthday."

There was a pause, then the door swung open again.

"Who shall I say is calling?" he asked, one bushy white eyebrow raised.

"A friend of Angelo," I replied.

"Wait here," he said, and closed the door in my face.

I waited for perhaps five minutes, and was about to knock again, when there was another step, and the door swung open.

The woman who stood there was perhaps the most elegant, beautiful person I had ever seen. Despite her age and a demeanour of deep sadness, she was more comely than any other such woman I had known; and I had known Lady Kyme, mother of Henry Fitzroy. For all she had a face marked by her years, each line added to her beauty rather than taking from it. Her lips were full, with no need for rouge, and her hazel eyes had such a look of warmth and kindness that I knew at once she was a person driven by love. And there as something else in her eyes—something I recognised...

I gave a small gasp, for there was no doubting it; I was looking into the eyes of Angelo.

My mama, he whispered in my ear. *Love her just as you loved me.*

I have a feeling I will, I replied. *But she has such a sadness about her; my heart aches.*

It is her birthday, and she does not have the necklace.

But I will give it to her.

But she also worries for me, her son. Have a care how you tell her of my death.

She moved towards me, putting one slippered foot on the door step, and I could see her even better as she came fully into the daylight. She was wearing a russet gown, trimmed with white lace at the sleeves and bodice, and a squared neckline that revealed the pale skin of her chest. The only jewels she wore were a pair of small silver earrings, and a silver chain across the grey hair she had pinned up.

"Who are you," she whispered, "that knows what day it is today?" She paused, looking me up and down. "And do you have news of my son, Angelo?"

"I do," I said, then reached into my bag. Her eyes widened when she saw the leather pouch I brought out. "But first, I believe this day you need to be wearing a particular jewel." I opened the pouch and lifted out *Il Fiume di Fuoco*. Her eyes grew even wider and she gave a small gasp. Her hand went to her mouth as she stared at the necklace. Its rubies shone beams of rich red light over her gown and her face, and the silver setting sparkled in the autumn sun.

"Where did you get..?" she began, but stopped as I slipped past her into the passageway, then reached round to put the necklace in place. She stood still as I did up the fastening, and when I came back to the step, she put her hand on the jewel at her neck. It was as if she could not believe it was truly there.

"Let me see it," I said.

Slowly she moved her hand away. The rubies sat against her pale skin, making her eyes seem a richer brown and her lips a deeper red. Even her grey hair seemed to take on some of their lustre. It looked as if the necklace could not exist anywhere else but on this elegant neck; as if any other person wearing it would seem an impostor.

"Truly lovely," was all I could think to say.

Then suddenly she gave a great sob; a cry that seemed to come from deep within her body as her eyes held mine. Two great tears appeared and began to roll down her cheeks.

Before I could react, I was pulled into her embrace, crushed by her arms around me. She rocked me back and forward; her tears on my cheek. "Thank you, thank you, thank you," she said in my ear, "whoever you are, I have no better words to thank you for bringing this to me."

Eventually she released me, and dried her tears with a small lace kerchief. "You had better come in, young man," she said with a sniff. "You have much to tell me of yourself and I would hear news of my son." She paused, "I have my life once more."

She touched the necklace again. "You have brought that back to me."

—0—

Signora di Luca sat me down in her parlour, making sure I was comfortably settled by the fire with a glass of wine in hand, before she leaned forward.

"Let us start with your name," she said, fixing me with an enquiring stare as she traced her fingers across the rubies at her neck. It was as if she was reacquainting herself with an old friend.

For a moment I wondered if I should maintain my disguise as a man, but one look at Angelo's eyes in her elegant face, and I knew that would not be appropriate. With this woman, I must swear to be honest. I must be myself.

"I travel by the name of Thomas Richardson," I replied in English. "But in truth my name is Mary Fox."

"I see," she replied in the same tongue. "I suspected as much." She regarded me a moment, then nodded. "Why Richardson?"

"My father was Sir Richard Fox.".

"You loved your father, such that you adopt his name." It was a statement, not a question.

I shook my head. "I never knew him; he died before I was born. I was raised by Sir Andrew, my stepfather, who hated me." She raised an eyebrow, so I continued. "He blamed me for the death of my mother in childbirth."

"Then you had a stepmother?"

I shook my head. "Nay. He never remarried." Instead there had been a procession of hard, uncaring women in and out of his life, none of whom had stayed long enough to become a stepmother. Sir Andrew once told me that none could replace my mother, who had been his one true love. Although I had never believed him capable of such a feeling.

"I see," she repeated, then gave me a long, silent stare. It was as if she was making up her mind to say something. "My son,

264

Angelo," she began, then stopped and swallowed hard. "My son…
is not with you, yet you have the River of Fire. He would never
have let it go, so I must therefore assume he is dead?" She spoke
in such an even, measured tone, that I had to bite my own lip to
stop myself from breaking into sobs on her part.

I must be strong.

I reached across and laid my hand over hers. "I am so, so
sorry," I whispered.

She nodded, with a calmness that spoke of great strength.
"How?"

I took a deep breath. "A man named Scoronconcolo was
travelling with us, and caught sight of the necklace. He must have
realised its true value, and killed Angelo for it." For a moment I
was back once again at that table. I forced myself away from the
image. "Scoronconcolo is a killer," I said. "It is what he does."

She leaned back and I let go my hand from hers. Her own went
to the rubies once more, and she swallowed hard. "But you got it
back?"

"I followed Scoronconcolo to Firenze, and was able to steal it
away from him." I paused a moment, considering if I should
explain more of the circumstances of the theft. I decided the less
said of that, the better. "I vowed to Angelo I would return it to you
by this day." And how close it had been – to the day.

She frowned. "But you say this man is a killer. How were you
able to take it from him?" She gave me a weak smile. "For all I am
forever in your debt that you did."

"I took a chance, when he was, er… otherwise engaged," I
said.

She nodded, and seemed to decide against asking further on
this. There was another long silence. "My son went all the way to
England to find it," she said eventually. "And he found you there
as well?"

"Yes. Once we retrieved it, we travelled together, down
through the Netherlands, Germany, Switzerland and
on to Milano."

And what adventures we had, Angelo observed in my ear. *A fight in the graveyard. A near marriage in Den Haag. A crossbow attack in the Switzer's alps. A forest fight with brigands. And of course, you becoming as drunk as a lord...*

Stories for another time, I admonished him. *Not now.*

As you wish, mio amore, he conceded.

"You went with him," his mother said, breaking into my thoughts. "Over, what—many months?" She paused, and leaned forward again. "Were you in love with my son?" she asked.

The question hung in the air, like a hawk hovering in flight.

You swore to be honest with my mama, Angelo whispered. *Tell her!*

"Yes," I said simply. "I loved him. I would have given my life to him and become his wife if he had asked."

My wife?

Yes.

Really? You mean that?

I do.

Angelo's mother sat back and gave me the best smile I had seen from her since we had first met. "Then you would have become my daughter," she said. "And I would have welcomed you to my family and loved you as much as my son clearly loved you, Mary Fox." She paused. "I would have become the mother you never had."

I had no words for this. If I had had a mother, I would have wanted her to be as much like this woman as possible.

Signora di Luca stood up and held her hand out to me. "And even though Angelo is no longer here," she said slowly, her eyes on mine, "I see no reason for this not to happen. I have lost a son, but in his place I would like to think I have gained a loving daughter?"

My breath stopped, and I thought for a moment I would faint.

Finally, after twenty years, did I have the mother I had so long sought?

By way of answer, I took her hand. She pulled me up towards her, and once again I was in her embrace. She held me tight, as if the bond between us was spun from the very threads of Heaven.

After a moment, I moved my head back and looked into her eyes. But it was Angelo's I saw.

This was the thing that broke my resolve, and I could no longer hold back my tears.

I had lost him.

A deep sob racked through my body, as if it would tear me in two.

This was answered by one from her, and within a second we were both clutching each other and weeping together; for the loss of a son, and the loss of a lover.

I cannot recall how long this lasted—whether it was a minute, an hour or a day. It mattered not. We stood together, arms tight around each other, until eventually we had both run dry of tears.

Mother and daughter.

I have nothing more to say, Angelo whispered. *I can leave you now in peace.*

A sound like leaves rustling in the breeze.

Angelo?

Angelo?

Nothing.

"He is gone," I whispered.

"I know," his mother said. "We will grieve for him together."

36
THE WRATH OF GOD

And that is where my story should have ended. Mary Fox and *Signora* di Luca—she said I must call her Mathilda—living in Pozzuoli as mother and daughter, growing together in a spirit of warmth, love and understanding.

But God had something different in mind.

It was late morning the following day. We were seated in the parlour in two armchairs by the fire. I had not long come back from the tavern where I had slept and Hestia was stabled. Mathilda had given me some flatbread and wine, and had just observed that I must come to live with her. I had agreed it would be lovely. Once we had discussed the arrangements, she sat back and observed me over her glass.

"You dress as a man," she said. "Is this how you wish to live?"

"It is how I have been for many years," I replied. "And Angelo said he was content."

"We always raised him to be tolerant of others. He was never one to judge."

I took a breath, and said something I had been thinking on more and more since my experience in Firenze. "Perhaps now I should begin to dress and behave more as befits my sex. I have usually travelled as a man, because it means I can pass unhindered. It gives me freedoms that a woman does not have."

"I understand," she said. "But do you still desire those?"

"Maybe not." I gave a small shrug. "Maybe what I want now is different."

"Then that is your choice." She smiled with a warmth that made her face glow in the candlelight. "And if you decide that is what you want, then I would love to clothe you in the finest gowns

I can afford." She paused, then added. "I have a seamstress that you must meet. It would give me great pleasure to help you find the true woman you are. My son must have seen your beauty; I would like to see it as well."

I smiled, seeing for a moment Angelo's reaction when I joined him at the table in Breda, dressed for the first time as a woman. "*Santa Maria Madre di Dio!*" he had said as he looked me up and down, "I could not have believed it possible!"

"Then yes, I would like…" I began, but my reply was cut short.

The whole house suddenly began to shake.

I faltered to a stop, unsure if such movement could possibly be real.

But it was. It was as if a giant's hand had picked the house up and was agitating it like a child's plaything. The wine in my glass slopped out onto the tiled floor, while ornaments and jars standing on shelves in a wooden case rocked and swayed. Mathilda and I watched in horror as some slid towards the edge, then came crashing down; smashing to pieces and scattering their contents across the floor.

A pair of candlesticks on the table beside me started sliding as well, the flames flaring as they moved towards their fall. I leaned across and caught one as it came down, but the other went past my hand and I gasped as it toppled over. By good fortune, the flame was put out as it hit the floor.

Then my chair started moving, as if the giant had decided that shaking the house was not enough, and was now pushing me across the tiles towards the fire. There was a shout from Mathilda; her chair was also moving. We both leapt to our feet before we were taken any nearer the flames. Her hand reached for mine, and we stood together in the centre of the room, swaying against the movement like sailors caught in a storm.

I became aware of the noise; a low rumbling sound like thunder, punctuated by screams from the street outside, while dogs barked and horses neighed.

"We must get out!" I shouted.

The door swung open, then slammed shut again, with the force to crush a man like a beetle. Mathilda shook her head. "Nay! We are safer inside!"

There was a snapping sound and a thin black crack appeared in the wall beside the fire. It started at the floor, then scurried upwards, breaking into a few smaller branches as it went. It was as if a sapling had become a tree in a matter of seconds.

The remaining pots teetered, then crashed to the floor, leaving the shelves empty, while an acrid smell of spices mingled with oils came from the carnage at our feet.

Mathilda's face was white in the light of my candle, as the house continued to shake for what seemed like hours. In truth, the whole thing took perhaps no more than two minutes.

Just as I thought we must take our chance and try to get outside, the shaking and the rumbling stopped, as suddenly as it had started.

Now the continuing screams and sounds of animals in the street were all we could hear.

Mathilda let go of my hand, and I realised how tightly she had been clutching it. As I put the candle down and rubbed some feeling back, her gaze swept across all the damage. "That was the most terrible one yet," she whispered.

I stilled my hands. "There have been others like this?" I asked. "How was there no such damage before?" The house had been too neat and well-ordered.

"One or two each day for perhaps a week now," she said. "But each just a brief and mild tremor. Nothing like that." She went over to the crack in the wall and ran a finger along it. "Pozzuoli sits on the *Campi Flegrei*, an area that often shakes, as if God must remind us of his presence. We are well used to such events, and think little of them." She turned back. "But nothing as bad as this has ever occurred. And if it continues, then belike they will get more often and even more destructive. How have we angered God so much that he must punish us so?"

I picked up the other candlestick, restored it to the table and lit it. "His anger has left us much to clean and tidy," I observed. "The sooner we begin, the better."

Glad of the opportunity to be helpful, I dropped to my knees and began gathering the pieces of pottery, which I put in a pile in the corner. I then found a broom and swept up the smaller shards, and as much of the spilled liquids as I could. Mathilda restored the furniture to its place, including the fallen chairs that had stood around the table. She produced a rough cloth to help with the liquids. After we had done as much as we could, we sank into our chairs.

"I would we have some wine," Mathilda said, holding a cracked, empty jug.

I showed her my broken cup. "If we had something to drink it from." For some reason this made us both laugh.

The door opened, and the old man who had first let me in the day before, appeared. I had learned he was Giuseppe, Mathilda's only servant. He clutched at the door frame for support, and stared at us with an ashen face that was whiter than his beard.

"There is much damage in the town, *Signora*," he said. "The street is full of broken roof tiles, and some folks have been injured by their falling."

Both our smiles were gone in an instant. Mathilda had been right to stay inside.

"Who is hurt?" she asked.

Giuseppe gave her a few names, and Mathilda nodded. "Go out and tell them to come to me in here," she said. "We can bind any wounds if needed." She got up and went to an ornate chest of drawers standing in the corner. It was made of a rich dark wood, with finely carved edges and handles in the shape of men's heads. She opened one of the drawers and rummaged inside. "I have some linen strips in here," she said. "When Angelo was a boy, he was oft giving himself scrapes and scratches. I still have the bandages I kept ready somewhere…" She closed the drawer and tried another one. "Of course, it has been many years since I last needed them…" She opened a third drawer and gave a triumphant smile. "Here they are!" She produced several rolls of yellowed cloth. "They may be old, but will still serve our cause."

There was a knock on the front door as she sat down; an insistent rapping.

"You must answer that," Mathilda said. "It may be someone who needs our help."

Giuseppe nodded and shuffled out. We sat in silence until he reappeared, closing the door behind him. "It is a young man," he announced. Then he frowned. "But he does not ask for you, *Signora,* and he is not wounded." His watery old eyes turned on me. "The man is asking for you, *Signorina.* He named you particularly. Mary Fox."

For a moment I could not think who this might be. A young man who knew of my whereabouts? Leonardo? But he was an old man. Scoronconcolo? But he had fled to Venezia. And neither knew my true name. Then I felt as if a cold wave had washed over me.

I knew who it must be.

"Do not let him in, Giuseppe..." I began, but it was too late.

The door was kicked open. A primed crossbow appeared.

Followed by Janet Crosse.

37
THE HEART OR THE SHOULDER?

Janet waved the crossbow, using it as if she was pointing with a finger.

"You," she snapped at Mathilda in English. "Stay where you are." She turned it on me. "You too, Mary Fox."

We stayed in our chairs.

She turned the bow on Giuseppe. "And you, sit as well." She indicated one of the chairs by the table.

"He has no English," I said, then told Giuseppe to sit as instructed, using Neapolitan. Mathilda said, "Who are you, and what do you want with us?" She gave a weak smile. "We mean you no harm, young fellow. Why not leave us in peace?"

"Leave you in peace?" Janet replied, the corner of her mouth turning up in a sneer. "Do you know what an evil serpent you have taken in? I cannot leave while this foul woman still draws breath."

Mathilda's mouth dropped open, and she looked across at me. "You would kill Mary?" she whispered, turning back to Janet.

"She accuses me of many crimes," I said, wanting to get my side of the story in first. "But I have an answer for each and every one."

"And will give such answers to Satan, ere long," Janet declared.

But Mathilda was not listening. "She?" she asked me. "Is this not a man?"

"Nay," I replied. "This is a woman by the name of Janet Crosse."

"I would warrant her dress is most unnatural," Mathilda said. She waved a hand at me, "were I not looking at my own dear Mary Fox in similar garb."

Janet's eyes narrowed, and I winced inside. I had no wish for

Janet to know that Mathilda and I were close, for it placed Angelo's mother in the gravest danger. Janet's grievance was for all the family members whose deaths she laid at my door, as well as that man Rutger in Switzerland.

Bringing harm to someone I cared for would serve her vengeance well.

"I have been here but a day," I said with care. "These people have been so kind as to take me in. That is all."

"Something they may come to regret," Janet replied with a scowl.

"They want nothing more than to care for people hurt in the violent shaking of God's wrath just now," I said. "Would you come between them and their compassion?"

"I would indeed," she replied. "The fate of such people is none of my concern."

Mathilda held up the linen strips, and again I winced at her unthinking good nature. "We would do naught but bind the wounds of those in need."

Janet was silent a moment, then seemed to come to a decision. "You," she said, swinging the bow at Giuseppe. "Use those linen strips to bind their wrists to their chairs." She pointed it at me. "Tell him, since you seem to have the ability to talk in their tongue."

I translated this for Giuseppe, and he came over and did as I asked. Once our wrists were secured to the arms of the chairs, he shuffled back to his own, and sat. Seeming confident in our incapacity, Janet put her bow down and came over to test our bindings. She lifted my wrist and gave me a slow smile. "I warrant you instructed him to keep them loose," she said. "Just as you must have told that constable in Firenze that I was holding you against your will."

I said nothing. But she was right; I had told Giuseppe to keep his knots loose. I gave a small sigh. It had been worth trying.

She drew the bindings tighter, making me grimace at the pain. But I remained silent, while she did the same to Mathilda.

I spoke up. "You were in gaol," I said. "How is it you are free and here now?"

Janet tested the bindings once more, then went back to her crossbow. "Through your mistake, Mary Fox," she said with another thin smile. "You struck a nobleman called de Ginori so hard he could scarce walk after, then you ran from him." She lifted the weapon and pointed it back at me. "He came to see me in gaol with one who speaks our tongue, and asked why I had tried to attack you. I listed all those you had killed, and he said he understood. He asked if I still wanted my vengeance, and I said by the Heavens, I did. If that was so, he said, then I was free to go, as long as I would come after you. He had my crossbow restored to me. Then he gave me provisions and a horse, telling me you said you were heading for this town. He bade me make good speed in pursuit." She gave me an impassive stare, her smile gone. "He said I should seek not just my own revenge, but his too."

"You seek vengeance against Mary, and it seems, us as well," Mathilda said. "But do you not see how God has vented his own wrath upon us?" She looked at the empty shelves and the crack in the wall. "He has shaken the whole town in his anger. We have suffered enough." Her voice became firmer. "Let us go, and be on your way. Vengeance is served."

Janet gave a hollow laugh, then shook her head. "His anger pales before my retribution," she said, turning the bow on Mathilda. "I have yet to begin." She lifted it higher, so it was aimed directly at my new-found mother's head. "If I kill you first, how will that make Mary Fox feel?" She settled the weapon and curled her fingers under the firing bar.

"No!" I shouted, "Not her! Kill me if you must!"

Janet Crosse turned her head to me, and I stared into eyes that seemed ice-cold and empty. Then she swung the bow across to me.

I looked down. *Lord, have mercy on my soul...*

There was a loud crack.

Then a scream.

I looked up.

Mathilda was staring beyond me, her mouth hanging open.

Giuseppe was slumped in his chair. His watery old eyes were open, but for sure, they could no longer see. The crossbow bolt had passed through his thin body, leaving a mess of blood that had burst from a hole in his chest large enough for a fist to enter.

Mathilda's eyes rolled up and her head slumped to her chest.

Janet gave a sigh as she wound back her bow and fitted a new bolt. "Your friend has fainted," she observed. "'Tis a pity, for I would have her be awake when I make my next shot." She tutted, as if she were but a matron observing a slovenly servant. Then she put the bow down and went over to Mathilda. "I think if I aim true, I can just nick her arm here," she said, indicating Mathilda's shoulder. "What say you, Mary Fox? It will give her pain, to be sure, and she will bleed from it, but it will not kill her." She put her head to one side and gave a small grin. "I warrant it will awaken her, so she is ready to receive the next few shots, each of which will do much the same." Her grin became a full smile, for all her eyes still seemed empty. "Then I can decide whether I deliver the final blow, or simply let her bleed to death, while you listen to every scream and cry."

She came over and put her hands on the arms of my chair, then leaned forward until her nose was almost touching mine. "When she is finally dead, and you have lived through the loss of one you seem to value, then you will know what I feel, Mary. You will understand. Finally, you will know. When you go to meet Satan, then you will know."

I had no words in response. I held her dark eyes, and kept my own steady.

Suddenly, she seemed to lose what little control she had. "Beg me, Mary Fox," she snarled. "Beg me for your friend's life! Beg me for your own!"

I kept my silence. Kept my stare. Kept the anger away from my face. Instead I made it flow to my hands, making fists and tensing them under the bonds. Wishing they were free. So I could put them around Janet's neck…

A feel of snapping. Fibres breaking?

I tensed again. Rolling my knuckles to push my wrists upwards.

More fibres breaking.

Mathilda had said the linen was old.

Another push.

Janet stood back. "Very well," she snarled, "let us continue." She retrieved the weapon, and pointed it at Mathilda. "I would you watch most carefully, Mary Fox, lest you miss how wonderfully true is my aim." Her eyebrows raised. "Of course, I might not be so skilled. What if I miss, and pierce her heart?" She gave a hollow chuckle, and it was as if she were a play actor speaking a part. She shrugged. "Then she dies immediately like the old man. I will need to practice causing my finer wounds on you instead."

I tensed my wrists again.

Janet swung the bow left and right. "The heart, or the shoulder? What say you, Mary Fox?" My continued silence seemed to anger her. "Speak, damn you!"

"Neither," I said. "Leave her in peace."

"Oh no." She seemed to come to a decision. "The heart it is. Let us be done with her, and you will be my sport."

Tensing. One. More. Time.

The bow was pointed at Mathilda's chest.

Her hand started to tighten on the bar.

Fibres. Breaking.

I yelled like a demon.

She snapped a look at me.

I sprang up from the chair. Threw myself at the crossbow.

The bolt flew.

38

THE RIVER OF FIRE

The shaft was standing proud in the wall behind Mathilda.

It had missed her.

A crack appeared around it, then another. Each one grew and spread away from the shaft, until the whole wall was crazed and large pieces of plaster fell away.

The whole house began to shake once again.

This time it was worse. Much worse.

Janet looked around, her eyes wide and her face paling. The case of shelves that had been emptied by the last tremor, now began to sway. It rocked forward, then back, then forward again, past the point of no return. It fell into the room as if a drunkard had collapsed. Janet stepped away as it crashed down.

There was a scream as Mathilda awoke.

Janet stumbled as the floor moved under her feet. With one last look at me, she got up, clutching at her crossbow, and staggered to the door.

"I will return for you later," she screamed against the roar of the tremor, then left.

I went to Mathilda. As quick as I could, I released her bonds. "Come!" I yelled. "We must get out!"

"What of the woman?" she shouted. "She will get away!"

I paused a fraction of a moment. The thought of Janet Crosse being free to come after us again made me feel sick. "Meet me outside." I named the tavern where I had stayed the night. "I will chase after her."

"Then go!"

I ran outside and looked both ways. It was hard to see past the many people who were rushing about with screams and shouts, but

I thought I recognised a bare head going towards the end of the street. Pushing my way through the panicking crowds, I followed Janet as fast as I could. I swerved as a roof tile crashed to the ground before me, almost causing me to hit a man and woman carrying a child. Another man was lying in my path, a pool of blood spreading from his head. I would have loved to have been able to stop and help, but there seemed little that would save him.

I reached the corner, and saw Janet heading towards the ruined Roman amphitheatre that stood in a field on the edge of the town.

Just as I set off after her, the earth tremor took on such force that I must drop to my knees, lest I fall. Up ahead, Janet was doing the same.

Then there was the loudest noise I had ever heard.

As I put my hands to my ears, God showed his true wrath.

A column of fire shot into the sky behind me, opening out as it rose like a canopy of black smoke and flames. The sky grew dark as the thick cloud spread, while more and more fire burst forth.

A strong sulphurous smell, many times worse than rotten eggs, burned through the air, making me gag and retch. A shower of small rocks fell to one side of me, then stopped. But I could not let Janet escape, so I picked myself up and ran on towards the ruins, my hand over my mouth and nose.

Another fall of rocks came ahead of me, with pieces of burning stone crashing to the ground like canon shot, so I must run to the side to avoid them.

I reached a row of arches standing side by side; each an entrance to a dark tunnel that must lead inside the Roman amphitheatre. I staggered to a halt. There was no sign of Janet. Should I run into one of the black tunnels, and risk her fearsome crossbow? Or stay outside and be hit if deadly rocks started falling again?

I chose one of the arches. It led to a passage, and I felt my way along in the darkness.

"Mary Fox?" Her voice echoed from in front of me.

I stopped and kept as still as I could.

"Mary Fox?" she repeated. Then there was a cracking noise, and the smack of a bolt into the stone beside me. I crouched low, and ran towards the sound, hoping to reach her before she could re-arm. I had nothing but my bare hands, but they itched to get around her throat. Meanwhile, I held them out before me as I ran.

I screamed as my hands smacked into a wall, which must have meant I had hit a turn in the passage. I glanced to my right. There was a faint glow where it came out into the centre of the amphitheatre.

A figure was silhouetted against the light.

I ducked back into the dark, just as another bolt hit the wall where I had been.

I ran back down the passage away from Janet, and stopped at the entrance. The smell of sulphur was even stronger, but thankfully no burning rocks were coming down.

As quick as I could, I slipped out and across to the next arch. I went in, then ran along the dark passageway. With luck I could catch her unawares when I came out.

I reached the end. Once more in the open, I gasped at the smell. Holding my breath, I ran across to the end of the first passage that I had run down.

Janet was standing just inside. As she saw me, she swung the crossbow round, and I dropped to my knee so the bolt flew over my head. It was as I hoped; for now she was vulnerable while she reloaded.

She was winding back the bow as I got to her. I knocked it from her hand, and pushed her to the floor. With a yell of triumph, I reached my hands towards her throat. But she twisted away, and flashes of light exploded as she hit my jaw. I grunted as the pain spread like fire, then she was up and reaching for the bow. I pulled her back, and managed to get a punch of my own to the side of her head, causing her to stagger away from the crossbow. I grabbed hold of it before she did, stood up, and with all my strength I hurled it away. It flew high into the air, then dropped into the open Roman arena.

With a scream of rage, she ran out after it.

At first the air was clear, but as she ran, a heavy fall of burning rocks started coming down. They were the largest stones I had seen so far; bright orange with fire, slamming into the earth with the sound of a thousand drums.

I watched from the cover of the arch as she dodged and weaved the rocks that fell around her, as if God was trying to hit her for all the evil she had done. She made it to where the bow lay, but before she could retrieve it, a rock hit her head. She staggered away, clutching at the wound; her hand turning red with blood.

It seemed that she had lost the understanding of where she was, and she turned round twice.

Then she staggered again, as another rock hit her.

This time she seemed to realise that she must abandon her weapon and run back to shelter.

But she seemed still confused by her injury; she went the wrong way.

Now she was heading towards a large pit in the floor of the arena.

There was a scream as Janet Crosse fell into it.

Just as she disappeared from view, the ground felt as if it was being shaken by a giant hand; worse than any tremor so far.

Then a wall to the left of the arena exploded.

A flow of rocks, burning red like a river of fire, burst through. It was moving a hundred times faster than a galloping horse, crashing and roaring so much that I thought my head would burst.

A wave of heat, hotter than a thousand ovens, reached my hiding place, and I scrambled back into the cooler passage.

The last thing I saw as I ran, was the burning river of fire filling the pit where Janet lay.

—0—

I waited for many minutes in the shelter of the other end of the passage, until the rain of rocks slowed and stopped. Drawing a breath before braving the sulphurous air, I ran out. The column of smoke was still there, standing beyond the town like a giant mushroom reaching into the sky

I ran hard to the tavern. It seemed to have escaped the worst of the tremor and the falling rocks, and I breathed a great sigh of relief when I found Mathilda inside.

"What of the woman?" she asked after we had held each other in our arms for many minutes.

"Perished," I said. "Swallowed by the wrath of God."

"The Lord has seen fit to punish her evil," she replied. "Giuseppe was a good man."

"Speak no more of her," I said. "We must flee this terrible thing." I did not know how long we had until the rocks started raining down again. I had no wish for us to fall victim to them as well.

"My husband's brother lives in Napoli," she said. "Can we ride there?"

"If my horse is still whole," I said.

We went out to the stables, where we were greeted by a wide-eyed Hestia. "The Heavens be thanked," I said as I stroked her muzzle, "you are spared." She whinnied in agreement. I put on her saddle and bridle, and mounted her. Mathilda climbed up a mounting block and settled behind me.

I walked Hestia cautiously out of the stable, but by God's grace, there were no stones falling at this moment.

"Quick," I said. "To Napoli."

39
A MOTHER'S LOVE?

Our journey to Napoli was made difficult and slow by the never-ending flow of people fleeing Pozzuoli. Hestia was forced to pick her way with care; past elderly men and women shuffling along; past fathers pushing rickety old carts laden with their goods; past crying children clutching at their mothers' hands.

And all the while, the great column of smoke and fire continued to rise ever upwards behind us, making the day turn to night and the sun seem a distant memory. Like most of the other travellers, we had bound scarves or rags about our faces, in an attempt to make the air less foul. It had little effect, with the sickening smell of sulphur forcing its way in. I had even taken an old sack from Hestia's stable and fitted it over her muzzle in the hope of helping her to breathe. I trusted she would understand, but she continually shook her head as if to dislodge it. Every now and then, she twisted round and gave me a look of accusation in her dark eye.

"Sorry old girl," I muttered under my breath on one such occasion, "but it was necessary."

Mathilda clung tightly to my waist, and except for some occasional words regarding our journey, she remained silent throughout the three or four hours it took us to reach the city.

I assumed she was lost in thoughts of Giuseppe, and how he had been so summarily executed by the cruel Janet Crosse. I grieved for her; Giuseppe had seemed a good man, for all I had known him for but a day. At least he would have felt no pain, before suddenly finding himself standing before the gates of Heaven.

My fear was that Mathilda would ask me of Janet's accusations.

Could she truly believe that I had not caused at least some of the many deaths of those that Janet had loved? I dared not tell her that it had been Angelo who had plunged his knife into the chest of Joan Cruddon. So I must take the blame for myself, or accuse her beloved son. Either way I would be abusing her faith.

Was this the reason for her silence; that she could no longer trust me? Even despite that I had returned the River of Fire necklace?

If I wanted nothing else, I wanted her trust. Even more than her love; for surely a mother's love cannot exist without that?

And yet, how could she? It had been because of me that Janet had come to her house and killed Giuseppe. So even if Mathilda absolved me of any blame from Janet's other accusations, she would have no doubt of my being the original cause of her servant's death.

These thoughts troubled my mind throughout our journey, until we finally came to a modest house on a street in Napoli, and climbed stiffly down from Hestia's back.

Mathilda's brother-in-law welcomed us both and sought to make us comfortable. Over the next few days, he and his wife gave us every care; providing what food they could, for it was scarce in the markets. No doubt this was due to the many people who had flooded into the city to escape the horrors back in Pozzuoli. And the darkness caused by the ever-present column of foul smoke that filled the sky all along the bay.

I kept my concerns to myself, waiting to see if Mathilda might broach the subject of our relationship. Yet she talked of everything else; busying herself with helping in the house, or searching out provisions in the market. She was always pleasant and attentive with me, although on occasions I did catch her giving me sideways glances that seemed troubled, as if she was trying to decide whether or not I was genuine.

It was as if the darkness caused by the smoke was stifling any talk of our feelings, and it was not until the wind changed and cleared the air, that the moment seemed right to have a meaningful conversation.

It was on the afternoon of the eighth day since we had arrived. Now that the sun was again in the sky, we decided to take a walk up a hill beyond the city's wall. Reaching the top, we sat down on the grasses. Before us was Napoli's harbour, with a few ships moored up. One was coming in to port, gliding across the blue waters with its sails cracking and tiny men climbing up and down its rigging like so many ants. Inland to the left was an enormous mountain; so high that it had some white clouds gathered around its twin peaks.

"It has the name Vesuvius," Mathilda said. She pointed in the other direction, to Pozzuoli, where another mountain had its own cloud of grey smoke still billowing forth.

"*Monte Nuovo,*" she observed. "A new mountain. It was not there before God unleashed the fire little more than a week ago."

I raised an eyebrow. "It has grown so quickly."

"Indeed." The silence hung between us, almost as heavy as the cloud of smoke. Then she took a breath, and said, "Much has happened, and most quickly, Mary, has it not?"

I turned and studied her face. It had such beauty; such kindness, that she was as close to a mother as I could ever want. But it had to be what she wanted as well, and the doubt was written plainly in the sadness of her smile.

"I can never repay your kindness, Mary Fox," she continued. "You loved my son, and I know he must have loved you. I would have had welcomed you as my daughter if you were his wife." She paused, then said the one word that in truth, I least wanted to hear.

"But…"

I nodded. "But, that is not how things are."

She stood, so I did the same. She put her hands on my shoulders, giving the smallest shake of her head. "Nay."

Even though I had known it would come to this, I felt a heavy weight pull at my heart. It could have been all I wanted; a happy, loving home here in this pleasant land, with a woman who would at last be the mother I had always yearned for.

But I knew it could not be; not after Janet and Giuseppe. Not after *Monte Nuovo* and the rain of rocks and rivers of fire that had built it.

She drew me into an embrace, and we held each other for some time. Then she stood back and asked, "What will you do?"

I had given this some thought already, and said, "I will resume my men's garb and ride to Venezia. Scoronconcolo is there, I believe, and I need to settle my account with him. For Angelo."

"I would you do." She nodded. "When will you go?" Then a small hopeful smile. "You will stay a few more days?"

But it was not enough. I shook my head. "Nay," I replied. "It is better I go as soon as I can. I will saddle Hestia and ride out at dawn."

She pursed her lips and nodded again. "So be it. I will never forget you, Mary Fox, and the kindness you have shown me."

"Nor I, Mathilda di Luca," I said. "I learned so much about you from Angelo, and now I have come to know you for myself, you will always be the mother I sought."

"And found?"

"Yes," I said. It seemed natural that we should embrace once more, and it was as warm and as loving as I could ever have wanted. I never would have it end, but I knew beyond doubt that it must. Eventually I broke away and stood back.

"Now I have to move on."

Together we held hands and walked back down the hill.

THE END

LOOK OUT FOR MARY'S NEXT ADVENTURE

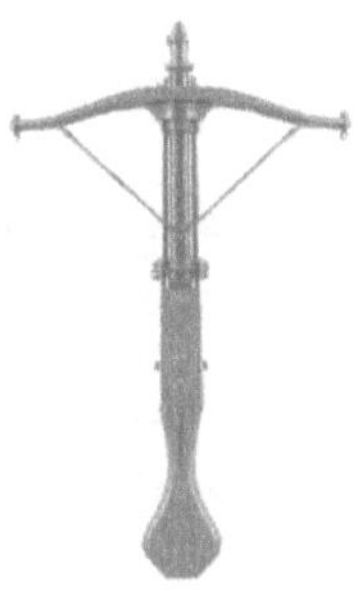

Sign up for Jonathan's newsletter to be the first to know about Mary's next adventure – and other news, at:
jonathanposnerauthor.com

AUTHOR'S NOTE

There are two key events in this book that actually happened.

The first is the assassination of Duke Alessandro de Medici by his cousin Lorenzino and the paid assassin Scoronconcolo on the 6th January 1537.

The other is the eruption of Monte Nuovo next to the town of Pozzuoli in the Bay of Naples. This took place 22 months later, on the 29th September 1538.

For the assassination, I was intrigued to discover that the Duke was lured to his death by the promise of an assignation with a lady by the name of Caterina Soderini de Ginori, wife of Leonardo de Ginori, and also sister of Lorenzino. There's no firm evidence that Caterina was actually present in the room when the Duke was killed, but it was the fact of her name being used that caught my attention.

By having Mary forced to stand in for Caterina, I could then make a small change to the known narrative, and place her there physically as bait for the Duke. As an observer, Mary can then describe the true horrors of the killing.

The events in the room that night are well documented, and I mainly used *The Medici: Godfathers of the Renaissance* by Paul Strathern as my source for this. It enabled me to tell the story of the assassination from the moment Lorenzino and Scoronconcolo came in, to their eventual ride across the city and on to Venice.

Scoronconcolo was an ideal villain for Mary—as a known killer, he fits the brief, and as a common man, he was never able (nor, I suspect, willing) to have his portrait painted. This meant I could describe him as I wished; imagining him in a way that showed he could be both evil and charming as necessary. I feel I might have been borrowing a trope from a certain British spy franchise there…

I understand Scoronconcolo was killed in Venice, possibly by Lorenzino. Although who knows? With Mary Fox on his tail and out for vengeance, it could be that she has a hand in his death… Watch this space!

As I said at the start of this note, the eruption of Monte Nuovo was 22 months after the assassination. This gave me a problem—should I keep the date and find a way for Mary to fill the time, or change the date, so there's a tighter timeline for her to get to Pozzuoli at just the right (or, as she might say, the wrong) moment? In the end I went for the latter. So if you're a historical purist, please accept my sincere apologies. Yes, I moved the eruption forward by nearly two years, but I had good reason and I hope you'll forgive me.

As part of my research I went out to Pozzuoli in May 2024, and spent a day walking around the town. I climbed as far as you can up the side of the mountain; it's so big that all you see is a slope, and it's only from the aerial views that the full crater is revealed.

I also went and stood outside the *Anfiteatro Flavio*, scene of Mary's final showdown with Janet Crosse, and noted the series of archways and passages that led in to the main arena. I made them a bit longer and darker for dramatic effect, but it was amazing to be looking at a building that is largely unchanged since Mary would have seen it.

Anfiteatro Flavio, Pozzuoli, May 2024

If you have any comments or questions, please contact me through my website.

jonathanposnerauthor.com.

Please also leave a review on Amazon, Goodreads or BookBub.

As an author it is always good to get feedback, good or bad.

Thank you in advance!

ABOUT THE AUTHOR

Before becoming a full-time author in 2021, Jonathan worked for many years as a marketing and advertising executive. He now lives in the South West UK, and when he is not writing, he enjoys walking, theatre and presenting regular shows on a local community radio station.

He is fascinated by Tudor history, and has written The Witchfinder's Well trilogy a series of three novels that address the question 'what might happen if you time-travelled back to the 1560s?' He has also written a prequel novel, three full-length musicals, a one-act play and two books of short stories.

For more information, visit his author website at
jonathanposnerauthor.com

Jonathan's books are all published by
Winter and Drew Publishing Ltd.

winteranddrew.com

The Broken Sword
Mary Fox's first adventure

You only discover what dangers you can overcome when you're tested to the limit...

Tudor England

When Mary Fox is ordered to marry a sadistic older man, she decides instead to strike out on her own.

As a woman in a man's world, no-one expects her to survive, but Mary is determined to prove them wrong.

Challenged to return the Broken Sword talisman and so break a centuries-old curse, she soon learns how to scheme, fight and outwit those who would drag her back to a life of servitude.

And in doing so, she becomes more than a match for any man.

Readers have said:

"Diabolically good! What makes this novel irresistibly readable is the emotional energy generated by the main character Mary Fox, her ups and downs, drawing parallels to our present times."

"I would highly recommend this book for its entertainment, historical authenticity and value."

"I thoroughly enjoyed this book. It draws you straight into the action from the first paragraph and the pace continues to the end. I found it hard to put down and was sorry when it ended. Very well written and easy to read, this is a great adventure story and I can't wait for the next one."

"If you like historical fiction, buy this book. You won't be disappointed."

mybook.to/MaryFoxBrokenSword

The Tudor Prince
Mary Fox's second adventure

A gripping tale of danger and deception that goes right to the top of Henry VIII's court.

What if you bear an uncanny resemblance to a missing prince?

1533. Mary Fox agrees to stand in for young Henry Fitzroy, the illegitimate son of Henry VIII. But then she uncovers a treacherous plot behind the prince's disappearance; one that goes right to the very top of the Tudor Court.

It's a plot to change the royal line of succession, and will almost certainly make England descend into another bloody civil war.

As Mary is pulled deeper and deeper into the deception, she realises she has to seize control and turn the tables on the plot's mysterious ringleader. But there's a twist; the man ordered to kidnap the prince is none other than Jacob Cruddon, Mary's bitterest enemy.

Can Mary defeat Cruddon and get out alive, or will he get his own revenge by killing her first?

Readers have said:

"Mary Fox brings it again. I love this spunky heroine and what crazy adventure, working as a double for the son of Henry VIII. I have loved reading the two books in the series and looking forward to the next one. Highly recommend."

"The Tudor Prince will have you rooting for the swash-buckling Mary from page one."

"I adored the first book but this one surpasses it! It's Mary Fox with a Tudor twist."

mybook.to/thetudorprince

The Witchfinder's Well Trilogy

Part 1 - The Witchfinder's Well

What if you fell through a time travel portal and landed in Tudor England?

How long before you say the wrong thing to the wrong person? Before you're accused of being a witch?

For Justine Parker it's almost immediate. She hardly has time to find her feet in a historical world that's hostile for women, before she's on the run from a ruthless witchfinder. He makes it his deadly mission to submit her to a terrifying trial.

And if that doesn't kill her, he'll burn her to death.

Justine needs to do whatever it takes to keep out of his clutches.But she can't do it alone – as a stranger in Elizabethan England, she needs help. Handsome Sir William could be her saviour – and even her lover – but his time is running out fast. A cruel twist of history says his own death is imminent.

Now Justine has to face a terrible choice – save herself, or change history and save her new love?

Unless she can find a way to do both.

Readers have said:

"A must for everyone who loves history and a must for everyone who wants to be whisked away to another time."

"An enchanting and un-put-downable read!"

"A good tale, entertaining, funny, informative, recommended, a good holiday book, one to go back to again and again."

" I couldn't put it down… a well-written book. Total enjoyment!"

mybook.to/WitchfindersWell

Part 2 – The Alchemist's Arms

Lady Mary de Beauvais seems to be the perfect 16th century woman, but she hides a dark and terrible secret - she is actually a time-traveller from 2015 called Justine Parker. So when she discovers there's another traveller from her own time, she sets out across Elizabethan England to find him.

But it's a search that leads her into dreadful danger – threatening not just Mary's own future, but the life of Queen Elizabeth as well. So Mary is forced to face her fears and take control – if she wants to save herself and those she loves, in this *"gripping adventure thriller"*.

Readers have said:

"Thoroughly recommend it."

"…this marvellous book was a winner for me… There's a good feel for the time and era, so history buffs will enjoy the rich tapestry of detail in this book."

"The numerous twists and turns keep you on the edge of your seat."

"Well written, kept you wanting to read page after page in one go!"

mybook.to/AlchemistsArms

Part 3 - The Sovereign's Secret

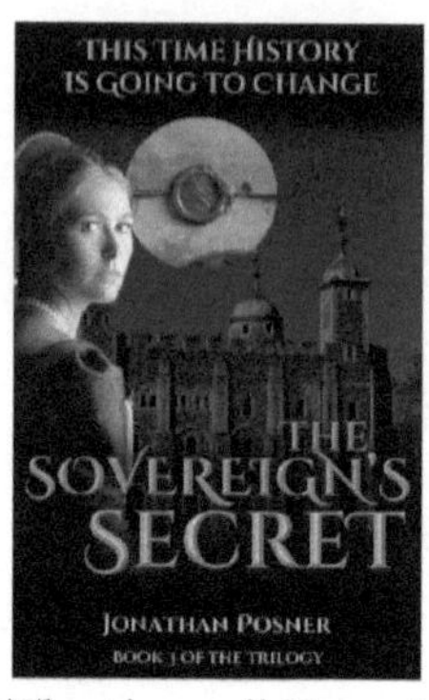

England 1575.

After involvement in an audacious assassination attempt on the life of Queen Elizabeth has tested Lady Mary de Beauvais to her limits – and beyond – all she wants is to do is live a peaceful life with her family.

Unfortunately her time-travelling past catches up with her, and she now faces the greatest threat to her life in Tudor England. That is until Francis Walsingham, the sinister spymaster, offers to send her on her most dangerous mission yet.

Can Lady Mary find the courage, the strength and the sheer determination to win through finally?

Whatever happens, history is going to change.

Readers have said:

"I liked that Lady Mary is a kick-ass heroine and the story has the odd bit of humour. The book is well-written and the historical detail seems pretty accurate."

"Be prepared for the fulfilment of the warning on the cover of "This time history is going to change." It's fun to see how [Jonathan] Posner brings this about."

"From the first page I was hooked. Well written, the book was full of excitement and at times I couldn't put it down. Most enjoyable."

mybook.to/SovereignSecret

Prequel - The Lawyer's Legacy

This fast-paced, action packed, historical thriller introduces Robert Wychwoode, the lawyer and spy-master of *The Witchfinder's Well* trilogy.

What if you uncovered a traitorous rebellion – but nobody believed you?

1535. Tudor couple Ophelia Williams and Robert Wychwoode make a great crime-busting team. They've cracked open a Cornish rebellion against Henry VIII.

But when it comes to stopping it – then they're on their own.

There's no doubting their bravery. Or their relentless determination. Or even their cunning and ingenuity.

But will it be enough?

Because the price of failure is death.

Readers have said:

"…it kept me on the edge of my seat and I just wanted to keep reading. Couldn't put it down!"

"Most enjoyable Tudor historical fiction."

"This was a fun read, especially in following the escapades of a 16th century woman who learns espionage…"

"…without giving anything away, there is an episode on board ship that had me on the edge of my seat. Well-researched and well-written; a joy to read. Highly recommended."

mybook.to/LawyersLegacy

winteranddrew.com

www.ingramcontent.com/pod-product-compliance
Lightning Source LLC
Chambersburg PA
CBHW030803210726
48290CB00002B/396